BAD CREE

BAD CREE

ᐊᑭᒫᐅᐧ

A NOVEL

JESSICA JOHNS

Doubleday
New York

All rights reserved. Published in the United States by Doubleday, a division of Penguin Random House LLC, New York.

www.doubleday.com

DOUBLEDAY and the portrayal of an anchor with a dolphin are registered trademarks of Penguin Random House LLC.

The epigraph "Auntie" by Edzi'u is used with permission.

Front-of-jacket photograph © Ramzi Chebbi / EyeEm / Getty
Jacket design by Emily Mahon
Book design by Betty Lew

Library of Congress Cataloging-in-Publication Data
Library of Congress Control number 2022933347
ISBN: 978-0-385-54869-4 (print)
ISBN: 978-0-385-54870-0 (ebook)

MANUFACTURED IN THE UNITED STATES OF AMERICA
1 3 5 7 9 10 8 6 4 2

First United States Edition

To Mom and Dad—

thank you for giving me every opportunity to dream this book into reality. I love you.

AUNTIE

by Edzi'u

Auntie is mood. Auntie is spirit. Auntie is prayer. Auntie is medicines. Auntie is dream. Auntie is hope. Auntie is smarten up. Auntie is feeling. Auntie is encouragement. Auntie keeps going. Auntie has no gender. Aunties save lives.   Embody Auntie. Be Auntie.   Say Auntie.

BAD CREE

∨⅄`

Before I look down, I know it's there. The crow's head I was
clutching in my dream is now in bed with me. I woke up with
the weight of it in my hands, held against my chest under the covers. I can still feel its beak and feathers on my palms. The smell
of pine and the tang of blood sting my nose. My pillow feels for
a second like the cold, frozen ground under my cheek. I yank off
my blanket, heavy like I'm pulling it back from the past, and look
down to my hands, now empty. A feeling of static pulses inside
them like when a dead limb fills with blood again. They are clean
and dry and trembling.

Shit. Not again.

I step gingerly out of bed, as though the world in front of me
might break, and turn on the light, wait for my eyes to adjust. It
illuminates my blanket on the floor, the grey sheet kicked into
a clump. Every breath I take is laboured, and when I blink, my
dream flashes onto the back of my eyelids. Running through the
woods. The snow glistening in the clearing. The crows covering
Sabrina's body.

Heart thumping in my chest, I kneel next to the bed, how I
imagine I might if I ever were to pray. "Come on," I plead into the
covers. "Where are you?"

I feel across the bedsheet for anything: blood, feathers, twig-small bones. My fingers shake and search by touch in between pillows, into every crease and wrinkle of the fitted sheet. I turn on the flashlight on my phone and use it to look into shadows, but I find nothing. My shirt, when I bring it up to my nose, smells like the outside in winter, like pine trees and sharp cold.

"You son of a bitch, come on." I kick the blanket to the side and put my cheek to the floor, scanning underneath the bed and bedside table. Dust and crumbs sit forgotten in dry corners. An old plate, mould forming along the ridges, lies next to holey socks. I close my eyes. My awake mind is trying to fog the dream over, shake it away, but I hold on to it. I know it was there, in my hand. As real as the floor still against my cheek, I was holding a crow's head when I woke up. I can still smell the blood in the bedroom air and feel where its beak pressed into my palm, right above my heart line. Throbbing and hot.

I think of the dream while I shower. I lather shampoo into my hair and rinse, watch the brown strands circle the drain. This is the third dream in three weeks. The third time I've brought something back with me.

In the first two dreams, I brought back branches. I broke them off the trees as I was running through the woods in a panic. The first time it happened, the branch disappeared as soon as I woke up and looked down at it. The second time, the moon was big and full outside, and I caught a glimpse of the flimsy stick gripped between my palms. That time, I held on tight, but it still disappeared. I had hoped that if I held on hard enough, I would understand how I could have a pine bough in my hands when the last pine tree I'd seen was a thousand kilometres away in Alberta.

I close my eyes and let the warm water stream against my

face, but I'm still shivering against the memory of last night. In my dream, I was in the middle of the winter woods, wearing only what I wore to bed that night: an old T-shirt and sweats. I cursed at myself for not following my idea after the last dream to wear shoes and something warmer to bed. At least it was better than the first dream, when I went to sleep naked.

I was surrounded by bone-thin pine, spruce, and balsam trees, browning at the base up to their torsos, sparse with white snow near the top. I let out a small gasp of surprise to find myself in the same woods again, my breath forming in front of me in an icy puff. There were no footprints in the fresh snow around me, as if I blinked into existence in that exact spot.

The wind whipped hard, carrying an icy whistle past my ears. In the moonlight, the trees cast shadows so tall they swallowed the land whole. My breath caught in my throat and the urge to run itched across my spine.

"Shit," I whispered to myself as I stepped in place, giving each foot a second's break from the freezing ground. The whistle from the wind, quiet at first, grew louder, until it was shrieking. This had happened in the two dreams before, too. A scream, like someone was on fire, came from a trail opening in the brush that snaked between the trees behind me.

I pulled my arms tighter around myself and crouched in place, trying to conserve my body heat. My arms were starting to redden, the frigid slap of the wind already working its way through me. I pressed my chin into my collarbone and squeezed my eyes shut. "One, two, three . . ." I tried my old trick of closing my eyes and counting to wake myself up from nightmares, but I knew it wouldn't work. It hadn't the last two times, either.

When the screaming started to get closer, I turned toward it and found myself facing the trail. Even though I was terrified, I knew I had to try something different. In the other dreams, I had run in the opposite direction, away from the sound, wading in snow through the woods. But last night, I walked the trail toward the sound, my feet crunching in the snow, the scream getting louder with every step.

The trail ended abruptly, opening into a circular clearing lined by pine trees. Icicles weighed down the branches, shaping them into clawed hands. And finally, I saw the sound's source: a body splayed on the ground in the middle of the clearing. Dark shadows blotted it like a moving Rorschach. The shadows grew and shifted, and I saw flashes of hair and limbs, but then, in a blink, they were covered again. It took me a second to realize I wasn't looking at shadows, it was crows. A whole murder of them moving over the body.

I open my eyes under the streaming showerhead and let the water sting them. My chest pounds with an ache and I sit down, the slightly clogged drain making the tub begin to fill around me.

Okay, wake up now, I had thought to myself in the dream. The crows' caws started to rumble deep, drowning out the body's long, endless scream. As they fluttered, I caught sight of the face and gasped. Horror crawled up and planted itself in my throat. My sister Sabrina lay unmoving, her open mouth unleashing the shriek that had been reaching deep inside my gut.

The shock that gripped me in place suddenly loosened, and I ran to her, my feet slipping on the frozen ground. I yelled as I got closer, startling the birds just enough for me to reach out and touch her face.

Sabrina looked like she'd been long dead. Her once-brown skin was now white, drained of all blood. Her hair was grey and stuck to the snow under her head. Her eyes were slightly open and milky white, looking past me. Her dry lips frozen into a perfect O. Her skin, too, was ice cold. Her clothes, a flannel shirt and jeans, were dishevelled and torn.

The crows were cawing so vehemently around me, it sounded like battle cries. They beat their wings in my face, trying to push me back, but I batted them away. Sabrina's scream never stopped, not even for a breath.

"Get away from her!" I yelled, tearing at the crows with such ferocity that feathers flew into the air and stuck to my sweating skin. Black barbs leaked between my fingers as I swatted and grabbed at the crows, their small bodies thrashing and pecking at my hands. I was losing myself in a swarm of black, but no matter how many I threw off her body, more seemed to materialize in their place.

And then I saw it. A hole as big as my fist just below Sabrina's collarbone. The bone-white of her sternum glistened against blood. A crow, perched on Sabrina's chest, was tearing at the sides of the wound, its beak coming away with skin and veins. I screamed and kept swiping at the crows until some finally started to fly away.

Sabrina's heart, exposed to the world, beat and beat and beat. The crow finally stopped its pecking to look at me. Its dark eyes reflected the moon above us, another hole in the chest of the world. Before more crows came back, I grabbed it around the neck, its feathers short and sharp in my hand, and with rage pulsing through my body, I bent its head backwards in one quick motion, breaking its neck.

The snap of bone splitting in two rang through the air as I pulled the head from the crow's body, blood covering my hands. Sabrina's scream stopped, and the few birds that were left took off like dust being blown back into the air. When I looked back down, Sabrina's face had gone slack. Her eyes and mouth were closed like a zipper.

I dropped the crow's body from one hand and reached toward her, but then I felt a tug against my spine, like an invisible rope pulling. Before I could touch her, the rope tugged again, harder, and I was back in my bed. The crow's head, its beak pressing into my palm and its warm blood on my skin, still in my hand.

At the thought of Sabrina, a cave I've tried to keep hidden somewhere deep in my body opens up. Her unrelenting scream echoes through me, stretching back in time. I sob in the bathtub, wet hair clinging to my cheeks.

After a few minutes, I grab the bar of Ivory soap and lather it between my palms. A stinging in a cut I can't see starts in the bed of my hand and travels through my arm, inches into my armpit, slides into my heart. I reasoned away the first two dreams. I told myself I was still dreaming when I thought I was awake. That it was all in my head. Now fear settles in me like sediment at the bottom of a lake. I can't reason this away anymore. The hurt is still in my palm even if the crow's head isn't.

I get out of the shower and slowly dry off. Take my time putting on clothes, an old band T-shirt and faded jeans, trying to slow my breath. It only kind of works. I hear a caw from outside my apartment window. When I pull back the curtains, I see three crows sitting on the telephone pole, easing into the backdrop of Vancouver spring.

That's something else about the past three weeks. The crows. All of a sudden, they're everywhere I look. They've started showing up on the telephone pole in my alleyway. Every morning, I wake up to their caws. I swear they're watching me. Through the windows, I can see their heads turn to follow me as I move across the apartment. A rush of guilt heats my neck as I remember the feeling of a spine snapping in my hands.

I skip breakfast and rush out. My body vibrates with adrenaline, but all that's around me are flowers and a breeze carrying the smell of the ocean a couple of blocks away. I jog to Whole Foods, passing old heritage houses that have been converted into four-plexes and apartments. It's my day off, but I know Joli is working and I want to see someone familiar, ground myself in reality again. When I walk into the store, I spot them at the far till. Their back is to me, their thick, dark hair straight and loose. They are ringing through an elderly couple wearing matching visors when they look back at me, like they could feel it when I walked in.

"Mackenzie!" they yell across the long rows of tills, startling the couple into a jump. They laugh and it comforts me like a blanket. I exhale a breath I hadn't noticed I'd been holding and walk over to them. "You're not even here this early when you're scheduled to be," they say, arching their eyebrows.

When I first moved to Vancouver, Mom reached out to Joli's mom, Dianne, a friend of a cousin who worked as an instructor at the Native Education College. "So you aren't alone," Mom said, but I knew it was more for her peace of mind than for me. Cree people aren't great at being subtle.

As soon as she met me, Dianne wrapped me in a hug so tight I forgot myself for a minute. She helped me find a small bachelor apartment—not an easy thing to do in Vancouver, where homes are empty and unaffordable and the cost of living is triple what it is in my hometown. But she knew a landlord renting a place for extra cheap since they started the SkyTrain construction next to it. Any maintenance on the building had stopped, since it would be torn down eventually anyways, so I try to live as small and quietly as I can in hopes they forget I'm there.

Dianne also got me to volunteer when she needed help at the college for a while. Best of all, though, was that she introduced me to Joli. Joli was my age, early twenties, and tall with a round face that drew in light like the moon draws in the tide. They and Dianne are Squamish. Joli reminds me of my older twin sisters,

Sabrina and Tracey, though they're nothing like either of them. It's funny what our minds will parallel when we want something bad enough.

For the first couple months in Vancouver, I spent almost every night having dinner with Dianne and Joli. Dianne lives halfway between Vancouver and Squamish, and Joli has a place in Vancouver with four other roommates. They moved out of their mom's house when they started doula training at Vancouver College. I ate a lot of meals at Dianne's house, laughing with the two of them. They are both so loud. Could call across the ocean and still be heard, I'm sure of it. But the loud comforts me. I know I'll never worry about losing them anywhere.

I walk up to Joli as they're handing off brown bags of groceries to the couple. They flip their hair and look me up and down. "That band hasn't played a show since the early 2000s."

I shrug. "Guess that makes them a classic."

Joli smirks and looks at me a little closer. "Everything all right?" Their eyes flit around me knowingly.

When I first got my place, Joli and I walked the back streets of Kitsilano together, looking for furniture. Rich people throw out perfectly usable things. As we sifted through chipped lamps and coffee tables next to recycling bins, they told me about their family, filling alleyways with the echo of story. They also showed me all the good pubs, the Vancouver bands to care about and the ones to ignore. They could read the city like my kokum used to read the land. Could tell from the cracks in the sidewalk how far we were from their favourite queer bar. Where to avoid because of cops. When I moved into my place, they gave me sage and an abalone shell. Said even if I didn't smudge, it was always good to have it just in case.

"It happened again, didn't it?" They can read it on my face. My fear must be etched all over. I nod, rub my palms together.

After the second dream, I told Joli about what had been happening. They are the only person who knows. "This time it wasn't a branch. It was a head. A crow's head."

"Hello, is this till open?" A customer has walked up to Joli's till, plopping his organic peaches down onto the conveyor belt.

"A head?" Joli whispers, their eyes widening. They ignore the customer behind them.

"The same thing happened as the last two dreams when I woke up," I continue. "As soon as I looked down—"

"Excuse me?" Peaches guy clears his throat. Joli doesn't turn around and instead keeps staring at me, waving a hand over their shoulder as if they were buzzing away a fly.

I look over their shoulder and shake my head. "I'll tell you everything after work. If you're caught ignoring a customer again, you're going to get fired."

Joli rolls their eyes and tsks. "Fine, but I'm calling you as soon as I'm done." They give me a squeeze on my arm before turning back to the till. I feel a wave of comfort at their touch. "Thank you so much for waiting," they say in their customer service voice. "Do you need a bag?"

I turn to head out the doors, looking back once more as I leave the comfort of Joli. I had planned on doing some errands today. Filing my taxes—late for the third year in a row—and getting groceries, but I feel exposed, an open wound walking around. I go back to my apartment instead. Inside, the exposed feeling doesn't go away. I prop my laptop on the counter and put on an old playlist, a mix of emo songs I've been listening to since high school, and start deep cleaning my fridge.

Since I moved in, the apartment has never been silent. I thought, at first, I'd love the quiet. My parents' house was always full of people and noise. Somebody was always in my business. I thought breaking away from that would be a relief. It wasn't, not even for a day. There was something about the absence of sound and the acute feeling that I was really, truly alone that left me on edge. Maybe my body wasn't at home in quiet. Maybe it needed the rumble and movement of voices and people.

Now I have playlists for every task, and I listen to audiobooks when I try to fall asleep at night. The books themselves don't matter, either. What matters is that I'm never alone, not for a second. Not even when I do eventually drift to sleep and could not possibly be aware of how alone I am anymore.

While I fill the sink with soap and hot water, I throw out old vegetables, shrivelled-up ginger at the back of the fridge, cans of half-eaten beans, a mouldy piece of cheese. But Sabrina's face, frozen and unseeing, keeps flashing across my mind. Her hair splayed against the white snow. Her sharp jaw angled to the sky. When the sink is half full, I start cleaning the dirty dishes that have piled up on my counter. The lemon dish soap can't mask the smell of winter and trees still fresh in my mind. I blink and see the crows again, covering Sabrina's body. Suffocate for a moment under the feeling of fluttering wings against my face. The feel of her frozen skin. The perfect O of her mouth while she was being torn open. I shake my head to dislodge the memory. When the dirty dishes are done, I pull out the clean ones from the cupboards and scour them, too. I wash every cup and plate I own until my knuckles are rubbed raw.

By the end of the day, I've cleaned most of my apartment. Everything smells like lemon and the artificial orange of Lysol. The three crows on the back-alley telephone pole are still perched watching me, cawing low to each other. The place looks cleaner than when I moved in. But my body still hasn't scabbed over.

Just after six, Joli calls. I pick up on the second ring.

"What's going on over there? It sounds like you're having the saddest party ever."

I turn down the music and dry my hands on a dirty tea towel. "Just doing some cleaning." I sit on my bed, grabbing my blanket from the floor. From here, I can still keep an eye on the crows outside. There's a beat of silence and I hear the jingle of Joli's keys. They'd be walking to their car after their shift.

They stay silent, waiting for me to continue. I sigh and tell them everything that happened in the dream.

"Oh," they breathe out, and there's no mistaking the sympathy in their voice. "And that's the first time Sabrina has been in the dreams?"

"Yeah," I say.

"Isn't it the anniversary—"

"This isn't some unresolved trauma shit," I cut in. "This is something . . . else. I woke up with a dead crow head in my hands, Joli."

"Okay," they say. "I have to say it again. You need to call your mom."

I sigh and pull the blanket up over my knees. When I first told Joli about the dreams, this was their suggestion. The thought of it makes my stomach clench.

"Or at least tell your Auntie Doreen or Auntie Verna," they rush on.

"I don't want to worry anyone," I say. I smooth the blanket across my legs. Calling Mom's younger sisters was a better option than calling my mom, though.

"Look, I don't know much about you Crees. But if these visions are—"

"They're not visions," I interrupt.

"You keep saying what they aren't. So what are they?"

"I don't know," I say, gripping the phone tighter.

"All the more reason to call someone. Are the crows still following you?"

I glance outside. "Yeah. Creepy bastards."

"Hey, don't go around cursing crows over there. Besides, you did decapitate one of their friends." They're quiet for a moment, and I hear their car rumble and start. "You call an auntie, or I need to talk to my mom."

"Don't tell Dianne," I say. Whether I tell my aunts or Joli's mom, it'll get back to my mom eventually. I sigh. "I'll call someone."

"Now?"

"Yes, now. Get off the phone and focus on the road."

"Go back to your sad music. Damn sentimental Crees."

I laugh and hang up, let the ease of talking to Joli sit in my chest. I close the living room curtains, even though the sun is only just starting to dip low in the sky, casting the world in a deep orange. I don't want to feel watched anymore. I stare at my phone for a few minutes before finally calling Auntie Doreen.

"What'd I tell you about calling on Thursdays, Mackenzie?" she shouts into the phone when she answers. I can hear the bingo caller's voice echo in the background. I look at the time again. It's an hour ahead in High Prairie. "Shit, sorry, Auntie. Bingo night. I forgot. This is important, though."

"More important than a ten-thousand-dollar dual dab? I don't think so." She hangs up, and I wait for her to call me back, because I know she will. There is concern in her voice. Even though we talk at least once a week, I know never to call on bingo nights.

"I was two numbers away and starting to sweat," she says when I answer her call a half hour later. "What are you calling for, my girl? Text me like a regular person."

"I've been having some weird dreams," I say. "Really, really weird dreams."

She laughs. "That's a bit vague."

I swallow into the phone. "This is going to sound fucked up

but stay with me." I sigh and blink, see the flash of pine boughs in front of me, and hear the crunch of snow under my feet. "I had a couple dreams where I was running through the woods, grabbing at tree branches and shoving them aside, trying to get through. But when I woke up, I was still holding on to sticks. Like I brought them back from the dream world. When I blinked, they disappeared."

She's quiet for a while, and I almost think she's hung up again, when she sighs. "I see."

I pace my small apartment, lapping the entire space in a few steps.

She's quiet and I hear the flick of a lighter, quiet talking and laughter from her end of the phone. She must be outside the Friendship Centre, smoking during the bingo break. I imagine her thin fingers pulling out a cigarette in the parking lot and lighting it. Smoke curling around her face and shoulder-length, permed hair.

"That's not all." My voice is quiet.

She inhales deeply. "Creator, what else?"

I tell her about what happened in the dream the night before. The crow's head and seeing Sabrina.

She's silent again and I listen to her puff on the cigarette. "And did you think I'd have an answer?" she says finally.

It's my turn to be silent now.

"My girl, I might be an old Indian, but I'm not a goddamn dream oracle. That's all really fucked up." She laughs her loud laugh and I laugh with her, feel the weight of the day lift off my body.

We're quiet again for a moment. "Auntie, do you believe me?" I ask.

She clicks her tongue and exhales, and I imagine her rubbing at her jaw, the way she does when she's thinking. "As a kid, you used to freak me out. Sometimes when you and your sisters would have sleepovers at my place, you'd wake up in the morning and your eyes wouldn't see me. Like they hadn't left the dream yet."

I suck in a sharp breath. Study my palm as I let what she's saying settle. "I can still feel the beak, Auntie. It's like a cut is underneath my skin."

The background noises start to slow and quiet. Auntie's every inhale is deeper than the last. Her short frame is probably leaning against the outside walls of the building, strong enough to hold it up if she needed to, nodding at her friends and enemies as they head back inside.

I keep pacing my apartment and glance to the closed curtains. "Also, this might be unrelated. But some crows have started following me around."

Auntie laughs again. "Unrelated? Crows are following you and then you murder one in your dreams. Keep your eyes on them."

"Joli called them visions," I say. I think about the dreams. The panic in my stomach as I ran. A feeling, deep somewhere, that I was missing something. "But they feel almost like memories."

"Are they?" Auntie asks.

"No," I say. "I think I'd remember Sabrina being attacked by a murder of crows. Or killing one with my bare hands."

"I need to think on this some more," Auntie says. "You should call your mom."

The back of my neck burns at the mention of Mom again, and I keep pacing. She and I haven't spoken in months. "Yeah, I've been getting that advice lately."

It's been three years since I moved away from High Prairie. Mom didn't like that I moved in the first place. Before I left, she came out to the back of the house to find me putting soil into a bottle. She shook her head and watched me. "Your body carries home just as much as the land."

I sat in the dirt and looked up at her, feeling small, a child again. "I know."

I watched her walk back into the house, her short, greying hair catching sunlight. Now here I am, far from home with a bottle of prairie soil still on my nightstand. It's the worst kind of loss for a Cree mom, splitting apart from her child. For her, it turned out to be the first nightmare of many.

"Well, if you don't call to tell her this, call to check in," Auntie says, her voice higher than usual. Trying to be casual. I nod into the phone, knowing she can't see me.

"I gotta go back in, my girl. Stella will steal my good dabber if I'm gone for too long."

We laugh again and it's all the medicine I need. I hear the scraping of her foot against concrete, stamping out her cigarette.

"Kisâkihitin," she says. "I'll call you soon. And tell me if it happens again."

"I love you, too."

When we hang up, she sends me a praying hands emoji and a shooting star. I respond with a thumbs-up.

I eat a couple of old chips from my cupboard for dinner, not hungry enough for anything more. When it gets late and I can't put it off anymore, I take my time getting ready for bed, scared of where sleep might take me. I slide my jeans off slowly. Pull my shirt over my head and hold the cotton in my hands. Rub it across my palms, soothing the faint burn under my skin. I stare at my hands until they blur before pulling on a thick sweater and sweatpants, a double pair of socks. In case the dreams take me again. I leave the light on when I get into bed and pull the covers up under my chin. It's only then I realize I'd been getting ready in complete silence, no music or audiobook playing. Outside, a crow caws.

I don't want to fall asleep for fear of where I'll end up. I think back to my conversations with Joli and Auntie Doreen. I know they believe me, but the way their voices changed when I mentioned Sabrina makes me doubt. They know as well as I do that in four weeks, it'll be a year since Sabrina died. I wish I'd fought harder through the crows, run faster, got to her earlier. Something crumbles inside me and I sob into my pillow. Not even in my dreams could I save her.

ᓀᐦ

You can always tell the time of day in Vancouver by the crows. In winter, they fly to roost in Burnaby at 5 p.m., at 8 p.m. in summer. They move through the sky like a thunder cloud, collecting more kin as they fly home.

I stand and watch from the entrance of my apartment as a murder forms on a thick, old cedar, much too early for the crows to be roosting. Especially here, right outside my place. The crows' calls slice in from all directions, from the city and the ocean, as they take over every limb of the tree, their bodies blacking out all the green of the leaves. A swarm of warnings. If I didn't know any better, I would swear it was the reckoning.

A man from my building, whom I know only from the laundry room, comes out front to watch them, too. "Must be an owl close," he says.

I don't respond but he clarifies anyways. "They'd only get together like this for an enemy."

I think back to my dream and a fact I've known forever. "They come together if one of their own dies," I say.

"Yeah," he says, "but not just to mourn. They gather for revenge. To find who killed their friend."

I want to tell him that nehiyawak have an enemy in ôhô. That they mean death for us Cree people, too. But I already know the white-man reaction to information like this. And I know the crows aren't looking for an owl, they're looking for me. As if on cue, all the crows' heads turn to look at me. In the quiet of their eyes, I see myself, and I'm aware with a knowing as deep as my history that they really, truly see me. Dread forms on the inside of my skin, claws its way up into the roots of my hair, raises goosebumps across my arms. I want to tell them that I'm sorry for killing their sibling in my dream, that I was only trying to save my own sister. But the dread cements my feet, shuts my mouth. The man doesn't seem to notice.

I turn away and start walking toward work. My breathing eases as I get further away from the crows. I keep my eyes trained on the trees lining the road and hear a soft caw following behind me, far enough back that it's never directly overhead, but close enough to make sure I know it's there.

When I walk into Whole Foods, the sound of the busy store envelops me, but I keep my attention on the crow that followed me here, perched on a tree branch outside the front windows, a black spot on my periphery. I startle when Joli walks up to me.

"Whoa, easy." They take a step back at my slight jump.

"Sorry," I say. "I didn't see you."

"Did you talk to your aunts or mom?" They study my face, combing their hair with their fingers.

"I talked to Auntie Doreen."

They pull on a hair knot. "And?"

"She's not a goddamn dream oracle, apparently. She needs to think on it."

Joli snort laughs. "Would help if she was."

"You're telling me."

"What about everyone else?"

"I don't know," I say. My throat tightens. "I don't really talk to Mom or Tracey these days."

Joli nods. The sad look on their face makes me want to hide. I see the crow flap its wings in the corner of my vision.

"We'll talk more after work," I say, not wanting to think about this anymore. "I'm almost late."

They nod and let me walk away without a fuss. I put my bag in the staff room and grab my till, bring it to my assigned checkout. I flick on the switch illuminating the number 8 above my head. I try to count my float, but my movements feel delayed. I have to think about switching the bills from one hand to the other before it happens. Over and over, I move money and count in my head. Every breath I take seems harder than the last, and I struggle not to look as the crow keeps moving between branches outside. I finally turn my back to the window and steady my eyes to my station, to the racks filled with organic mints and gum.

Auntie's words ring through my head like a homing beacon: *You'd wake up in the morning and your eyes wouldn't see me. Like they hadn't left the dream yet.* I used to have weird nightmares when I was a kid that I called my darkness dreams. In these dreams, I would wake suspended, floating in space. I could open my eyes and see the darkness around me, but I couldn't move my body. I'd just float and look around, try to breathe and figure out if I was still asleep or dead. Sometimes things would visit me in the dreams. A shape of a person would come and push on my chest, bugs would fly around my face, shadows inked against the dark. But the dreams would always end, eventually. I would breathe and count to ten, jerk my body awake, and lay in a sweat on my bed, refusing to allow sleep to take me again.

When I was nine, I had a darkness dream where rats were eating Sabrina. I was suspended then, too, hanging in a void.

Sabrina floated in front of me, her eyes wide. Rats—hundreds of them—crawled across her body. They ran over her stomach, nibbling at her skin. They chattered and hissed to each other, talked low about where they wanted to burrow. I tried to move toward her by using the breathe-and-count method, tried to pound my fists and beat the rats away. But nothing worked, I couldn't move. For hours, the rats crawled across her skin, through her hair, while we floated in nothingness together. I tried to tell her with my mind that it would all be okay, that the dream would be over soon, but her terrified eyes just saw the rats, the blood from their bites forming beads across her skin.

Finally, I woke up, screaming, to Sabrina crying at the foot of my bed. When I held her against me, I felt the heat from her body. My mom came running into the room, panicked eyes looking into every dark corner. Sabrina told her rats chewed through her stomach, and Mom lifted her shirt, ran her fingers over smooth skin.

The next morning, Dad set rat traps around our rooms. Sabrina got a fever so high, Mom had to take her to the hospital. She stayed there for two days with an IV drip, tubes attached to her veins. On her second day in the hospital, a rash formed across her chest and she struggled to breathe. The doctors said it was an allergic reaction to something but Mom didn't believe them. Me and Tracey stayed in the hospital bed, slept on either side of Sabrina, keeping watch. Tracey said in her dream that night, she had felt the bites, too. Mom told an Elder, and they gave her a dreamcatcher. She hung it above the hospital bed, slept on the couch in the room, believed us.

When her temperature finally went down and the rash started to go away, Sabrina came home. Dad cleaned up the empty rat traps from our room and we watched her closely for weeks after that, afraid that at any moment the rats would take her again. She seemed a little harder after that, even then, her jaw locking shut like Mom's after something bad. I wish that was the worst thing that ever happened to her.

The dreams I'm having now are different. I can move and speak. But both types feel like a warning, a deep siren of something to come.

The crow's caw from outside brings me back to reality. In front of my till a line has formed.

"Hello?" A woman impatiently waves her hands in front of my face. My legs shake, and I hold on to the side of my station.

"Sorry." I start to ring through her items without really seeing them.

When someone dies, you stop remembering them fully. When I try to conjure Sabrina in my mind, I only see her in parts. I see the dark split ends of her hair. Her hooked nose. Her hand as it gripped a paintbrush, moving it across a canvas. Her arm reaching out to poke a cousin, teasing them into giving her bites of their food. But I can't remember her whole and complete all at once.

As usual, the thought of Sabrina, in parts or not, brings an ache to my gut. The last time I had a darkness dream was the night before she died. She and I were suspended in the void again and I couldn't move, but this time I watched as a frost crept over her body, until she was completely white except for the blue of her veins. The ache now is more than a missing. It's the same hollow feeling of total helplessness I had when I watched as Sabrina turned to ice in front of me.

At the end of my shift, I'm more tired than usual. I lock up the front doors and grab my backpack from the staff room, spot Joli waiting by the back door. Their sharp eyes tell me I look as exhausted as I feel. They put the back of their hand to my forehead before I have a chance to stop them. I push it away lazily.

"A little warm. You should rest."

I grab their arm and we walk out of the store together. "I'm fine."

"Let me give you a ride home, at least."

"I live four blocks from here."

"I know that. But it's late and you're burning up."

"You just said I'm a little warm."

They look at me like I'm a child giving them attitude and then nod to their car in the parking lot, pulling their keys out of their tote. Behind them, I hear wings beating against air.

"Okay, okay," I say, trying to act calm. "Let's go, then."

In their car I tell them more about the call with my auntie. "I just need to wait until she comes up with a game plan," I say, as if the problem is hers now. Joli nods but doesn't say anything. It starts to sprinkle rain as I get out. Joli waits until I get inside the building's front doors before they drive away.

Inside my apartment, I lock the door behind me and double-check my patio door is locked, too. The wind picks up against the windows. The whistling reminds me of Sabrina's scream. I think I hear scratching on the patio, but when I look outside, there's nothing, just my small camping chair with the broken arm and an empty planter. The scratching comes again and I think I see something move in the darkness. A shiver crawls across my back. I close the curtains, fear bubbling in.

The rain starts falling heavier, and I fill the kettle with water, find a tea bag in my bare cupboards. I'm still so tired, but my body is in panic mode, trying to figure out where the danger is.

I replace the half-full bowl of water in the corner of the apartment that catches the leak when it rains. I wrap myself in my blanket. The blue and white patches are starting to tear at the seams and the cotton insides are coming out in tufts. I grab my laptop from my nightstand and go to my photos, a niggling feeling in the back of my head.

In the photo album marked "home," I start to scroll. I scan the old photos. The most recent is from three years ago. I look into the faces of my mom and dad, Sabrina and Tracey, cousins, aunties and uncles. Even though they're fraternal twins, I'm always shocked at how different my sisters look. Sabrina's angled face, long hair, her body tall and built like a tree, like our mom. Tracey is short, her shoulder-length hair always pushed back like it had somewhere to go. Her big cheeks reach right up into her eyes when she smiles, beaming in any direction she looks.

Sabrina was born first, and she came out like a gunshot. At least, that's how Mom tells it. She was quick and didn't fuss. Frowned as she got cleaned up. Tracey made a whole show of it. For an hour she worked her way out. Tried coming out upside down and sideways. Took her time to get it right. When she finally arrived, the cord was wrapped around her neck so tight she was purple. The doctor said if she was in there much longer, she would have died, so it was lucky Sabrina came out as quick as she did.

When Mom laid them next to each other, she thought they'd hold hands or move toward each other, the natural pull of having formed in a body together. But they didn't reach out. They just stared and stared like it was the first time they'd ever met. Two pieces of skin on either side of an open wound considering how to reconnect again.

Even though my dad isn't their birth father, I see him in the bridges between their eyes. They furrow their faces in the same way, a permanent wrinkle between their eyebrows, like they're always scowling, or thinking. Tracey and Sabrina were a year old when my parents got together, and then they had me a year later. Dad always loved us the same. Maybe it was because he was raised by a stepdad, too. He knew the kind of love that existed beyond blood. I didn't know me and my sisters had different dads until the kids started saying it at school. Mom was mad, but Dad said we should know. I don't know how I missed it. My light skin, the way I was treated better everywhere we went. "We always knew," Tracey said to me one day. "Of course you didn't. It's easy to miss something if you're never targeted for your difference."

The kettle whistles, and in the dark kitchen I pour my tea. My feet stick to the laminate floor as I stir in a spoonful of sugar. I double-check the front door is locked again before feeling my way back to bed.

The leak has finally let go, and the calming *tick tick tick* of water dripping into the bowl starts to drone. Outside my window, I hear a flutter and the scratch of claws on wood. My breathing goes shallow. I turn on my music again, trying to drown out the sound, as if it would mean it isn't happening.

I pull my laptop back over my knees and keep scrolling until I come across photos of my family at ayahciyiniw sâkahikan. Mom and Dad on the shores of the sprawling water. My sisters cutting cattails growing out near piers. Aunties holding fishing rods in one hand and babies in the other.

There were a thousand lakes in Alberta, but when we said "the lake," it could only ever mean one. Ayahciyiniw sâkahikan is the first left turn after the "Leaving High Prairie" sign when you head south out of town. The gravel road leads past marshland, cattails standing at stern attention in small ponds and creeks. After Grouard, the hamlet where our kokum was stolen away to residential school, the first right down an even smaller dirt road leads to the lake.

My first-ever memory is of being at the lake. Me and my family spent almost as much time there as we did at our own house, especially in summer. It's only a twenty-minute drive from High

Prairie, but to us it felt like a different world. It signalled the end of nine months of winter, it meant campfires, sleeping against the curve of the lake, picking wild daisies.

Being by the lake is different from being by the ocean. The ocean announces itself, the steady sound of waves letting you know it's near and ready. By the lake, the noise comes from everything around it. Trees rustling in the wind, birds and bugs chirping. The lake itself, though, stays quiet unless big winds or nearby boats disturb the water into lapping the shore. It watches more than it speaks.

Most people camp at the lake's provincial parks and public campsites, but that costs money. Our camp spot was the same every year: through a hidden turnoff into the bush. After a short walk through the trees, there was a perfect clearing right next to the water. Three jack pines grew out from the waterline, their trunks forming together at the base, which you could spot from miles away. It was mostly sand and rock, with a flat area for setting up tents and a fire. We were far enough away from other people, but still close enough to walk to the other campsites, if we wanted to.

Trails spread through the woods like mycelium underground, like veins across a body, connecting everything in every direction: to and away from the lake, running along the length of the water, and sometimes, I swear, right up into the sky. We probably walked every one of those trails a hundred times, but that doesn't mean we ever grew tired of them.

I keep scrolling and find more family photos. I enlarge an old photo of me, Tracey, Sabrina, and my cousin Kassidy, Auntie Doreen's daughter, in the blue wagon kokum got for us one summer. The memory of the day kokum brought us the wagon burns bright in my mind. Kassidy was eight, I was nine, and Tracey and Sabrina had just turned eleven. It was our first time out on the lake that summer. Me and Mom, the aunties, Kassidy, and my sisters had come out earlier to set up camp. The uncles were getting our food for the weekend and Dad was still on the road, driving in for the weekend from an electrician job up north.

By the shore, me, Tracey, and Kassidy were digging holes next to the water. Sabrina sat against the cluster of jack pines, reading a book about trees. She was already reading at a grade-seven level and read anything about plants she could get her hands on. I don't think I ever saw her that summer without a book in her hands.

We looked up when we heard a crunch coming from the trail that led to our campsite. Kokum emerged from the woods like a creature from the deep. With a cigarette in her hand, she swatted at the mosquitoes in front of her while pulling a giant blue wagon behind her.

Kokum was shorter than all of her daughters, though she didn't look it, and she was all teeth. Her real teeth rotted out as a kid, and when she got her dentures, they were too big and too white for her mouth. I think I fell in love with her teeth first. How they were so even and moved to the sound of the room. She used to call them a weapon. "Stronger than regular teeth," she would say. "Can bite right through bone. Don't ask me how I know." Her party trick was putting her teeth in our water cups when we weren't looking, laughing when we'd spot the enamel staring back as we put our lips to the glass.

She wheeled the wagon over to the campfire and whistled at us, even though we were already watching her. We normally were, whenever she walked into a space. She waved her hand in front of the wagon like a magician, the smoke from her cigarette curling around her body.

We all dropped the sticks we were using as shovels and ran over to her. Sabrina left her book right on the ground.

Mom, hearing the whistle, came out from inside one of the tents she was setting up. "Holy, where the hell did you get that?"

Kokum smirked over her shoulder at my mom while her grandkids circled her in hugs. "Kokum has her ways."

Auntie Verna popped her head out of a tent next to Mom's. "There's no way that's going to fit all those kids. They're not babies anymore, you know."

"Watch your tongue," kokum said, taking a drag of her cigarette. "These babies will fit just fine." I breathed her in as she talked to my mom and aunties. Even with all us kids pushing against her, she was sturdy like the trees she just came through. Her chest moved under my head as I pressed into her harder.

"Okay, let's take this out for a spin." She grabbed Sabrina by the hand and helped the rest of us get into the wagon. The cigarette, mostly ash, dangled from the side of her mouth, moving up and down as she talked. She started wheeling us back to the trail.

"Don't worry about us," Mom yelled, "we'll make sure to get everything cleaned and set up."

"Thanks, my girl." Kokum waved behind her. "We're just gonna walk for a couple High Prairie minutes." That's what kokum used to call walking the trails through the woods.

Mom rolled her eyes. "Well, how long is that?"

"The minutes take as long as they need to!"

A minute to her was the distance between two trail openings on the lake. No two openings in particular. It was just the amount of time it took to get from one trail leading from the woods to the water and the next one. Sometimes these openings were only a few feet apart, sometimes they took forever.

This is how I learned the trails around the lake, how I started to make myself a part of their paths. Before we had the wagon, we'd just walk, and she'd point out plants and what they could do, tell us stories and jokes.

"Wapanewask," she said once, pointing at the ground to a yellow stalk sprouting tiny, white flowers growing in a plume. "Your mom's favourite. Fitting. Yarrow is stubborn, like her. Only grows where it wants, doesn't take orders from anybody."

Sabrina wrote down everything kokum told us about plants. She even drew sketches and, eventually, started painting them. Me, Kass, and Tracey were more interested in her stories.

Sometimes she'd take us on a long walk right before we were supposed to be leaving, when Mom and the aunties were packing up the campsite. By the time we got back, it would be late.

"We only walked a couple minutes!" kokum would say when Mom got mad at her.

Mom shook her head. "A couple minutes, my ass," she said as she started to unpack, setting up camp again for us to stay one more night.

"It's not the only way to measure time," kokum said once. "Sometimes time is measured in the days between phone calls with your kokum, which should never be very many. Sometimes it's the measure of a heartbeat."

The wheels squeaked as kokum took us down the trail for the first time in our new wagon. After a couple minutes, the trail forked. Going straight would lead us to the road where we left the cars. Kokum took us right, where the lake turned into marsh, and then into rivers and creeks that opened like fingers spread right through Grouard. The water was connected to everything, even though from our campsite we could only see a fraction of it.

Me, Kassidy, and Tracey fit comfortably in the wagon next to each other. We could have fit Sabrina, too, but she wanted to walk next to kokum, help her pull the wagon and look at the plants up close.

Kokum swatted at a mosquito on Sabrina's arm. "Damn mosquitoes are bad this year," she said, rubbing where she just hit.

"They just love that Cree blood." She looked back at us in the wagon and winked. We all giggled, but I laughed the loudest, the way kokum taught me.

Once, I had laughed with my hand over my mouth because my teacher told me an open mouth was a rude mouth. Kokum gently moved my hand from my face and told me to laugh like I was blowing air into a giant balloon, as open and as hard as I could. She said that if my teacher ever told me to cover my mouth again, I should tell her and she'd take care of it.

We rode along the trail, kokum smoking and telling us stories about the lake, pointing out areas where she used to bring the aunties and Mom when they were just kids like us, the size of the fish they used to catch, the time they saw maskwa and her cub. The moss and trees muffled our talks, like we were in a cozy room together rather than out in the open.

We'd stop every now and then when she'd point out a flower or plant. Sabrina stroked the newly bloomed petals of a wild rose. "Okiniyi," she said, and kokum nodded, proud. It was still early summer, but the pink of the roses could be spotted everywhere through the trees.

Whenever we passed a trail that opened back to the lake, we'd catch a glimpse of water and count out loud together: one, two, three High Prairie minutes.

"Always do this if you go for a walk," kokum said, "to remember how far you're getting from your campsite. Count the trails to the water, remember the minutes." She talked and talked and pulled Sabrina close, trailing her hair with her hand. She looked back at us in the wagon when we got too quiet, and she'd always look right at me. She had the softest eyes, and when she held me in them, I knew that no one else in the entire world could ever love me like she did.

Kokum was pointing out a ohtihmina vine, the small strawberries still a while off from flowering, when Sabrina let go of her hand and walked forward, staring into the empty trail in front of us. Kokum stopped and looked up after her.

"What is it, my girl?" Fallen pine cones and sticks crunched under her feet as she closed the distance between them.

"I think mosum is walking with us, too."

If kokum was surprised to hear this, she didn't show it. "What do you mean?"

Our mosum had died from a heart attack a few years earlier. He was a big, soft man who was always chewing tobacco and making kokum laugh. Even though kokum was always laughing anyways, she never laughed as hard as she did with him. Sabrina described the man she saw. A tall, brown man in a red shirt, which is what gave him away. Mosum wore that red shirt on every important occasion, the loose collar and three buttons undone from the top, a gold cross hanging in the centre of his chest.

"Mosum is standing right there," she said, pointing. "He's laughing into the sky, but the sound is coming out like thunder. Does anyone else hear it?"

When no one answered, she looked scared. Somewhere in the woods, a robin sang.

Kokum smiled the scare away and pulled Sabrina into a hug. "It's okay, my girl. Mosum is just telling us a storm is coming." She looked into the sky then and we all looked up, too. The sun beat down hard against thin wisps of white clouds. They were spread out in impossibly straight lines around the sun, a rib cage around a heart. Otherwise, the sky was clear.

"Let's head back, count the minutes as we go," she said.

Kokum turned the wagon around and pulled us back down the trail toward our camp, faster than before, not stopping to point out plants or tell stories. The squeaking of the wheels quickened with each turn, and we all counted the minutes at each glimpse of water. The minutes seemed to shrink, like time was an elastic band someone let go after pulling it too tight for too long.

After the final minute, just as we got to our trail and turned down toward the water, we heard a rumble from above. The air hung heavy as we left the brush and broke into the campsite. We jumped out of the wagon and left it by the trees, running toward the tents. Mom and the aunties were tying off a tarp between a couple trees when they saw us.

Kassidy was running slower than the rest of us, so kokum scooped her up. The rumble sounded again, louder and closer. The heat held above our heads like a broken thought. The sky snapped just as we made it under the tarp, the rain pouring around us in buckets.

"Just in time," Auntie Doreen said, pulling Kassidy from kokum's arms and into her own. "You're damn lucky you didn't get caught in that. That came out of nowhere."

Kokum held me and my sisters in front of her as we all looked out into the sky, now rolling with thick storm clouds. Lightning cracked and we counted out loud together until we heard the thunder come after it, measuring how far away the storm was. After each line of lightning formed above us, we only counted to three before hearing the thunder. Deep in my chest, I felt mosum's laughter move like a wave from the base of my spine and out my own mouth.

I stare at the photo of me and my cousin and sisters in the wagon, so many years of walking High Prairie minutes not yet stitched into our skin. Then I scroll down to another photo from years later, the summer before I left for Vancouver. It was the last summer we spent together, taken right in front of the three jack pines. I'm in between Sabrina and Tracey, my arms around their shoulders. The sun is big in the sky and we're not smiling.

In the photo, the lake stretches like it's spreading its arms around us, too. The water is never-ending, touching the clouds on the horizon in the distance. Sabrina's face looks back from my computer screen. I zoom in on her and see something I never noticed before. Right below her left collarbone, a cut, already scabbed and healing. A long, deep red against her brown skin. Dimpled, like a piece of her had been pecked out. In the reflection of her eyes, I see the tree line of pines and fir behind her. The woods, with every trail and story we knew as well as we knew ourselves.

A thought lodged in the back of my gut comes loose: *These are the woods from my dreams.*

σⁿⅭ

I sleep fitfully, thinking about kokum and the photos. In the early hours of the morning, I lie in bed, exhausted, listening to the sound of rain leaking through my ceiling, slowly dripping and filling the bowl.

The winter before I left High Prairie, kokum died. Kokum had moved from her old farm outside of High Prairie to live with us after she was diagnosed with end-stage liver cancer. In the year she became a part of our home, time both stopped and sped up. We had her forever and only a minute. She was alive, full, present, and then she shapeshifted into nothing. There was no measure of time that made it make sense.

An Indian dying is like a balsam fir getting chopped down. Trees for miles and miles feel the pain under the soil. They send their reserve nutrients through the root network to the stump, which closes over with bark like a scab. Eventually, the stump turns into a nursery, a home for new growth, for something else to take shape. This isn't the same as healing or being reborn, but it's the closest we'll ever get.

But there was no comfort when kokum died. Family came in from everywhere, trying to give us their strength, and still it never felt like enough. Older relatives spoke about death with reverence.

Cree people know that this life is just one stop on a longer road. But I couldn't bring myself to understand like everyone else seemed to. Kokum was my parent, just as much as my mom and dad. She was a part of my life, like waking up and going to sleep at night. And then all at once, she wasn't. Sabrina and Tracey were the only other ones who looked the way I felt: empty, gutted, alone.

Even as the cold of winter dissipated into spring and then summer, our hurt stayed. Everyone tried to pretend we could go on as before, but the hollowness stuck. I left for Vancouver in the fall, hoping that not having to see my own hurt on their faces anymore might offer some relief. I thought that I could leave the bad behind. But I guess the bad isn't a thing you can run from, because it's not a thing that can be held. It doesn't announce itself, there's no siren or beacon. Instead, it's a steady beating, like a heart or a drum. It's a sound that lives in the body and grows down into the ground.

That's the best and worst thing about being connected to everything: you are a part of it all, but you can't choose what gets sent out into the world. Or what can find you.

Light streams in from outside as the day breaks, speckling my bedsheets. I want to move, get out of bed and start the day, but every time I blink, I see the wood trails I grew up walking, the same woods from my dreams, and the scar on Sabrina's chest.

A shadow of wings passes through the light. When I stand, my bones crack as if I've been sleeping for a hundred years. My brain is fogged and I stutter around the apartment. The exhaustion from the past three weeks is catching up with me. I call in sick for my shift and start to hack out a cough for real. It comes out in a dry, deep caw.

Joli texts, asking if I'm okay.

I'm fine, I respond. *Just wanted some time off work to do some running around.*

Five bucks you're still at home, they text back.

I'm out! Shopping.

Prove it.

I sigh and share my location, allowing GPS to snitch on my lie. There's a beat before Joli responds. *You owe me five bucks. You ok?*

Self-care day, I text back instead. *I'll call you later.*

I look up crow facts online and devour all the information. One website says that older sibling crows will help their parents raise the newborns. A pain starts to inch up my neck, planting itself in my jaw. In school, I used to follow Sabrina and Tracey around like my life depended on it. I didn't make friends easily. It seemed like too much effort when I already had my sisters and cousins, people to love me no matter what. They took me with them wherever they went, fierce in their love, like I was a part of their bodies from the very start.

I order takeout and pace my apartment. I stare at my mom's number on my phone and press the call button but hang up before it can ring. I wash my face, balancing my phone on the edge of the sink, almost hoping it will fall and crack. I think about calling again but keep pacing the length of my apartment instead, counting the steps between my front door and the patio. Finally, I lie back in bed and call her. With the phone against my cheek, I close my eyes. It only rings once before she picks up, like she was waiting for it.

"Hello?"

The sound of her voice is an ache.

"Hey, Mom." My voice cracks into the phone. "Did Sabrina have a scar under her collarbone?"

"Good afternoon to you, too." She sounds tired, worried.

"Sorry. Hi. How are you?"

She's quiet for a beat. "Okay."

"Sorry, Mom. I haven't been sleeping well. Did she?"

She's silent for another moment and I hear her take a sip of coffee on the other end of the phone. I imagine her at her usual spot at the end of the kitchen table, her arms wrapped around herself in her robe, the phone cradled to her ear.

"No," she says finally. "Not that I can remember."

Blood rushes to my face. "Okay, I'm sending you a photo. It's from our last summer at the lake, before I left. Zoom in on Sabrina's collarbone. What is that?"

I hear the rustle of Mom's robe as she shifts in her chair, the tick of her nails on her phone as she opens the photo message. She breathes in a deep sigh, as if to steady herself. Sometimes, I have to do that, too, before I can look at photos of Sabrina.

She tsks. "Yeah, that looks like a cut, but I don't remember it. Or her having a scar in that spot. Maybe it's a glint of the sun or something."

"A glint of sunlight on her skin?"

"Maybe it's something on the camera?"

"Well, it's a photo of a photo on a computer, it makes it look all weird, let me send you—"

"Did you ever end up going to that grief counsellor Dianne recommended?"

My grip on the phone tightens. When Sabrina died, I didn't go back home for her funeral. Mom convinced Dianne to try to get me to go to an Indigenous counsellor she knew, but I never went. "No."

"Grief comes in waves, and the anniversary of her death is coming up."

"That isn't it, Mom."

"You said you haven't been sleeping." I hear the worry creeping into her voice again. I'm silent on the other end of the phone for too long, thinking about whether or not I should tell her about the dreams. She inhales sharply, probably from turning or moving too fast. Pain is woven into her body, built into her blood and bones.

"You should retire soon," I say.

She laughs. "Retire at fifty? What world are you living in?"

Mom works at the detox centre in town. She was first there as a patient, when we were kids, when she couldn't stop taking pills that helped her sleep. Now she's a nursing assistant and the work is heavy, on her body and her mind.

I sigh. "Do you ever have weird dreams?" I ask.

I hear the creaking of the old kitchen chair as she leans against the table. I imagine her cracked hands running through her hair. "I taught myself how to stop dreaming when I was a young iskwew. My dreams were always bad, and always true."

I freeze. "How?" I ask. "How did you stop dreaming?"

She laughs. "Sheer will, my girl. You've got stubborn blood running through you, too."

"But they were always true? What do you mean?" I press.

Mom's quiet again, and I hear cups clattering against shelves. She's gotten up from the table, is putting dishes in cupboards, already moving away from our conversation. Another sharp intake of air and something crashes to the counter. She must have moved too quickly, a muscle pulling the wrong way.

"At least go down to part time."

Mom snorts into the phone.

"They have a full staff and extra volunteers," I say.

The line is quiet while she deciphers what I'm really trying to say.

"Tracey is doing fine. She works with me at the centre on weekends and is still playing music."

Tracey started drinking in high school, but it didn't get bad until the year kokum lived with us while she was sick. She got sober a few months after kokum died, then relapsed last year when we lost Sabrina. Mom got her the job at the detox centre, since that's what helped with her own sobriety. She says Tracey has been sober for months now, but I haven't spoken to her since she found out I wasn't coming back for Sabrina's funeral. I'm too scared to hear what she would say. I can't face her knowing that I had a chance to come home, to hold some of the pain left in the wake of our sister's death, and I didn't. I'm happy she's doing better, but I don't blame her for relapsing. It's the bad that has been passed down and passed down and passed down, that weaves itself into the marrow of our bones. A bad inflicted on us, one we have no business carrying. But it's heavy. And we're all just coping with it in the ways we know how.

"You can always ask her about this scar of Sabrina's. If anyone will know for sure, it's Tracey."

In the quiet of the connection between us, we both know I won't.

"Jesus," she says. "You two are so much alike, you'd think you were the twins."

I laugh. "She'd hate to hear you say that."

We talk for a few more minutes. Clipped questions and answers about our lives. But it's strained. We never talk about my not coming home when I should have, but the fact of it is always there.

"I'll let you get going," I say when the conversation starts to grow quiet. "Give Dad a hug for me."

"Sure," she says, a sadness in her voice. "I'll ask him about Sabrina's cut, too. In the meantime, get some sleep, okay?"

"Okay."

"And call more often. I love you."

The next day I call in sick from work again and start watching superhero movies and taking notes. After my call with Mom,

I've been thinking about my dreams. Maybe I was looking at them in the wrong light. What if, instead of being something awful, the ability to bring things back from the dream world is a power? I order takeout for breakfast and lunch, make a mess of the kitchen I cleaned only a few days ago. I lie in bed, watching shows on my laptop and barely moving. By the end of *Superman, Spider-Man, Batman,* and *The Avengers,* I've written down "with great power comes great ???" and I've made a list of possible ways one might acquire a power:

1. bitten by a bug
2. parents died or I get a bunch of money somehow
3. non-consensual scientific experiments
4. industrial accidents
5. aliens/gods (what's the difference?)

I know I can rule a few things out. My parents are still alive and I have no money. I haven't been in any accidents, and I can't recall being the subject of any experiments, scientific or otherwise. A bug bite is the only thing that could have happened without my knowing.

I strip off all my clothes and stand an inch away from the mirror by my bed, examining my body. My skin looks even more pale in the dull, pulsing glow of lamplight. I lean closer, running my hands across the acne scars on my face. The ditches and curves that move with my mouth are familiar, but I feel like I'm seeing the rest of my body for the first time. My shoulder-length brown hair, thick and oily from being unwashed for so long, seems darker, more coarse than usual. Stretch marks line my belly and underneath my arms like something on my skin is about to sprout. I hear the crows on the telephone pole chattering to one another.

Darkness from outside inches into the apartment. My stomach twists in guilt at the day wasted watching movies and living in memories of dead people. Still naked, I cut a magnifying glass out of the bottom of a plastic pop bottle from my takeout, an idea I found on the internet. I hop in the shower and sit hunched in the tub, catching a little bit of water in the cut-out bottle. I trace the bottle bottom over my legs, starting a meticulous search of my body.

I see myself close-up, maybe for the first time ever. I envision my body cut up into sections and go over the magnified version of my skin, bit by careful bit. I feel bigger with each minute I spend looking. I find freckles and beauty marks that I've never seen. I don't know how to distinguish what has been there for years from what might be new. I'm shocked when I recognize nothing.

I turn the water hotter and plug the drain, so the tub starts to slowly fill. I abandon the makeshift magnifying glass in the water and instead start to feel, running my hands over every bump and fold on my body from my feet to my scalp. I stare at my hardened knees and the lines on my palms. Press on the parts that still hurt—the underneath hurt that you can't see. I think about the superhero movies and wonder why I started on research that points to the answer being something outside myself, something that happened to me, instead of something that was inside me all along.

When the water fills high enough to cover me, I get out. I list everything I've found on my body in a notebook with the date. So next time I have to look, I won't be surprised again.

I'm lying in bed listening to an audiobook on the inner life of bees when I hear the noise from my kitchen. *Shuk shuk shuk*. I press pause on the book, unsure if the sound came from the recording. But then I hear it again, crawling out from the shadows—*shuk shuk shuk*—and I feel my body tense in fear. I recognize it right away: coins in an empty tobacco tin. Three shakes in the darkness.

As a kid, almost every night, kokum, mosum, Mom and Dad, and the aunties and uncles would gamble together. Play poker until the sun stretched out in the morning. No matter where they were—my parents' house, kokum's trailer, the lake—they'd play. All they needed was a table and a deck of cards.

Kokum always started the games. She'd disappear down the hall and then we'd hear it: the rattle of coins she kept in her Player's tobacco tin. She'd shake it as she walked down the hallway. *Shuk shuk shuk.* Nice and slow, a signal and a warning. That gave the aunties enough time to move the kids to the living room, where blankets on the floor made our beds. *Shuk shuk shuk.* Just enough time for Mom to grab the worn-out deck of cards from the kitchen drawer.

Kokum would stroll into the kitchen, *shuk shuk shuk,* shaking the tobacco tin. She'd put on her cowboy hat with the leather band that wrapped around twice, held in place by a silver buckle, a glint from the silver casting beams of light on the ceiling as she tipped the hat over her eyes. She'd put the tin of change next to her, pull out quarters and loonies for her buy-in. She was the resident banker for the house, trading in everyone's bills for coins so they could play, too, keeping stock of who owed what.

My sisters and cousins and I would watch from pretend sleep while the kitchen glowed with cigarette smoke and the boom of laughter, listen to the flip and shuffle of cards and glasses filling with liquid. We'd watch as a grocery bag full of dry meat got passed around the table through the din, hands stretching to dip their pieces in a brick of butter. Slivers of meat left behind in the yellowed slab sticking out at all angles. They'd smoke and tap cigarettes into a glass tray, ash growing into hills of snow.

Instead of sleeping, we taught ourselves how to play poker and rummy. We practised shuffling and dealing with our own deck, how to move cards through our hands to the floor and suck them back up like magic. We recited all the good and bad jokes to each other, copied how the adults threw their heads back in wide-mouthed laughter, and tried to guess how much of a fortune was in kokum's Player's tin that started and ended the night.

"Who wants to buy in?" Sabrina whispered one night to a circle of small, chubby faces looking up at her from underneath sheets and sleeping bags.

We probably didn't even have to whisper. It was hours after the aunties had put us to bed, and the cackling from the kitchen filled every inch and corner of kokum's trailer. A bright cone of light lit up the floor where the curtain that separated the living room from the kitchen was slightly open, giving us just enough light to see each other's eager eyes.

Tracey pulled out a deck of cards from her blanket and Sabrina stuck her hand underneath the couch. After a few seconds of fishing around, she came out with a big container of Tums. She gave it a little shake, coins clinking inside.

My cousins laughed and held their hands out to Tracey, clumsily shuffling the deck.

"We don't have any money," Kassidy said to Sabrina from beside me. She scrunched up her nose and shrugged into her pillow. Sabrina smiled. She was tall and gangly. Her pyjamas, which fit fine a couple months ago, were now too tight. She had callused elbows and was all edges, like her bones were waiting for her skin to shed. She flipped open the whole top of the Tums container and poured out some of the coins inside: pennies, nickels, dimes, and a couple quarters, dusty with the white powder, spilled out into the middle of the circle. Sabrina divided up the money at random, making sure each of us had four coins.

"The game is pass the ace," Tracey said, looking like the jack of spades with a sheet pulled over her head. She dealt us one card each. "Winner doesn't get anything, but the loser has to go out there." She pointed with her chin to the door leading to the kitchen. A couple of the cousins gave out low squeals, and Kassidy stifled her laughter and moved closer to me. The warmth of her body was like a heater at my side.

Tracey and Sabrina shushed everyone and took turns explaining the rules. Shadows rippled across their faces as they spoke, commanding the circle of children around them.

I don't remember winning or losing, just playing and eventually falling asleep with cards in my sticky hands and the sound of my family all around me, as if they sprouted and grew from the floor and the walls.

Shuk shuk shuk. The sound comes again from the darkness of my apartment. This isn't the first time I've heard it here. It started happening about a year after I moved in. Sometimes, it will come from the bathroom or right outside my front door. Sometimes, I think it's happening in my head. I'll wake up to the smell of Player's blues and the slap of a hand on a table, flourishing a straight to beat a three of a kind. *Shuk shuk shuk.* I'll wake up and rub my eyes, peering from my bed into the dark kitchen, and I swear sometimes I've even caught a glimpse of a silver buckle glinting in the shadows.

I imagine kokum there, in my kitchen, or my doorway, signalling to me she's on her way. But she never appears with the deck of cards. She never walks out of the shadows, like her death was just a bad joke she's been waiting to reveal all these years. I worry that this place, the solitude of my life in this apartment, in this city, has turned my memories monstrous. That loneliness can make once-beautiful things terrifying.

ᓄᐊᐧ·

When I wake up in the morning, I take a walk down to the beach to clear my head, to try to get the empty in my body to fill. That might be the worst thing about death: it doesn't stop anything. The world keeps moving, even though the pain is just as real as the day it settled in.

The sun peeks out from behind the mountains. I don't know if I'll ever get used to feeling so closed in, surrounded by mountains and the sea. The world looks so small here, like I'm standing in a bowl.

I hear the crows before I see them following me down the street, and I feel the day spill. I pull my hood up and start to run, disappearing into alleyways and looping through side streets. If one of them falls behind, they call to another to take their place, swooping past me, smelling like cedar and rust. Sometimes, when they're close, I can hear them talking.

My apartment is on a hill, up a winding street from the water, and as I run, I see slivers of the ocean between rooftops. Every time I glimpse the water, I count it like a High Prairie minute. My kokum never saw the ocean in her lifetime, and I wonder what she would think of its vastness. Of its never-ending blue.

My phone buzzes in my pocket. I pull it out and see my cousin's name, Kassidy, light up the screen. I slow my run into a walk and answer, out of breath.

"Hello?" Kassidy laughs her hello the way she laughs her way into every room, announcing herself before she's actually there. I hear the bark of her dog, Atim, too, so I know they must have been playing before she called me.

Even though Kassidy is a year younger than me, Tracey and Sabrina used to swear she was always around. As if we all flashed into existence at the same time in the same place.

"Hey, Kass," I say, smiling at the sound of her voice.

"What the hell is going on over there?" she asks. She says it with a piece of her laugh still on her tongue, but her tone is serious.

"Same old, same old." I kick at a rock.

"Really?" she says. "So you usually wake up with a crow's head in your hand?"

I stiffen. "Your mom told you?"

She sighs. "Only because—"

"It's not made up," I cut in. "Or whatever else she might think." My throat tightens. There's a sting behind my eyes but tears don't form. For a split second, I regret telling Auntie Doreen anything.

"Easy," she says. "I don't think it's made up! Neither does my mom."

"Who else have you guys told?" I ask. The sun is hot on my face, but a burning is coming from somewhere else. For some reason, I feel ashamed.

"I see the future in my dreams." She blurts it out quickly, like it's a breath she's been holding in. In the background, I hear Atim bark again, trying to get her attention.

I stop in the middle of the sidewalk. "What?"

The barking continues on her end of the phone. "Quiet, Atim!"

Kassidy yells, the phone muffled. The barking settles and I can imagine him looking up at her expectantly as she sighs into the phone. "It's why my mom told me about you. Because she figured I'd get it. I mean, I'm not out here killing crows, but . . ."

"What do you mean?" I hear the flapping of wings in the sky above me, but I don't look up. "What do you mean you see the future?"

I hear Kassidy swallow. "It started out as small, weird déjà vu moments. Things in real life happening that I already saw in a dream. But I thought it was just coincidences, you know? Then like two years ago, I dreamt I was driving the highway between High Prairie and Peace River. As I was coming up on a hill to an intersection, a truck didn't stop at the stop sign and T-boned me. I woke up screaming, hurt ringing through my body like I've never felt before."

She pauses and I stay quiet, beads of sweat forming on my forehead.

"A week later, I went to Peace River to see my friends, completely forgetting about this dream, right. And then I'm driving home and I'm coming up a hill to the same intersection in my dream, and I remembered. I felt the hurt in my body again, like a reminder, and I hit the brakes. Not five seconds later, that same truck comes flying past that stop sign, but I was stopped and just watched it drive by."

I feel out of breath as she talks, even though I'm still motionless on the sidewalk. "How long has it been happening?"

"For as far back as I can remember," she says, without any laughter in her voice now. "I told my mom a long time ago, but I haven't told anyone other than her, and now you."

"Not even your dad?" Kassidy is Métis on her dad's side.

She sighs into the phone. "You know how tightly wound up

in the church my grandparents are," she says. "I love my dad, but he'd probably just think I was possessed or something."

"Does it still happen?"

"It happens all the time. That was the only life-saving one, though. So far."

A relief starts to form somewhere in my body, like moving water over rocks, so I start walking again. I hold the phone softer to my ear. "What does this mean?"

From the tone of her voice, Kassidy sounds relieved, too. "I don't know. I've been living with this my whole life, basically. But whatever is happening to you sounds different."

When I get to the end of a street, I see a lone crow perched on a sidewalk bench, as if waiting for me. The goosebumps form again, and my breath catches in my throat. "Crows are following me."

Kassidy laughs. "Not exactly what I meant the last time we talked and I said you needed to make more friends," she jokes, and the lightness returns to her voice, making me feel lighter, too.

"I think you should come home," she says. "Maybe it's something we could figure out together."

I stare at the crow for another second before I cross the road, the beach finally coming into full view. The crow lets out a low murmur in its throat and I hear it behind me, the click of its talons as it flies from light pole to light pole, following. The thought of not feeling so alone with all of this makes my pulse skip. But thinking about going home scares me almost as much as the dreams do.

I don't say any of this out loud. "I'll think about it," I say. "Look, I gotta go."

She sighs into the phone. "You don't sound good."

"I'm just tired."

"Tapwe," Kassidy says. "Call me later, okay?"

We hang up and I count myself down to steady my breathing. Kassidy can see the future in her dreams. Even though whatever is happening to me isn't the same, it's something. Would this be easier to figure out together? Is this even something we can figure out? The smell of ocean salt drifts into my nose as I cross a patch of grass to the beach. I try to shove these questions to the back of my mind for now.

The delay in my body I've felt for days clings to me like static as I take off my shoes and dig my heels into the sand, feel the still cold beneath the surface. I have to walk out a fair way to get to the water, the low tide exposing dead crabs and the small holes in the sand where the live ones hide. Limp seaweed and shells look less impressive without water. I find a couple of shiny ones and pocket them, give my thanks to the sand.

The waves sound like how regular dreaming feels. Rolling and endless. I go in up to my ankles. The shock of cold sends a flicker through my body, and I feel like I'm coming back into myself. When I was six, my parents put me in swimming lessons with my sisters and Kassidy. Sabrina and Tracey had already been in lessons for two years, so they were in a different part of the pool, and Kassidy was placed in a more advanced group. She'd been swimming in the lake since she was a baby. I was tougher to coax into water. I was put in the lowest group, told that I could be a good swimmer if I learned to trust the water, to let myself go at least enough to float. When I dunked my head below, the pressure on my ears felt like sucking, like I would lose myself in it. It made me feel too alone.

I cried to my sisters and Kassidy that day, told them I wasn't going back in. So every week when Mom would drop us off at the pool, we would go inside and wait behind the doors. After she drove away, we'd walk to the corner store and get one-cent candies, play in the empty field behind the pool, and wait. Just before she came back, we'd wet our hair with an outside tap and wash our tongues, stained from coloured pop rocks. I never learned how to swim but I still wonder what it feels like to be held by another body without fear.

When I turn my back from the shoreline, I see three crows waiting on a bench by the grass, their eyes following me. I consider walking further out into the water where they don't seem to go, but I don't know which I'm more afraid of. As I start to walk back to the grass, my body lags again.

I find a spot underneath an old cedar and sit in the shade, watch the waves wash up on the sand and suck themselves back. I rest against the tree trunk, sink my sand-covered feet back into my shoes, and pull out my phone. I look through old photos of Sabrina, try to find ones where I can see her collarbone. The wind picks up and the cedar sways. I look at its roots poking out of the soil at my feet. Kokum told me once that jack pines have roots up to sixty feet long. "Sturdy like nehiyawak," she said. I wonder how deep cedar roots can go.

The rustle of the branch above me sounds different from the wind, and I see a flash of black feathers through the branches. Seconds later, something falls next to me on the ground. I gasp, thinking at first that the crow has dropped dead right next to me, an omen I don't even want to think about. But the object is smaller, in the shape of a green and white crescent moon. It's a watermelon rind. Chewed down so much that there's no pink flesh left.

Then I hear the sound of two crows speaking low to each other, a language that lives in the back of their throats. A third crow, the only one that's fully visible, appears on a lower branch. It lands and stares at me. I focus my breathing, and though the hairs on my arms are still poking through my shirt, I remember something I read on the crow website: they give gifts to their kin. I open up my Cree dictionary app and look up the word for *crow* in nêhiyawêwin: *âhâsiw.*

"Âhâsiw," I say out loud, looking up at the bird. At once, the crows caw and take off into the sky. One of them shits, the white splat landing in front of me. A woman walking by looks at me like I'm the one who just took a dump in public, and she walks away a little faster.

I don't know what I was expecting. "Âhâsiw," I whisper again to myself. My mouth works around the unfamiliar word. It sounds like it feels: a discovery. I look at the watermelon rind again and shake my head. I search "crows following people" on my phone and watch videos of crows attacking when people have gotten too close to their nest or newborn crow babies. In one, a particularly ornery crow follows someone for blocks, swooping and cawing to scare them away. But these crows aren't attacking me, and they don't seem to want to scare me off. They're just there. Watching. I watch the videos while the salt air and the sound of the wind against the cedar boughs move through me until slowly, without warning, it lulls me to sleep.

When I open my eyes, I'm at our family's camping spot on the lake. The sun is low and the summer heat sticks to the ground. The three jack pines sway in front of me and the water is still. Calm sifts through me, the type of calm that only ever happened here, next to these woods. A breeze picks up and the trees curve like a body bending.

A wave of sadness and joy rises in my chest. It's been years since I've been back in this spot, by this lake. I almost smile before I remember my last dreams, and my pulse quickens. I study the woods more closely, looking for any sign of winter, but the trees are green and brown and full. I listen for the sound of screaming. Nothing but wind and the chirps of birds and insects. *Of course. The one time I fall asleep wearing shoes, I'm not in a pile of snow.*

And then from behind me, I hear it. The sound of shoes on rocks and splashing water.

When I turn around, I'm face-to-face with myself and my sisters. They walk straight toward me in the shape of an arrowhead, Sabrina at the front and dream-Mackenzie and Tracey slightly behind her to the sides.

Everything slows. A yelp escapes my mouth. Sabrina's face lights up with the lowering sun. Her long, dark brown hair falls across her shoulders and down her back. There's a hollow, a sadness in her eyes, too. She pulls her flannel shirt tight around herself as she walks, crunching across the rocks next to the shore. The shock of seeing her fully alive freezes me in place. Air empties from my lungs.

"We're only going for ten minutes," Sabrina says. The sound of her voice drops me to my knees. My heart feels like it drops, too, and tears sting the corners of my eyes. I grip the ground underneath me. Seeing her alive feels like a relief and a shock all at once.

"I'm not walking forty-five minutes to a shitty party to stay for ten minutes," dream-Mackenzie says.

I wipe my eyes and force myself to look away from Sabrina. Dream-Mackenzie walks closer to the trees, rolls up the sleeves on her oversized jean jacket as she goes, looking from the woods and back to her sisters. She walks hunched, unsmiling. I feel like I'm looking at someone I don't even know.

"There's never been a bad party at the gravel pits," Tracey says. She pulls out a mickey of rye from her coveralls and takes a sip. Her eyes are already glazed, a thin film hardening to keep herself safe. Dream-Mackenzie drinks next, while Tracey runs her hand over her round face, gesturing for the bottle's return as soon as dream-Mackenzie is done.

Tracey walks barefoot, shoes held with hooked fingers. She loops and zigzags into the water and back onto the shore, leaving trails of footprints that look like art. She's quick and quiet, and I know by the way her eyes dart across the ground that she's looking for the shine of dropped jewellery or forgotten wallets left by campers or people thinking they had found an untouched part of the beach.

A seagull with a patch of feathers missing limps across the rocks and doesn't startle when dream-Mackenzie, Tracey, and Sabrina walk by. Scavengers are always as tough as they look. The woods hold old and new nests that leak feathers through the sticks and leaves.

Rocks dig into my knees as I watch the three of them come closer. I shakily will myself to stand. There's an urge, somewhere deep in my body, that wants to run to my sisters and hold them. To press my head into the nook of Sabrina's neck and never let go. But I stay frozen. The fear that I felt in my past three dreams inches up my legs before the realization hits me: this dream is actually a memory. I'm seeing something that has already happened.

I remember this night three years ago, this conversation as the three of us walked away from our family campsite. This was our last night on the lake the summer before I left. We were going to a party at the gravel pits, a spot in the woods by the public campsites, an abandoned place cleared away years earlier for a pipeline that was never built. All that was left were piles of gravel and deep pits dug up and never covered, where kids our age would throw pit parties, sneaking out of their family campers and tents, beer and liquor tucked away in their coats. That's the thing about abandoned places: they get reclaimed one way or another.

There were two ways to get to the gravel pits from our campsite. One was to follow the shoreline toward the public campsites and then cut away from the water, north along a service road to the pits. This was the way we were walking now, the long way that took nearly an hour. The other way was to cut through the woods, taking the trails northeast. This was a straight line to the gravel pits from our campsite, so it only took about twenty minutes. But you had to know your way.

This night, we were going to meet up with Kassidy at the gravel pits. She usually stayed at the family spot but had come out with friends staying at the other campsites.

I watch as the three of them walk closer to me. While they talk, they look at each other and everywhere else aside from me.

Finally, I find my voice. "Sabrina!" The sound comes out like a crack of thunder.

No one looks at me or seems like they heard anything. They just keep walking toward me, talking low to one another. I take a moment to look for any sign of a scar on Sabrina's chest. Her skin is smooth and dewy from the sun, but there is no scar.

When they're close enough for me to touch them, I reach out. "Wait!" I yell again. Looking at my outstretched hands, I realize for the first time that I'm still holding my phone. Stunned, I squeeze it a little harder. I've never brought anything from the waking world into a dream before. I look up just as my sisters are walking through me.

I feel as though a gust of air has reached inside and blown up my lungs. A static energy like my whole body is a limb that's fallen asleep courses through every inch of me. Light and vibrating, I wince. Just as I start to think it's more than I can stand, it's over. Tracey, Sabrina, and dream-Mackenzie walk on, leaving my stunned body in their wake.

Shaking, I put my phone in my front pocket. I'll think about it later. I touch my legs and torso, then my neck. I feel solid under my own hands. But they just walked through me like I was a ghost.

"Hey!" I yell, and sprint to catch up with them. I try again, reaching out to grab Tracey's sloping shoulder, and then Sabrina's broad one, but the same thing happens. My hand goes right through them like I'm made of vapour, and the static vibration runs through my arm like it's been zapped asleep.

My heart sinks. I'm so close and I can't even touch them. I reach down and pick up a handful of rocks and sand and throw them into the water. The water ripples where they sink. When none of them notice, I pick up another handful of rocks and sand and throw it at them, but it goes through their bodies. Again, none of them notice.

"What's the fucking point of this?" I yell, my voice choking out of my throat.

I sigh and surrender to walking behind them invisibly, watching their feet crunch over sand and rocks, listening to the murmur of them talking. The last time the three of us were together in this place. Their hair swings to the rhythm of their gaits, sometimes interrupted by the breeze. The sun is starting to rest on the curve of the lake, beams reflecting off the water like it's made of gold. Clouds cover the sky in patches, heavy and low.

My cheeks stiffen against a sudden chill, and I look down to realize I'm walking in snow.

"What the fuck," I whisper, and my breath comes out a cold puff in front of my face.

I look at my sisters and dream-Mackenzie. They're still walking toward the cloudy summer day, the lake silent at their feet on one side and the trees swaying in the breeze on the other. But snow sprouts from every footprint they leave behind in the sand. I walk in their frozen wake, the summer sounds of earlier replaced by the blanketing silence of cold. And then suddenly, the cracking sound of a whip comes from the lake as it snap-freezes over.

My sisters and dream-Mackenzie don't notice a thing as the wind picks up, the slight breeze turning into a howling from the woods. I hold still as the familiar dread from the past three dreams washes over me.

And then I feel it. A knowing in my periphery like I'm being watched. I turn to look out onto the lake and I see her. Sabrina, with her sharp face and long hair pulled in front of her shoulders, stands on the now-frozen water looking in my direction. Unsure if she can see me, I slowly raise my hand. She cocks her head to the side and gestures toward me.

I look back to the three figures walking away, the carpet of winter behind them, and again, to the Sabrina on the lake. How are there two of her?

Before I mean to, I'm walking toward the Sabrina on the ice. I step carefully so I don't slip, but I don't slow. A burning need inside me pulls me across the lake until I stop, red-faced, a few feet in front of her.

Up close, she is not the same Sabrina as the one who just left me behind on the shore. She looks more like the Sabrina from my last dream. Her skin is pale and wrinkled. Her hair is a mix of brown and grey pushing up from the roots. Her eyes are deep brown, but look waxy, like they're covered in a soapy film.

"Can you see me?" I ask. My voice quivers, either from the cold or the fear.

She smiles but it doesn't reach her eyes. Her lips crack at the strain. She says nothing.

I study her face, trying to figure out why I don't feel the urge to reach out to her like I did with the other Sabrina on the shore. I don't move. "Why are there two of you?"

She keeps staring at me with the same smile. The sides of her mouth are cracked with cuts and look sore, like she's been standing in the cold for too long. Her neck and shoulders twitch, like a bird ruffling its feathers. She cocks her head to the side again and a strand of grey hair falls across her face.

Then I see it. Peeking out from under her torn shirt, a glint of a scar just below her collarbone. I look down at her jeans, ripped and fraying. It's then that I realize she's wearing the same clothes as Sabrina was in the last dream. The same thing Sabrina on the shore was wearing, except they weren't yet dishevelled like this.

"How did you get that scar?" I try.

She keeps looking at me, her face unmoving.

"How?" I ask again, and take a step toward her. As I do, the ice underneath us sags. I freeze in place. I'm so close I can smell her.

Her mouth pulls into a smile so wide a cut on her bottom lip opens and a stream of blood rises, flowing in a perfectly straight line down her chin. Her arms seem frozen at her sides, and I notice her fingers, from the tips to their base, are so raw they look painful to touch, like they've been chewed through.

She brings her leg up and slams it down. A soft pop comes from the ice underneath us, fractures like lightning spreading out around our bodies.

"Please," I whisper, as if making my voice small will make us lighter. "Don't move."

The smile falls from her face. In another second, she lifts her leg and brings it down, harder.

"Don't!" I plead. I reach out to grab her hands, to keep her from moving, and I'm surprised when they don't go through her. I gasp. Her hands are stiff. The raw, exposed skin of her fingers is sandpaper against my skin. The wind from the woods picks up, carries across the ice lake, whipping her stringy hair across her face.

She raises her leg again and her gaze bores into me. Before I can think of what to do, she's brought it down again.

The last thing I see before the ice breaks is her mouth forming a perfect O. Right before the water sucks us under, she releases that same endless scream that has been haunting my every waking moment.

My mouth fills with lake, and the shock of freezing cold slows my body. I open my eyes to try to find Sabrina in the water, but the cold stings them closed again. The pressure against my eardrums feels like two hands looking to hurt. I hold my breath for as long as possible, trying to kick my legs upwards to the surface. My heart pounds in my head as I feel the oxygen in my body running out. I keep kicking, but the surface never comes. Unable to hold my breath any longer, I open my mouth and swallow water in a gasp.

I wake up against the cedar tree, drenched from head to foot. The blue of the ocean glints at me before I gag, folding over onto the grass. I heave and vomit fresh water, gasping on the ground and shivering uncontrollably. In front of my vomit, the watermelon rind is crawling with ants, its decomposing corpse half devoured by the insects, already part dirt.

ᓂᐱᐊᐳᒡ

I'm holding the lake in my belly. Soaked, I somehow start to make my way home, throwing up a couple more times along the way. Water and bile pool in the middle of the sunny sidewalk. I shiver uncontrollably from cold, though my chest and stomach burn hot. I focus on my breathing. Every inhale is slow, but I'm thankful I can fill my lungs again. I fumble my phone out of my pocket and try to turn it on. It's dark and silent. Dead from water damage. My heart starts to hammer in my head as I stare at the blank screen.

Finally, I make it back to my apartment and strip off my clothes. I look at myself in the bathroom mirror. I'm pale and wet hair clumps to my face. When I open my mouth, I hear the ice from the lake cracking. I start a hot shower and the water bites against my body. I sit in the bathtub and shake, now out of fear more than the cold. The memory I was brought back to, our last night together at the lake, burns in my mind. I think about my fingers going right through my sisters. The static feeling. Seeing Sabrina. I feel cut through, opened and raw.

When I get out of the shower, I dress in layers. I move slowly through my apartment, scared that the floor will crack into water underneath me. I close all the curtains, blocking the crows speckling the telephone wire outside. I dry off my dead phone and bury it in a bowl of rice. I turn the heat up and, too exhausted to wash anything, throw all my wet clothes and damp towels in a corner. I empty my cupboards, looking for crackers or anything that will fill my stomach, even though I'm not hungry.

When I take my phone out of the rice hours later, it won't turn on. My body feels like it's still in the water. I try to shut my eyes and lie down on the nest I made in my bed, but the world moves and sways. I listen to the sounds of outside, cars honking, a siren going off, and try to think of a way to call an auntie or my mom. But I don't have the energy for anything beyond just lying here.

I nod in and out of sleep, confusing the haze of awake with dreaming. When I do actually sleep, I can't tell how much time has passed. The buzzing at my apartment door grinds in my head and I think I'm dreaming that, too. When I finally move to answer, my voice is hoarse. "Hello?"

"Mackenzie, let me up." Joli sounds relieved and annoyed.

I buzz the building open and unlock the front door, move back to my bed.

Joli stops in the doorway to take everything in. They move slowly across the room to my nest, flick on a lamp, and keep their voice soft. "Mack, are you okay?" They sit at the edge of the bed and run their hand over my arm and forehead. "You're on fire."

They go to the kitchen and come back with a cold, wet towel and press it to my head.

I hold the towel in place as I sit up. "Is this real or a dream?"

Joli looks at me in their worried way and then glances around the apartment. "It's fucking boiling in here." They get up and turn down the heat on the thermostat. Then they open the curtains a small crack. It's grey outside and getting dark. I've slept the day away.

I pull the blankets closer, move my eyes to focus on Joli. "How many days has it been?"

Joli walks the apartment, taking in the clothes littering the floor, the upturned kitchen, cans, condiments, and takeout containers all over the counters. They start picking up and folding some of the dry clothes discarded in a pile. "I've been texting and calling. Why does your location say you're in Alberta?"

My head spins in a memory of drowning in water, of feeling completely alone. I move to the edge of the bed. "What?"

Joli pauses folding a pair of pants, runs a hand through their hair, and gestures east. "You still have your location shared with me from yesterday. I checked it today when my calls were going right to voicemail. It says you're in Alberta, at some lake."

I think about reaching for Joli's phone seconds before my arm moves, and then I cross the short distance to them. "Show me."

Joli knits their eyebrows in confusion as they pull out their phone. They tap into my contact info. On the map, the location icon representing me is a circle with my initials, MW. In the middle of ayahciyiniw sâkahikan, MW hovers over the water, surrounded in blue. Like I'm floating.

Ice cracks in my ears and I feel like I'm drowning again.

"What's going on?" Joli asks. Fear laces their voice.

I go back to the bed and grab my phone from underneath the covers, the black screen reflecting my body's outline. "My phone is here. It died this morning."

Joli grabs the phone like they need the feel of it as proof but then gives it back to me just as quickly, like it's cursed. "That's weird." They pick up another discarded article of clothing on the floor. "Maybe it's a glitch. Satellites in space can fuck up, too."

They say it too nonchalantly, like they are trying to convince themself. But the knowing sits at the corner of my eye socket, a black speck of understanding that is still too far away to see clearly. Joli audibly sighs. "It's still way too hot in here and it stinks. I'm opening some more windows."

I feel myself sink further into my pillows while Joli moves around the apartment, opening a couple windows just a crack.

"What is this?" Joli turns their attention to the table and holds up the makeshift magnifying glass.

"It's a tool for survival, don't throw it out."

They shake their head and put it back down. "Have you eaten anything besides takeout?"

"Joli, I was there. On the lake."

They stop looking around the apartment and stare back at me. "How?"

"In my dream."

They come back and sit next to me. "What happened?"

"You know how I said these dreams weren't visions? And they obviously aren't regular dreams, either. I think they are memories. It was like I was taken back in time."

If this surprises them, in an act of grace, Joli doesn't show it. They nod for me to continue. I rush through the story, realizing how much I need to get it out, say it out loud. Fear opens up inside me, something in my stomach breaking.

I swallow again and search Joli's face for any sign that I've lost them. That they don't believe me. But instead, they're leaning forward with intensity. "You almost drowned?"

"You know I can't swim. I got pulled under. I think I woke up just in time."

Something else flashes across their face. Sadness and anger. "These dreams can hurt you."

I exhale deeply and nod my head. "It hurt like real life." We both sit in silence for a minute and let the realization settle.

I look at my phone's blank screen again and barrel forward. "And you know how I've been bringing things back from my dreams? This time, I did the opposite. I fell asleep while I was holding my phone and I took it with me. And now it's got water damage and, apparently, it's saying I'm still there."

The room fills with a cold chill and their shoulders tense. "Well, we're gonna have to get it fixed. You should talk to your family."

My mind flashes back to the phone call before I fell asleep on the beach. "I talked to my cousin Kassidy," I say. "She's seen stuff happen in her dreams that have come true."

"Whoa," Joli says. "Like the future?"

"I guess so."

"So this dream shit runs in the family?"

I think about Kassidy keeping her dreams a secret and my mom stopping her own, whatever she meant by that. I wish I knew more about both of them.

"You guys need to be careful," Joli says, their voice serious and quiet.

"I can't really help what happens in the dreams. I don't have a lot of control."

"I don't mean in the dreams. I mean in this world. Be careful who you tell. My grandma told me once about my uncle who started having visions." Joli's eyes trace the ceiling, seeing something other than my apartment. "He told the wrong people, got taken away from his family, locked up in white rooms." I stare at them.

"This place wasn't built to believe us, and white people will try to stamp out anything they don't understand." Joli's eyes hold mine. "What about this memory?"

"What do you mean?"

"You said the dream, at least the first part of it, was a real memory. What happened that night?"

My head starts to pound and the burning in my chest rises up again. I try to remember what happened after we got to the gravel pits: I know there was a party, heat from a giant bonfire, and fear. Something in the deep dark of the woods. But the memory collapses into itself, ink so smudged I can't make out the words. My thoughts get hazy behind the pounding. I hesitate. "I'm not sure. It's the last time all of us were together at the lake. Before I moved."

They eye me, and my head throbs harder. There is something else about that night, something just out of reach.

"It was right after my kokum died," I say, slowly piecing together the timeline. "Everything from then until I left to move here is a mess."

They nod and rub my arm again. We sit in silence for another minute and then they get up. "Let's get this"—they gesture to the upturned apartment—"sorted out." When I groan and lean back into my bed, they clarify. "It's something we can control. This apartment, this space. Something we can focus on that's manageable. We're going to the store to get some groceries. And then we need to do some laundry."

I don't move and give an exasperated exhale.

"Kid, I love you, but you've got to be part of picking yourself up, too," Joli says.

"Don't you have finals coming up? You have enough going on. Go home, I can take care of myself."

They gesture around the apartment again. "Clearly, that is not the case. I brought my flashcards. You can help me study."

We come to an agreement: they'll run out to get food for dinner while I do laundry and clean up the apartment. It's the best we're both going to get.

When they leave, the room feels empty and I turn on some

music to fill the silence. I drink some water, trying to ease my throbbing head, but the liquid tastes like bile in my mouth. The weak light from outside snitches, exposing every corner of my dirty apartment. I want to feel closed in again, hidden, but I get up.

Joli makes a vegetarian chili with a salad when they get back. They listen to a podcast while they cook, making it sound like the kitchen is full of people. The smell of roasted pepper and garlic settles in the air as they flit around, alternating between stirring a pot and organizing my cupboards.

"I'm pretty weak, you know. You should probably throw some meat into that chili," I yell from my freshly made bed. I am picking up all the clothes off the floor and sorting them for laundry.

Joli pokes their head out from behind the wall that separates the kitchen and the rest of the apartment. "You should be grateful I'm cooking for you at all. I should just leave you to rot in your gross apartment."

"Hey, it's much less gross now!"

I sniff a pair of socks and, unsure, throw them into the dirty laundry pile. I move slowly. The pain in my head has eased with Joli around. They come over with two bowls, hand me one, then sit on the chair next to my bed to eat. We dig in while they tell me about school. I didn't realize how hungry I was. For food and for company.

"You still look pale, but at least you're fed," they say.

I take our dishes to the kitchen. When I come back, they feel my forehead. "I think you're on your way back to a normal temperature. Leave that damn thermostat alone."

"Okay."

"Hey," they say seriously, "we need to do something. This dream stuff is no joke."

I look at them and see the worry etched all over their face.

Behind them, out the window, the crows take flight. One after another, they form patterns of three dark flecks in the sky.

"I know," I say. "Thank you for checking in on me. You could have definitely left me to rot."

"I'd never." They laugh and put their arms around me. I almost sob at being held, at the feeling of their skin on mine, a physical reminder that I'm not something they can pass through.

"We need to sort out your phone, though," they say as they pull away. "If your aunt goes too long without hearing from you after you told her about this dream stuff, from what you've told me, she's likely to show up with some fire."

"I'll figure it out first thing tomorrow," I say.

We clean up the rest of the kitchen, and afterwards I help them study with their flashcards. They get every question right, but we still go through them a few times. Only after I promise Joli I'll do my laundry and be in bed early do they get ready to leave. "I'll see you at work tomorrow. We can talk more about everything then if you want."

I hug them and push one of the containers of leftover chili into their hands. "If I'm not fired for missing so many days, I'll be there."

With Joli gone, the apartment is back to empty. I finish sorting my laundry, and as I'm putting the clean clothes away in my dresser, my phone lights up, the blue of the screen shining across the room.

I run over quickly and fumble with the charger to plug it in. "Please," I whisper, as if to help it along. "Please work."

After a couple long minutes, the phone background flashes and stays lit. I breathe a deep sigh of relief. I have eleven messages. I sit at the edge of my bed and check them—most are from Joli, but a couple are from Auntie Doreen, Auntie Verna, Mom, and a few from my boss, asking if I'm coming to work tomorrow. I text him back right away, tell him I'm feeling better and will be in. I call Joli.

"It lives!" they yell into the phone when they answer.

"Just came back from the dead. I thought it was a goner for good."

"You won't have to spend a bunch of money replacing it now."

"Good, 'cause I don't have any. Can you check my location? See if it's still . . . weird."

Joli's quiet for a second and the phone is muffled. "Okay," they say finally. "It's fine! Says you're at home."

I sigh, relieved. "Okay, thanks, see you tomorrow."

I leave the phone plugged in and I'm gathering up the rest of the dirty clothes to take downstairs to the laundry room when my phone lights up again and the message tone sounds. A text from an unknown number: *nehiyawak who don't know how to swim should keep away from water.*

My hands start to shake. I look at the area code, but it's not one I recognize. I text back. *Wrong number.*

I stare at the blue speech bubble and feel the heat rise in my face. The pounding starts again in my head as I watch the blue dots come and go. *I don't think so.*

Who is this?

You know who this is. You're not listening.

My stomach drops. Joli is the only one who knows about my last dream, about almost drowning. I know as I type out my reply that it's wrong, but I press send anyways.

Tracey?

The blue dots appear for a little too long and then disappear. After what feels like forever, a message appears.

Close. Same womb, different sister.

σdĊ·ᴙˋ

Instead of throwing my dirty clothes in the wash and going back up to my apartment, I close the door to the building's laundry room and turn off the light. Squatting in front of the washing machine, I rest my back on the cold metal and listen to the water whirring behind my head, imagine waves crashing against a shore.

Two floors up, my phone sits in my kitchen drawer, turned off, tucked away underneath tea towels and washcloths. I breathe in the smell of the laundry detergent and place my hands against the cool tile. I'm shaking uncontrollably. I try to reason away the text messages. I just need one explanation other than that they're from my dead sister.

I'm hiding in the laundry room like I hid in this city after Sabrina died. I had already been living in Vancouver for two years and hadn't even been back for a visit yet. One warm night at the end of August, my phone lit up over and over and over with calls from my mom. I didn't know exactly what I was going to hear if I picked it up, but I knew in my gut it was big and bad, so I ignored it.

When I finally did answer, the next morning on no sleep, I knew I wouldn't go back home for the funeral. After losing kokum, I knew what living in a grieving house was like. I knew the never-ending lonely that hung in the halls and in every corner, how the upturned earth of our world would smell. I knew our lives wouldn't be the same once Sabrina became a slit in the ground.

We were warned about kokum's death before it came. She tried to prepare us for it, talked about death like it wasn't already in the room with us. She detailed her passing through into another world as if she were describing a trip to the grocery store. She made it out to be mundane, so boring that when death actually came, I was shocked by the ugliness of it.

I thought if I stayed away after Sabrina's death, the ugly would pass me by like a car that has some better place to go. I didn't know how wrong I'd be.

I stay in the safety of the laundry room for the whole half-hour wash cycle and then put my clothes in the dryer. I curl up on the floor, stuff a pair of abandoned jeans under my head, and listen to the sound of wet clothes against metal and the hum of the dryer. Still shaking, I fall asleep in seconds.

When I wake again, the cycle is over and drool sticks to my cheek. It's the deepest sleep I can remember having in a long time. I'm relieved that I didn't dream. I feel weighed down, anchored to the world. I pull my laundry from the dryer and take it up to my apartment. The sun is already rising. I was in there all night.

I avoid looking at the drawer where my phone hides, as if I can pretend it's not there. I take my time putting away my clothes, try and fail to stop thinking about the messages. Outside, I hear the crows cawing on the pole and I try to listen in, see what the day holds for me.

It's the most I can do to make a cup of Red Rose tea before pulling out the phone again. I blow on the steaming water while I stare at the blank screen. I turn it back on and wait for the white light to flash. When the phone background appears, I stare at the messages app at the bottom of the screen, but no new notifications pop up. I wait a minute before feeling sure, and then go into the app again.

At the top are the messages from the unknown number. I didn't dream them, and they didn't disappear. With a shaking hand, I press the call button on the number. Slowly, I hold the phone to my ear. There's silence and then three clicks. A robotic voice tells me the number I've called is out of service. I exhale and hang up. I go into my contacts and scroll to Tracey's name. I stare at it, as if that could be enough to reach her.

When I was ten, Tracey taught me how to head butt: use the top of your forehead, aim for the bridge of their nose or jaw. At twelve, she showed me how to punch without using my fist, which could easily break or bruise. Your elbow is one of the hardest joints in the body and gets more leverage than a cocked fist. "If you have to use your fist," she told me, hand on my shoulder, "grip a lighter so you don't break your fingers." On my eighteenth birthday, sitting in our hometown bar, she showed me how to open a beer bottle with my teeth, pointed out the bottles that were best to hit someone with. Imports have the thickest glass. Domestics break too easily, which can cut you or shatter into an eyeball. Other tips I picked up from her in passing throughout the years: If you're in trouble, use a fake name or name of your enemy. Leave first and quietly, so no one knows you're gone. Tracey knows a lot of things, but the thing she's always known best was how to keep herself from hurt. That's how I know she wouldn't pick up if I called.

My phone rings, shocking me out of my thoughts. Auntie Verna. My stomach tightens and I answer, my voice coming out in a croak. "Is everything okay?"

She laughs. "Everything is fine, my girl. Just had a feeling, thought I'd call and check in. How are you?" Her voice drapes over me, an arm wrapped around my shoulder. I wonder if any iskwewak have answered a call outside of the hours of noon to five without feeling a sense of panic. From outside my window, I hear the beating of wings.

"I'm okay. Been having a weird few days. How are you?"

"Just got back from your mom's, we're getting the garden ready."

Auntie Verna lives alone in a one-bedroom apartment a couple blocks from my parents' place, so she usually walks over to visit every day. If you didn't know any better, you'd think her apartment was a craft store. Her walls are lined with plastic containers from Walmart: bins, drawers, cabinets. Filled to the brim with every colour of fabric, cotton, and yarn, every size of bead and gem. She has an entire corner by the kitchen table reserved for tanned hide, usually from moose and deer she and her friends harvest in the fall. She's never been married and saves all the money she makes from selling her beadwork, knitting, and quilts at craft shows to go on yearly trips to Vegas.

"Hope it does better than last year," I say.

"Mmm." I imagine her nodding, her long hair swaying with the gesture. "How are you doing, really?" Her voice is deep and soothing. She's a high school counsellor, and this is the tone she takes with students who are having a hard time. Even though I know what she's doing, I feel at ease.

"Some things have been happening in my dreams . . ." I start. I tell her everything: bringing things back and forth from the dream world, nearly drowning, my phone location showing up on the lake, the messages from Sabrina, and, of course, the crows following me.

She's silent while I speak. When I'm done, I hear her readjust the phone against her ear, know her hands are holding more than just me: a bowl, knitting, beads.

"You remember the scar on your mosum's side?" she asks.

"His animal was maskwa. He was a good hunter and trapper and knew every trail north of High Prairie, every body of water. He never killed maskwak, though. When things got rough for us and we couldn't afford much, he started taking moniyaw hunters through the bush. They paid him well and killed whatever they wanted. Maskwak, too."

I nod into the phone as if she can see me.

"Maskwak started to follow your mosum. He saw the big bear droppings, fresh, on his regular walking trails. Bearberry bushes picked clean," she continues, talking low into the phone. "One day, a maskwa grabbed him. Didn't kill him, just took some of his ribs. It was a painful message."

What kind of messages were these, then? I wonder, but don't ask out loud.

"Am I a bad Cree?" I ask instead. The words hang between us. I can see Auntie's kitchen where she sits: The stool pulled up close to her crafting table. The laminate floor. The smell of bread in the oven.

"He was a good hunter," Auntie responds. "But he wasn't living in a good way. If he was, he would have been as good a hunter as kokum." She laughs big, the sound wrapping into me on the other end of the phone.

"Auntie, how could Sabrina message me? That can't be real."

She scoffs into the phone. "Our ancestors and spirits have been speaking to us in a million different ways for thousands of years. You think they would have a hard time figuring out texting?"

I'm silent at the simplicity of the statement. How easy belief in my truth comes to her.

"The only thing I'm worried about"—Auntie hesitates—"is the water."

When I described the drowning dream to her, there was a quiet over the phone that I only now recognize as fear. When I told her

I woke up and vomited the water, she let go of the breath she'd been holding throughout the story. And if an auntie is scared of something, that means it's truly terrifying.

"Does that mean I can die in my dreams?"

The silence spills into my eardrums again.

"Auntie, what if I die?"

"You aren't going to die, my girl." She says this matter-of-fact, like it's all the reassurance I'll need.

"But what if I do?"

"I think you need to come home." Her voice is soft with the suggestion. She's trying not to let her fear slip through, but I can feel it. "I'll talk to Doreen and your mom. We'll all pool together some money. I'm on summer holidays, so I can spend some time around the house."

"I'll talk to my boss." It's all I want to promise.

"Listen, my girl. This is serious. These dreams, the crows. It's all telling you something. You need to listen."

The thought of going home after so many years, after not having gone back when Sabrina died, is terrifying. But there's a seriousness in an auntie suggesting you do something.

We catch up on a few more things, my mom, town gossip. Before she hangs up, Auntie tells me she loves me and to stay inside for now, knowing it doesn't matter. Dreams can get you anywhere, but sometimes the illusion of safety is better than nothing.

I hang up and rummage in my closet for the cookie tin with the bundle of sage and the abalone shell that Joli gave to me all those years ago. When they gifted me the medicine, I smiled in what I hoped was a grateful way. I didn't want to tell them that I had never smudged before, that I'd never seen kokum, Mom, or any of my aunties do it, either. The night after they gave it to me, I YouTubed how to smudge and watched a white yoga instructor smudge her studio, chanting self-love mantras. I burnt my thumb on the lighter from holding the flame too long. I didn't fan the bundle right, so it kept going out. I couldn't concentrate on a mantra, especially one about loving myself. My thumb blistered and bulged red for a full day afterwards.

Dianne and Joli smudged at their place one time after we had dinner. I pretended not to pay too much attention, but I watched on desperately. I copied what they did, movement for movement, and when I got home, I wrote down everything I saw and heard.

I smudge now by myself for the first time since the YouTube incident. I repeat *go away go away go away* under my breath as I fan the embers, because kokum told me once that a prayer can be anything, so I guess that means it can be a plea. When the smoke goes out, I wait and wait to feel changed. I wait to feel anything, even something small, like a blister on the tip of my thumb. Nothing comes.

My shift doesn't start for another hour, but I leave early, decide to walk the long way. The cherry blossoms have been blooming all over the city since spring, reminding me that beauty is always here, even when I'm not looking. I hear the telephone-pole crows following behind me as I start down my street, but they don't get too close. I think about the watermelon rind they dropped at my feet and I'm surprised to feel more comforted than scared by their presence today.

I stop in the middle of the sidewalk to look at a low-hanging blossom branch dipping toward the ground. A pink petal falls. In the gutter, a hornet crawls out of an empty, half-crushed can of Coke. I think about a time at the lake when we were kids. It was early summer and shot blue. Me, Sabrina, and Tracey came across a bees' nest in the trees and swatted it with sticks. When the swarm leaked out of the layered-paper hive, Tracey ran first.

I froze, the fear sticking my feet into the earth. Instead of running, Sabrina pushed me to the ground and threw herself on top of me. She covered my ears with her hands so I wouldn't have to hear her scream.

Back at our campsite, Mom and Auntie Verna picked out the stingers with tweezers while kokum rubbed aloe leaves on her skin. Someone sang to her. They cradled her like a baby. She whimpered and hung her wet face. Instead of being grateful, I pinched my own skin to look like bee stings and cursed Sabrina under my breath for not running away, too. I don't know why I thought love was something people could run out of, like there might not be enough left for me if Sabrina got some.

At work, no one asks why I was off for the past few days. I get a couple of tight-lipped smiles as I pass people, which tells me a rumour or two has probably formed. Joli eyes me from their till as I walk the aisle toward them. They ring through a woman while studying my face. I stand off to the side by the rack of natural oils.

"You look almost human again," they say.

"Excuse me?" The woman looks up from texting and Joli waves her off, keeps looking at me while ringing through some bulk quinoa.

I dig my name badge out of my pocket and pin it to my Whole Foods–brand shirt. "I still don't feel right. Like I'm being eaten from the inside out."

"Maybe you need some more time in the real world."

The woman looks from Joli to me and audibly sighs. "Remember to double bag the vegetarian lasagna. Last time the bag almost ripped biking home."

"Of course it did," Joli says, still looking at me.

"Oh yeah, and my phone. It's, uh, still kind of on the fritz," I say, glancing around us.

"That'll be thirty-five dollars and sixty cents," Joli says to the woman.

She shakes her head and pulls out her Visa from her leather purse. She walks away with a huff.

"You're welcome," Joli says to her back, and then looks at me. "Why do you look like you're about to tell me some bad news?"

I give a small smile at my friend's intuition and lean against their till. "I might try and go back home." I wasn't entirely sure about this, but I wanted to try the words out on my tongue. See how they felt when they came out. Out the window behind Joli, three crows pick through a garbage can.

Joli nods. "Good." They straighten the pens on their till and move the rubber bands next to the brown grocery bags. "I think that's good."

"I have to tell Brandon first, though. And I've already taken a bunch of sick days."

Brandon is our manager. He likes to quote white feminist books and brings all his Tinder dates to the same bar a block from the store.

"Well, if he makes any trouble about it, tell me. I can work doubles and we have more than enough people to cover."

"You shouldn't be working doubles."

"How much are flights?"

"Aunties are on it."

"Leave me a key, I'll water your plants."

"I don't have any plants."

"How long are you planning on going for? Do you still have a suitcase?"

"Joli, I love you."

Joli sighs and looks to the line forming behind me. "Damn sentimental Crees. Go, you're already late."

I smile again and start toward the back of the store. Brandon is looking up recipes for puff pastries when I walk into his office. When I ask him for time off, he closes his laptop and looks at me carefully. "You were just off for quite a few days."

"Yeah, sick. It wasn't, like, a holiday or anything."

"Right, well, it really screwed us, you know. Finding last-minute coverage isn't easy."

"I know, that's not what I meant to do, I just—"

"This isn't reliable co-operation, Mackenzie."

In a staff meeting a few months back, Brandon kept talking about "reciprocal responsibility" and "reliable co-operation" within the workplace. He probably read the phrases in a management textbook and thought it sounded professional. Though I think they mean something different to him than they do to me.

"Right, well, I feel like I've always been reliable."

He makes a show of taking out the schedule and alternating between sighing and huffing between pages. I stay quiet, as if that might help.

"It just won't work," he says finally. "It hurts me to say, you know it does." His bony arms cross over his chest and his moustache, pulled into wax points on either side of his mouth, moves as he frowns.

I nod and want to say nothing, want to head out the door and go to work, stay hiding. I could tell everyone I tried and I'd be telling the truth. But the text messages from Sabrina flash in my head and lake water rises like bile in the back of my throat. "I didn't take time off when my sister died," I say instead of moving.

He'd already written off our conversation, opened his laptop again, and was back to scrolling. He looks up.

"I didn't take one day off. I need a few weeks, and I know we have the people to cover."

A muscle in his neck twitches. The mention of death has made him uncomfortable, like it does for people who never want to be confronted with it. He clears his throat. "Fine," he says. "I'll work something out. You'll be lucky to get a couple weeks."

I nod and give him a flat smile. "Thank you," I say, though what I want to do is grab his laptop and smash his head in with it. But he'll be more likely to help me if I'm nice. If I act sweet. If he feels like he's the saviour here. "I'll be leaving in the next couple days."

As I leave his office, I don't feel any relief. I pass Joli on the way to my till and nod, give them a real smile, one that says I won a small battle. They whoop out loud and scare a customer grabbing his bags. I tense, but in my gut, I feel a settling, an eddy forming against a rock.

I text Auntie and let her know I'm good for a flight anytime. She responds with two thumbs-up emojis and says she'll book it for the day after tomorrow.

I hesitate before typing my reply. *Thank you for getting Kassidy to call me. It helped. Can you tell my mom and Tracey? I want them to know what's been going on . . . I just don't know if I can say it all again.*

She replies right away. *Of course, my girl.*

I leave my phone in the staff room, not even looking at it during my break. At the end of my shift, Joli is waiting for me at the back doors and I tell them when I'm leaving.

"I'll come over tomorrow to help you pack."

We walk out the doors and through the parking lot, waving to a co-worker behind us who is locking up.

I kick a jagged rock. "Sure, but I'm not bringing much."

I see Joli look at me from the corner of my eye. In the distance, crows speckle the sky, hundreds of them, heading to roost in Burnaby. "I know going home is complicated," they say. "But the answers must be there. They have to be."

Their response eases me. Maybe this is how to put an end to the dreams and whatever is happening to me.

Joli puts their arm around me and pulls me in close. "And if all else fails, you have me."

A guy in a loud car drives fast through the alleyway, too close to our bodies, and yells something at us out the window. Joli flips off the back of the car and runs their hand through my hair in one smooth motion. I lay my head on their shoulder and take a deep breath in. They ask if I want a ride home, but I insist on walking. I walk them to their car, and then keep heading toward my apartment.

"Text me when you get there," Joli says before closing the car door behind them.

I take the long way back again and don't check my phone. The crows follow and I don't try to ignore them. When I get to my apartment, I heat up last night's leftover chili and listen to a podcast about meditation and mindful thinking to help people sleep. The host speaks in a quiet British accent that I know is meant to be calming, but it only irritates me. I download some meditation apps because I can never get meditating right on my own. It always feels stressful trying to quiet my mind. I pay attention to every cut and curve of my plates as I do the dishes. Watch the bubbles form with the hot water. I try to take deep breaths in and out as I work, hoping that this is what the British host means when they talk about being mindful, though I can't be sure.

When I finally check my phone before going to bed, the only new message is from Auntie Doreen with my flight info and ticket. *Non-refundable. No backing out now!* Followed by seven heart emojis.

My stomach drops, but I text her back with a thumbs-up.

I think about texting Sabrina. Just to talk to her again, even if it's terrifying and weird and I have no answers. I would tell her

I'm sorry for never coming home when she was alive. That I still think somewhere deep down, despite it being illogical and impossible, I'm to blame for everything bad that happened. I want her to text me back with hatred. Yell at me. Tell me how selfish I am. But the truth is, if it's her, if it's really her, she would never say any of that. She'd tell me she loves me. She would only try to make me feel better.

My head feels heavy. For a while I lie there thinking about how full I am from Joli's food and listening to the crows' caws. Exhaustion spreads through me and I almost forget I'm afraid to fall asleep. I'm wondering what it would feel like to let thoughts just pass me by like the calm British voice said, until I'm pulled into a dreamless sleep.

U<d'''

The "Fasten Seatbelt" light blinks on as the plane starts its
descent into Edmonton. My insides roll with thunder.

The day before had gone by in a blur. Joli helped me pack,
like they said they would, but mostly we drank whatever booze
we could find in my cupboards. We listened to old emo music,
which Joli barely even complained about, ordered Chinese food,
and plotted Brandon's death. For a night, everything felt normal, like it had all been a nightmare and I was just finally waking
up. The telephone pole had been empty of crows all day. The
quiet left behind in their absence made my skin crawl.

I spent the hour-and-a-half flight staring out the window at the
snow-tipped mountains, thinking about the marvel of something
so big suddenly appearing small, just because of distance.

The day kokum died, I woke up to Sabrina sitting on the edge
of my bed. It was a quiet winter morning. Everything was still.

"I heard the phone ring at five this morning," Sabrina said.

As soon as the doctors had moved kokum from our house into
hospice, we knew whatever hope we had that she'd still make
it was gone. For the whole last month she was there, a family
member was with her every hour of the day and night. The small
couch in kokum's room quickly turned into a guest bed. We all

walked through the world like it was made of glass, certain if we made any wrong move, we'd plummet right through. Phone calls were the worst of it. They'd always be nurses or family members telling us about another close call.

We didn't need to say anything else that morning. We got Tracey, who was already lying awake in her bed, and went down into the living room, where Mom and Dad sat waiting for us. The cold, stale air ate through the space between us. Nothing in Mom's face gave away that she had just lost her own mom. "We knew this was coming," she said calmly. "It was time."

Kokum had told us at the start of fall that she wasn't going to see another winter, though the doctors thought she might be lucky. She died a few weeks after the first snowfall.

The three of us swarmed Mom, hugging her from every angle. Her body was stiff underneath us and she waited only a minute before picking us off her like lint.

"I'm fine," she said. "I'm more worried about you all."

Mom made the calls while Dad cooked breakfast. She even called the family members she didn't speak to anymore, for one reason or another. She mostly spoke softly, but every now and then, her voice got firm. "That's enough now," she said. That meant the person at the other end was losing it in a bad way, but she still spoke longer to them than to anyone else.

The next few days were a blur of friends and family. Most of the funeral stuff was already planned, Mom and the aunties had made sure of that. One thing Cree people are supposed to do when we're grieving is stop. Stop work, stop the everyday of our lives. We're supposed to rest. But Mom refused. She was always moving, always going. She didn't let herself slow in those days, even for a minute. When I told her to take a break, she said, "If I rested for every person we've lost, I'd never start up again." I didn't know how to respond, so I said nothing.

The only thing kokum wanted a say in was where the funeral and wake would be held. She wanted it at a hall in Keg River, a four-hour drive away, even though she hadn't been back there in years. She wanted to rest where she was born.

Tracey said she didn't want to see kokum's body at the wake, but Mom convinced her. "You'll regret it if you don't," she said. "You don't want to live with regret."

On the morning of the wake and funeral, Mom and Dad drove up earlier to help set up, and Sabrina drove Tracey and me in her car. We were silent most of the way, watching the snow-heavy trees flicker past the windows.

We stopped in Peace River to fuel up. Tracey and I pulled our jackets up against the chill as we jogged inside the gas station while Sabrina leaned against the pump, rubbing her mittened hands together to make heat. It smelled like oil and outside cold. We were walking the aisles looking for road snacks when three men came up behind us. They wore full coverall Carhartts, an oilfield company logo I recognized from town stamped over their left chest pockets. One wore a toque under his hardhat. Another tapped a fresh tin of Skoal between two fingers. When we moved to let them pass, the man with the Skoal feigned going the other way and put his hands up in mock fear of running into us. He laughed at his own joke and then looked back and forth between me and Tracey when we didn't laugh back.

"Smile, girls," he said, tapping his tin a few more times. "It's not so bad." The guy wearing the toque and hardhat behind him gave a snort and walked around us. The third guy paused in the aisle, unsmiling.

I knew the kind of smart reply Tracey would normally throw back, but as I instinctively turned to stop her, she was already replying "sorry." She shifted her eyes to the floor, then grabbed my hand to pull me away. We left the store without buying anything.

In the car, she sat in the back seat and stared out the window. I tried to catch her eyes in the rearview mirror, but she avoided my gaze for the rest of the drive up.

Me, Tracey, and Sabrina clasped hands as we stared into kokum's casket. She looked cold, and I felt the sudden urge to find a blanket. To tuck her into this bed of hers. Someone placed five cards, each one overlapping the other, between her hands folded on her chest, like we were sitting down to a game and she was just resting her eyes. Like she'd be up any minute. I wanted to lift up the corners and peek, see exactly what kind of hand I'd need to beat.

I knew I was bad for not feeling more reverence about death, for not holding the understanding of how it worked for nehiyawak. All I could see was a deep crater in the ground and the people left behind grasping at the edges.

Sabrina sucked air in through her teeth, like she'd just been stung.

"She's so small," she said, staring down into kokum's casket.

And she was right. Kokum was a seed in a mound of dirt. How far away from her was I that she could look so small when all my life she had been a mountain?

The rumble of the plane touching down on land shakes me out of my memory. When I step out onto the tarmac, the prairies pull me in. The air smells like wet leaves and jet fuel. The sky opens up for miles in all directions, and for a minute, I just stand and stare, as if it was all taking me in, too.

At kokum's funeral service, Mom hugged every crying relative. She nodded at the stories but told none of her own. She handed out tissues. She did the speaking parts of the service that no one else could. She said we weren't going to stay the night, even though almost every family member told us to. She said it was because of the long drive home and I believed her.

At the end of the service, I walked through the parking lot of the hall to start Sabrina's car, get it warmed up for the drive to the cemetery. The snow bit my ankles and the cold seeped under my layers, like only a prairie winter knows how to do. When I walked past Mom's truck and saw her sobbing against the steering wheel, I only looked for a second before rushing away.

That is how grief lived in our house every day afterwards. In the dishonest light of day, we tried to turn everything normal. We painted on smiles in front of people, waited for the winter to thaw, like it might break down the grief, too. But it stayed. Whatever thin good was still clinging to our lives stayed just out of reach.

The following summer was the last we spent on the lake. But even by then, I knew I couldn't stay in High Prairie anymore. The bad inside me was spreading, eating me up. So I left. I left them all. And now I'm supposed to enter that house again. Where the loss of our family has doubled. Kokum and Sabrina, two of its organs. I think coming home is the right thing. But my chest stays clenched and knotted. The trepidation has just as much to do with guilt as with fear of what I'll see. What kind of sorrow was the house holding in its bones now?

"Follow the painted lines!" An airport attendant wearing a fluorescent vest brings me back to reality again, pointing in the direction of the airport with one hand, waving the other hand at my face. I nod and keep walking, shivering a little at the crispness of the air, despite the sun. The tarmac is wet in some places, cold in the shadows, the signs of Alberta opening into summer.

I turn on my phone as I walk through the airport to the exit. Five messages from Auntie Doreen telling me to text her when I land and then updates on where she's waiting for me by the baggage claim. One is just a photo of her view from where she's standing. I go into my messages from Sabrina—still nothing new.

I hear Auntie before I see her. "My girl!" Her voice carries through the crowd and I see her hand waving. She comes into full view as I slip past other travellers rushing to their own loved ones. Auntie Doreen's curly hair has more strands of grey than when I last saw her. She stands beaming at me. When I reach her, I collapse into her arms. She smells like cigarettes and coffee.

"Oh, my girl, my girl," she repeats as she holds me, slowly rocking back and forth. I feel like a child again. Without realizing it, I start to cry.

"Okay, that's enough. Let's get your bag and get out of here, I'm parked illegally."

I laugh and wipe my wet face with my sleeve. "Damn, it's good to see you."

"Yeah, yeah, that's what they all say."

Even though she bats me away, her arm never leaves my side. It stays tightly wrapped around my waist as we wait to get my bag off the carousel and walk through the airport. Outside, Auntie Doreen's old purple van, which she likes to remind us all was where Kassidy was conceived, is parked at the five-minute passenger pickup spot. Cars move around the van, while a parking attendant circles her vehicle, trying to make out the licence plate number through the caked-on mud. Auntie quickens her pace.

"Call off the search!" she yells as we get to the van. She motions for me to hurry, opens the passenger door, and pushes me in. In another quick movement, she opens the back door and throws my bag in the back seat.

"Ma'am, you can't—"

"I know, I know, we're on our way." She waves at the parking attendant like she's shooing away a fly. "You should be wearing a jacket out here, it's chilly in the shade!"

She jumps into the driver's seat and squeals out of the spot. Mud flies in the air behind her tires. I watch the attendant in the side-view mirror and laugh. "Auntie!"

"What? You want to pay twenty bucks to park for five minutes? Damn rip-off. Callin' me *ma'am*." She scoffs and checks her rearview mirror. A small dreamcatcher and a gas station air freshener sway as she changes lanes without signalling.

"Okay, my girl. We have a three-hour drive until we're home. We're either listening to Garth Brooks or talking, your choice." She pulls out a cigarette and lights it, keeping the other hand on the wheel.

The sun breaks through some clouds and I feel the heat of it full on my face. In the back of the van, empty McDonald's and Tim Hortons bags litter the floor, and I can smell Atim, who must be back in High Prairie with Kassidy.

I look at the sky for any sign of birds, but it's clear and empty. The thunder in my body dulls to a soft vibration. "So everyone knows what's going on with me, right?" I ask. "I mean, why I'm coming home."

She takes a drag of her cigarette. "Yes," she says. "I told your mom and Tracey, like you asked. So now we're all caught up. And we're all here for you."

She catches and holds my eye and I nod. Auntie finishes her smoke and reaches over to hold on to my arm while she drives. We pass through the city until the buildings start to thin, and then we're out of it completely. I breathe in the scenery I know so well: giant, bubbling clouds, treetops, and a never-ending sky. The hair on the back of my neck prickles and my gut clenches. Sometimes, something this open and honest is terrifying.

"Okay, well, give me town gossip or something. Shit that doesn't have anything to do with dreams."

We talk and listen to Garth Brooks turned low, the CD that still skips in all the same places, as the two-lane highway turns into single-lane roads, until, eventually, there's nothing but us and the green ditches wider than the road we're on. We pass freshly tilled fields, readying themselves for the rolling canola and wheat that will grow soon. The drone of Auntie's voice is heavy on my eyelids, which flutter to attention as the car swerves and gently hums over the rumble strips every time she moves to light up a fresh smoke.

We stop in Swan Hills so Auntie can gas up and I can use the bathroom. I buy us both a hoagie sub, some jerky, and a Snapple to share. Our convenience-store snack reminds me of road trips to the city with Mom or Dad. Me and my sisters would be in the back, passing around the jerky. Back then, it felt like we spent just as much time in the car as we did anywhere else. When you live in the middle of everywhere, it feels like you're always in a car trying to get somewhere else.

We pass Kinuso, where Auntie Doreen bought Atim all those years ago. Driftpile, then Joussard. Small signs point to dirt roads that aren't named, only numbered. Turnoffs that come up on us too quick. Places you'd miss if you didn't know where to look. Time seems to slow, memories of places collide with what I see now, like I'm living in the past and the future all at once.

Driving through Edmonton, I saw things already changing, taking shape from the last time I'd been there. Construction in progress, roads fixed and made bigger. Out here, I can still point out the potholes that will never get filled but all the locals know to avoid. I notice some roads that used to be for well-site access are now closed. Their old signs jut out from the ground, grass and bush already growing up to close them over. It's like I've appeared in a world everyone outside of it seems to have forgotten about.

The smell of pine and dust brings us past Sucker Creek and Auntie gives me the side-eye, squeezes my arm, which she hasn't let go of. "Want to go say hi to the lake?"

I look at the road ahead of us. A right turn would take us past a worn-out signpost with a write-up about the signing of Treaty 8, down a road that passes Grouard, and then to ayahciyiniw sâka-hikan. A left turn would take us to kokum's old farm, where my mom and aunts were raised and kokum lived until she had to move in with us when she got sick. Driving straight takes us to High Prairie.

I grip my seatbelt. "Kind of just want to get home," I say.

Auntie nods and gives me a gentle look, a glint in her eye I can only describe as knowing. "I'll bring the lake to you, how 'bout?"

For the next half hour, Auntie tells me stories about the lake. I know them all, but like all the stories my family tells, even the old ones are spun new again with each telling. Something always added, changed, like everything is, over time.

"Cree memories are long, and they swim in that lake," she says. "I'm sure the lake remembers that time when your kokum fell asleep floating on the blow-up mattress . . ."

We pass the "Welcome to High Prairie" sign and into the out-skirts of town. A lumberyard and a gas co-op greet us first, long-haul semis stare at us from the near-empty lot. Buildings that had opened when I was a teenager for oilfield offices are now gated, closed up, and dark.

Auntie notices my head turning to follow them. She pauses her story. "They're trying to sell these buildings out here since the companies have left, but no one wants an office or store so far from town."

I nod and she continues talking about kokum on the lake. We pass another gas station and crawl past the A&W before we see the first house. Then another. They sprinkle in until we reach streets lined with single-story bungalows, trailers, and town houses. Rusted trucks and cars without wheels sit on front lawns. There's more road than sidewalk and the ditches are a checkerboard of mud and brown grass. Some house numbers are spray-painted onto their front fences.

We snake our way deeper into the heart of town, a couple turns off the main highway, like a rabbit hole leading into a nest. The streets are wide and the original high cut-out storefronts with chipped paint look like old saloons. You'd think you walked onto an old western movie set where any second Doc Holliday would walk out, drunk and looking for a game of cards.

But the streets are empty. Hotels and motels flash neon vacancy signs that look too dim in the bright of day. Everywhere is quieter than I remember it.

As we pull up to my parents' house, Auntie is nearing the end of her story. She doesn't finish it, but I know how it ends. The wind took kokum on her blow-up mattress, moving her to the middle of the big lake. The same lake her ancestors had been living around for thousands of years, the same lake she grew up knowing. She woke up, disoriented, shocked that something so familiar could still surprise her.

My parents' white house sits soft against the blue sky, like it's floating in water. The gated-off yard separates our world from the street around it. Two windows look out from the side of the house. Auntie puts her van in park and gives my arm one final squeeze. I wish she wouldn't let go. Atim meets us at the gate. His black hair is peppered with grey, just like Auntie's. He breathes hard, his tongue hanging slightly out of his mouth.

We open the gate and Auntie Doreen scoops up her dog with an excited flourish, like they've been separated for a year instead of a few hours. The mound of dirt in a garden bed at the corner of the yard looks fresh, dug up by Mom and Auntie Verna the other day to ready it. Three crows perch on the branches of the birch tree next to the garden. I hold my breath when I see them, surprised at the relief their presence spurs in me. As I walk up to the back deck, I feel the rush of the past few days catch up with me. Like when you're following an ocean wave and know when it's going to crash, but the force of it knocks you back anyways.

"Followed you here from the coast?" Auntie asks, nodding to the crows. She's only partly kidding.

I shrug, but a small smile escapes.

"When we were young," Auntie says, pulling out another cigarette and putting it between her teeth, "kokum told us that crows were tricksters. Big teasers, too smart for their own good. Just like nehiyawak." She flicks her lighter, and the tip of her cigarette sparks into a deep cherry on her inhale. The smoke circles her head and into the sky.

"If the timing of them being here is some sort of joke, it's not very funny," I say. I place a hand on the rail of the front steps, feel the weight of the house in the wood grain.

"Maybe it's not a joke," she says. She takes a couple steps up the stairs, pausing again for another drag.

"Whenever I used to see a crow and proclaim bad luck, kokum would give me trouble," Auntie says. "She said crows can bring good or bad messages, and I was an ass to assume."

We walk up the rest of the steps that still creak in the same spots and stand by the smoking can in the corner of the deck, the wood under our feet more worn here than anywhere else. I want to tell Auntie that I wonder what kind of messages the crows could be carrying, but I stay quiet. I don't know if I want to hear her guess.

"Okay," she sighs, sucking in her last drag before flicking the butt into the can. "Are you ready?"

I take one last look at the crows and nod. I feel the house move, like its muscles are tensing. I brace myself as we open the back door.

Me and Auntie step into the back entranceway and the smell of home shocks me. I want to let my body fall, press my face into the damp carpet and heave, but there's no time for that before a swarm of cousins envelop me. They sweep me up into hugs and kisses, voices yell from stairs and hallways. Someone takes my bag, and my coat is peeled from my body. I laugh and wipe away a tear from a cheek that isn't mine. I wait for the tightening in my chest to loosen.

"Awas, all of you." Auntie shoos the cousins away like she did the airport attendant. "Let Mackenzie catch her damn breath, holy."

I laugh as the faces disperse, until there's only one left in front of me: Tracey. She's taller than I remember. Her hair is shorter, though, the shortest I've ever seen it. It's longer on top of her head and swept thick to one side, tapering off above her temples and shaved above her neck. The room dims around her a little, like she's spotlit. Her cheeks plump into a smirk.

"Don't know why they're all making such a fuss," she says. "You being here means one less bed for them to sleep in." She moves forward to hug me and I hesitate. Scared that I'll go right through her like in my dream. I'm rigid with surprise when we connect. I grab the back of her sweater to make sure she's real.

"Hey," I exhale into her neck. I want to say more. That I've missed her. That she smells different, like the pages of a new book. But I only hug her for a second before pulling away. "Where's the rest of them?"

The room comes into focus again. She furrows her brow, looking for a moment like Sabrina. "The same place they always are," she says, pointing with her chin toward the kitchen.

"Am I invisible here or what?" Auntie holds out her arms and Tracey hugs her, too, squishing the dog between them. Auntie whispers something to her I can't hear. By the time I look to the kitchen and back again, Tracey is gone. I forgot what it's like to watch her disappear. She's always slipped in and out of rooms so easily, like water leaking through cracks. She learned all the ways to stay hidden, how to walk with her feet moving toe to heel, how to breathe soft and gentle, how to close doors with the handle turned so the latch doesn't click a sound into the night. You never knew where she was until she wanted to be known.

Auntie nods in encouragement and I follow the noise of laughter into the kitchen. My parents' kitchen is the smallest room in the house but somehow manages to fit everyone. Auntie Doreen moves past me, still holding Atim, and takes the last empty chair closest to the stove. Kassidy sits at the kitchen table and hugs her mom and Atim when they walk by. Steam rises from the big pot on the stove.

Cousins spill out from every countertop and corner. Next to Kassidy on the other mismatched kitchen chairs are Auntie Verna and my mom and dad. I look more and more like my dad every day. Rugged, oval face, deep worry lines around our eyes like sideroad ditches. The cousins who met me at the door filter in and out, too. They're all talking loud, fussing over one another, flitting back and forth from cupboards to the table. Kassidy jumps up when she sees me and her yell fills the kitchen, louder than any other sound. Her smiling cheeks push her eyes into a squint. She bounds over and wraps me in a hug.

"I swear I didn't believe you were coming until now!" she says into my ear. Her long hair falls into my face, lands in my mouth as I open it into a smile. Holding her feels like a light turning on. When kokum told me that cousins were our siblings just the same, I already knew. Just like I knew that our aunties were our parents, too.

Over Kassidy's shoulder, I see my mom get up from the table. She is straight-backed, her weathered hands rubbing her jaw,

Sabrina's jaw, kokum's jaw, and then through her short, spiky hair. Kass lets go of me as Mom starts to walk over. Her strides are quick and sure, like she's built right into the house.

She pulls me into a hug and holds me tightly. She smells like the stew cooking on the stove. I'm surprised at the softness of her, despite all her sharp angles. I want this embrace to mean everything between us is forgiven, that the years of heartbreak can be healed. But for all a body can do, it can't dam a river that runs too wide.

I'm relieved when Auntie Verna's voice breaks us apart.

"My girl!" she screams. "When did you sneak in here?" She pushes back her thick-rimmed glasses as she studies my face.

"Did you not hear the ruckus by the door?" Mom yells back at her sister. "It sounded like a tsunami hit." When Mom lets go of me completely, I think I see her hand fly to her face and wipe a tear away. Too quickly, though, so I wonder if it happened at all.

"I can't hear anything over you and your loud-ass family," Auntie Verna throws back as she bounds over from the table, a blur in her matching yellow dress and cardigan. Her hug is as comforting as her voice, its waves passing through her body into mine.

"They're your loud-ass family, too," Mom says.

From behind my back, Auntie Verna pokes Mom and then darts away. The kitchen erupts with laughter as Mom starts to chase her around the kitchen. Auntie Verna tries to hide behind an uncle, but he moves out of the way, knowing better than to get in the middle of them. Mom grabs Auntie Verna from behind and she shrieks in laughter.

"I'm old now and I'll still kick your ass," Mom says.

As they start to play fight, the swarm begins again. I'm wrapped up in another cousin's hug, and then an uncle's. By the time I reach my dad, he's crying and not trying to hide it. We hug for a long time before I settle in next to Auntie Doreen by the stove. Dad gets up to do the dishes and be closer to me, while Auntie stirs the stew. Atim paws at her feet. She looks like she has an extra set of arms, weaving her way through people to get to cupboards and drawers. She gestures with a vegetable or a spoon to anyone within eyeshot when she needs something passed to her that she can't reach.

I watch my family as they eat, laugh, and talk. The reminder that this is the everyday of this house settles in the lonely place in my mind. I pick at a fresh bun left on the counter so I have something to do with my hands. I breathe in the familiar yet new buzz of my family and wait for a comfort that does not come. Behind the bright dome of the kitchen, grief still stretches like bruises into dark hallways. The urge to run into them pulls at me. Underneath it all, there's an uneasiness I recognize, maybe one that hasn't left.

Kassidy's laughter pulls me back. My cousins' faces glow as they talk and tease each other. I already feel forgotten. The feeling I had after Sabrina saved me from the bees, that there's not enough love to go around, creeps in. This is what I've been missing out on for all these years, and instead of feeling a part of it now, I'm still an outsider looking in. Something deep in me screams with a wanting, the bad part that expects love without having been here to love back.

I look out the window to the backyard. The sun is lower in the blue sky, already smudging into pink, but I know it's hours yet before it disappears. In the birch tree, the crows sit still and quiet.

I pull out my phone and text Joli, telling them I'm home safe and sound. Out of habit now, I go into Sabrina's messages. I look around the kitchen again before Auntie Verna walks over, her long hair swaying. She hugs me, the warmth from her cardigan settling across my skin. It's only then I realize how tired I am.

"You haven't slept in forever." A statement, not a question. She pulls away and takes my head in her hands. She looks deep into my eyes, and I think she's about to tell me something when some cousins run by, bumping into her as they pass. She shouts something at their backs before turning to me again. "You should crawl on into bed."

I look at the stew next to me and then to my dad. "I'll save you a bowl. Hide it in the back of the fridge," he says, kissing my forehead.

I make the rounds in the kitchen, hugging and kissing everyone good night.

"You're in the craft room upstairs," Mom says. "Want me to walk you up?"

The craft room is Sabrina's old room. Mom never calls it that, though. Hearing her say it in person feels like a sliver sliding into thin skin. "No, it's fine. I know where it is."

She gives a tight smile and a nod, then turns and pretends to tidy up the counter. I look around for Tracey as I head upstairs, but she's nowhere to be found.

Sabrina's old room looks completely different. Where her piles of books, journals, and drawings of plants used to fill her desk, now there is a sewing machine and a basket of fabric. Mom even got rid of her four-poster bed and replaced it with a single, blow-up mattress on the floor. Zippers, yarn, and a bag of buttons litter the carpet, but otherwise the room is bare. Sadness blooms inside me when I realize I still expected it to smell like Sabrina.

The mattress has been made up nice with extra blankets and quilts. Two pillows and my old baby blanket that kokum made are stacked on top. I collapse into the bed, the day settling over me all at once. The anxious feeling I've had since I walked into the house sits at the corner of my eye. It's not as dark and silent as it was after kokum's death. Instead, it's as if the bad has been patched over, pushed to the side. Even in this room, there's no evidence Sabrina ever lived here. I wonder what's worse: living in the deep marrow of grief or pretending the person you're grieving never existed in the first place.

I stare out the window, watching the low clouds against the pink and red of the setting sun that make the skyline look like it's on fire. Noise drifts upstairs and I hear my family in the room, even with the door closed. Still, I find myself turning a podcast on before nestling into the blankets. The emptiness of the room spreads and settles around me, but when I close my eyes, I can see what it looked like the last time I was in it. Sabrina sitting on the edge of her bed, her walls covered in photos. When I breathe in, I think for a minute I smell the dried flowers that used to hang from her window, but then it's gone and I know I imagined it. I desperately want to sleep, in a way I haven't since all the dream stuff started. And not because I'm tired, but because I just don't want to be awake anymore.

A bright light stings my eyes when I open them again. Panic flowers in my chest as I shiver against the cold. "No," I groan, squinting against the light. In all the past dreams, the moon was never this bright. I sit up and my heartbeat calms as I realize where I am: still at my parents' house, in Sabrina's old room. The covers are thrown off onto the floor next to me, the cold of the morning sticking to the walls and mattress. I shiver again and grab the blanket, wrapping it around myself. Finally, relief like aloe vera on a burn. I slept all through the night. I didn't dream.

Elated, I head downstairs, trailing my fingers on the walls. In the kitchen, Mom, Auntie Doreen, and Auntie Verna are sitting at the table having coffee, while Kassidy and Tracey sit behind them on opposite ends of the counter looking at their phones. Tracey glances up, catches my eye, and gives me a small smile. I give a tight-lipped one back. I wrap my arms around Auntie Doreen's chest, put my cheek to the back of her head, and glance out the kitchen window. On cloudless days, I swear the prairies are closer to the sun than anywhere else in the world. Not because of the heat. It's the size of the floating orb when nothing else is around it. Beating like a heart dropped into a blue, blue ocean.

"How'd you sleep?" Mom smiles from across the table. I give her a stiff, quick hug.

"Better than I have in a lifetime," I say, proud of the truth in it. I take a sip of Mom's coffee. It's more sugar than coffee, just like she's always had it.

"Awas, get your own," she says, but lets me drink more anyways.

"Any crow dreams?" Auntie Verna asks.

I glance up at Tracey, who's watching me intently. I can't read anything on her face. Kassidy looks up from her phone. "No, nothing. It's been a few days, actually."

I glance out the window again to where the crows sit perched on the birch tree. Concern is still painted across everyone's faces.

"Really, I think the dreams are done now. I don't know, I think I just needed to come home." I hold up my right hand as I speak, like I'm swearing on the bible, and I remember it's the same hand I could feel the crow's beak pressing into for days afterwards. I want my words to convince them as much as I want them to convince myself.

Everyone's expression softens a little, except Auntie Verna's. I can't tell what she's thinking as she looks me over, like she's tracing the outline of my body with chalk. She squints, pushing the bottom of her glasses up with her cheeks. "I don't think dreams are that simple, my girl," she says. She settles back into her chair.

"What do you mean?" I move closer to her, deflating a little.

"Let me tell you about my dreams," she says. And as always, we all turn to listen.

"As a kid, I used to dream in single colours. I'd fall asleep and dream I was walking the thin dirt road to kokum and mosum's farmhouse. Everything from the dust floating in front of my face to the blades of grass in the ditch would be a different shade of blue. I'd dream in blue every night, until out of nowhere, I'd dream I was swimming in a sea of red. Weeks would pass in red before I'd dream I was flying in green. I've dreamt like this for as far back as I can remember, before I knew the names of the colours or thought to ask if this was even normal."

As Auntie Verna talks, the air moves around her like a lazy river. Her eyes catch ours in turn. There's a depth to them like she's seeing more than just us. Though she's the youngest of her sisters, Mom always said that Auntie Verna was older than her years. Always watching, careful of the world around her.

"I started to notice a pattern to the colours," Auntie Verna continues. "When they were at their sharpest, most vibrant, I knew I had to be careful in real life. That's when strange, bad things would happen. It's when the coyotes would move closer to the house at night, their howls deep and loud like they were right outside my window. We'd wake up in the morning to a dead chicken or two in the coop. It's when the kids on the school bus would notice the smallness of me and my sisters, start to get brave like the coyotes. I had to have my guard up after these dreams, watch after everything with a little more attention. There was a heaviness to the world, like everything could break at any moment.

"When the colours in my dreams were dim, slight hues, I could relax a little more. I still had to be careful, because we always had to be careful, but the world felt less tight. I didn't have to keep an eye on my sisters every second on the playground, and we could sit on the deck after dark without worrying. I could breathe without a hand on my heart, move around a little easier."

I watch Mom grow slightly more tense as Auntie talks. It's not visible on her face, but her hands grip her coffee cup harder. Her back straightens. I want to reach for her, rub her back, smile at her, but I just cross my arms again, turning my attention back to Auntie.

"I noticed that the colours meant something, too, but even they changed meaning without any clear pattern." As Auntie talks, the lazy river of energy enveloping us starts to quicken. "Sometimes orange was a safe colour, telling me that in real life everything was okay. Sometimes it was a sign of rage. Blue could mean I was moving on a good path, but sometimes it meant I had to slow down. I'd dream in the colour, then wake up and have to really think about what it meant. About what felt right. The knowing doesn't live in my brain, though, like most people think. It lives in my gut.

"There were times I didn't listen to what I knew to be true, and I paid for it when I woke up. One time, in eleventh grade, I dreamt of my best friend, Sam, in red. I saw Sam on a red road, surrounded by red trees, in the passenger seat of a red car kicking up red dirt. Before I woke up, I knew in my gut that it was a warning. The next day, Sam told me she was skipping school for the rest of the week and hitchhiking to Grande Prairie to meet up with her boyfriend. As she spoke, I saw a redness start to glow from her skin, like a shroud sprouting from deep in her pores and seeping out. I told her I didn't think it was a good idea, that she should wait for the weekend and I'd go with her. But she didn't listen. She kissed me goodbye, and I just let her go. That was the last time I ever saw her."

Auntie pauses to swallow, the river she's conjured around her slowing to an eddy. Behind her big glasses, her eyes glint with liquid, though no tears fall. Auntie has told me about Sam before.

Every time we pass a poster of a missing girl around town, the
torn pieces of paper yellowing at the edges, she tells a different
story about her friend. But she's never told me about the dream.

"The dreams have saved us, too," Auntie says. She tucks her
long hair behind her ears, catching the arms of her glasses. "They
might have saved your mom. One time not long after Sam was
disappeared, I dreamt a deep green lake swallowing Loretta up.
Up until then, green was usually good. It felt like a poultice on
a wound. But this time, my body was telling me different. When
I woke up, my stomach hurt and was bloating like I'd just swallowed a gallon of water. A few days later, the dream was still
sitting on the edge of my mind and these two wanted to go down
to the lake."

She nods at her sisters and I glance over at Mom, who has let
go of her cup and is now holding on to the kitchen table like it's
a life raft. Auntie Doreen's curly hair bobs as she signals for her
sister to keep going.

"It was a hot summer day, the sticky kind of hot that spreads
across the prairies like syrup." Auntie's eyes are somewhere else.
"Loretta and Doreen were putting on their bathing suits when I
told them we needed to stay home. I could see the green glowing
from Loretta's skin, like algae stuck to a rock. I cried and cried,
said they shouldn't go to the lake. They both brushed me off,
told me to smarten up and get my suit on. But I just cried even
harder, dropping to my knees and sobbing into the floor. There
was something in my pleading that made them listen. So we stayed
home. We found out the next day that a kid from town drowned
in the lake."

Auntie Verna pauses. I feel nauseated, and now I'm holding on
to the edge of the kitchen table, too. Auntie Doreen bows her head
solemnly. Kassidy and Tracey have made their way from the coun-

ter to the chairs next to me, like they got caught up on the tide and floated there. They look straight ahead, their faces pale. Mom is still unreadable, and her voice surprises me when she speaks.

"All those kids who pulled him to shore," she croaks. "Friends of ours. They were alone with the body for hours before they could get help."

Auntie Verna nods at Mom and puts a hand over hers. She squints her eyes, her cheeks pushing her glasses up further on her face again. After a minute, she looks at me. "Don't write off these dreams too quickly, my girl," she says. "If mine taught me anything, it's that you have to pay attention."

"I didn't know," Mom says. She's still gripping the table.

"I've only ever told Doreen," Auntie Verna says. "I knew to listen to the dreams, but I never knew how to talk about it. Not really."

Mom presses her lips together and gives a small nod. "I know." She looks like she's about to say something more, but then Auntie Verna looks at me.

"My girl, I've been dreaming about you for the past three nights."

My mouth goes dry. I feel the pulsing of my own heartbeat in my head.

"In the dream, you're flickering, like a light that's about to go out. You're there and then gone and then there again." The river of energy in the room is back and it's crashing toward me. "In the dream, and when I look at you now, you're red red red."

⊲ᓕᑊᓯ ᔪᐤ

In my parents' small bathroom, I crouch on the floor and scroll through my phone. I breathe slowly, feel the air sift through my body like it's sand. After Auntie Verna finished telling us about her dreams, I rushed out of the kitchen like it was on fire. There's a soft knock on the bathroom door.

"Mack." Mom talks low. "You okay?"

I try another breath and lean harder against the wall. "I'm good. Everything's good."

She sighs on the other side of the door. I can tell she wants to press, to keep talking, but there's more between us than just wood.

"Look, I gotta go do some running around. Auntie Doreen went out but she should be back soon. Dad's just at work." She's trying to be a comfort.

"It's fine, Mom. Thanks."

She pauses another second by the door before I hear her walk away. Whispers between Auntie Verna, Tracey, and Kassidy seep through the walls but I can't make out what they're saying. *It doesn't matter,* I think. *The dreams are gone, they're over. They have to be.* I repeat this to myself, waiting for my breathing to even, but it doesn't.

Finally, I will myself to stand. I turn on the tap but don't put my hands under the water. I just listen to the sound pouring into the sink and stare at myself in the mirror. I search the air around my body for any sign of colour, red emanating from my skin, but I see nothing. I continue to breathe slowly in and out.

When I go back out into the kitchen, Mom is gone. Kassidy is outside with Atim, and Auntie Verna is going through the cupboards, pulling out baking ingredients and bottles. Tracey sits at the kitchen table, alone.

"I'm making waffles and eggs, my girl," Auntie says a little too cheerily. "Won't be long."

Tracey keeps her eyes on me as I nod at Auntie. I don't have the heart to tell her I'm not hungry.

"Quick game before breakfast?" Tracey asks.

I almost laugh at the shift in tone. "Yeah, sure," I say. "It's been a while since I kicked your ass."

A shiver runs through me as we move into the living room. It's colder in here than the kitchen, the shadows in each corner press into the walls like rot. The pullout couch faces our old TV, empty chip bags and Gatorade bottles litter the coffee table. Blankets are piled in the corner, ready to be made into a bed for whoever decides to land here.

We settle onto the couch, the cushions so worn they sag in the middle, pulling us together. Tracey turns the TV on with the remote, the batteries held inside by duct tape, and *Mortal Kombat* flashes ready. She passes me a PlayStation controller.

We've been playing this game since as far back as I can remember. As kids, me, Sabrina, Tracey, and the cousins would play king's court. Whoever won would keep playing, and whoever died would lose their turn and have to give up the controller to the next person in line. Tracey usually won.

As we wait for the game to load, I study the pictures on the wall next to us. They still haven't changed from when Mom first put them up. Pictures of the family, at the lake, at home, out at kokum's farm. She would always add photos without taking any old ones down, so it's basically just a collage, snapshots of different years of our lives. There are no new photos, though. The most recent ones were put up a year before kokum died.

Tracey watches me study the wall. "Can't believe in a few weeks, it'll be a year since Sab died."

I stare at a photo of Sabrina and Tracey when they were three. They're smiling into the camera as kokum kneels next to them, a fish as long as they are held between them. I would have been just a baby.

I steal a look at Tracey, her hands sure around the controller, relaxing into it like it's a part of her. The last time I saw her in person was three years ago. Around the same time as in the dream-memory. She looks younger than I imagined she would after so long. Her face catches the light from outside.

"Are you still mad? That I didn't come back for Sabrina's funeral?"

I don't mean to ask the question, but it comes spilling out like water from a broken tap. It's the question that's been sitting at the back of my mind every day for almost a year.

I look away from her to the TV, not wanting to see her reaction. On the *Mortal Kombat* home screen, our icons select the characters we always choose: mine picks Kitana, hers Johnny Cage.

If she's surprised by the question, she doesn't show it. "Who said I was mad?"

I catch myself. Tracey had always been quick to anger. "I figured . . . since we didn't talk . . ."

"I don't know." She sighs and picks a fighting arena. "You just didn't show up. You didn't show up for her."

When I didn't come back for Sabrina's funeral, I found out that

I could never hide completely. My family still found ways to reach me. They all called. Aunties, uncles, cousins, family friends. They called and cooed and tried to say everything they thought would be a relief. They kept talking about luck.

The night Sabrina died, she was making a quick trip to the store. She got in her car, put on her seatbelt, and had the keys in the ignition before a blood vessel erupted in her brain. It was lucky, everyone said, that she hadn't been driving, putting other people on the road in danger, before she had the aneurysm. It was lucky, they said, that it didn't happen in the house, traumatizing everyone inside. Lucky it was only my mom who had to see her, a half hour later, when she looked out the kitchen window and saw Sabrina's car still parked in the driveway and something slumped over the steering wheel. Lucky it was just her and no one else. The timing. How lucky. Like someone had planned it that way.

Timing wasn't the luck of it, though. The luck was that we lost Sabrina all at once, instead of in pieces. One thing they don't tell you about when someone you love dies because of a sickness is that death happens in a million different ways in the lead-up to the actual moment. We lost kokum one bit at a time as she got sicker and sicker. When she got too weak to hold her cards, we lost the air around her and the aunties playing crib. When she couldn't stand for long anymore, we lost the smell of her baking. When the machines took over breathing for her, we lost the sound of her booming laugh filling any room. Of course, people cried about not getting to say goodbye to Sabrina, but there's nothing very good about a goodbye. I got to say goodbye to kokum before she died and I didn't get to say goodbye to Sabrina, and neither one gave me any peace.

I see in the way Tracey runs her hand through her hair and shifts her eyes that her body, too, doesn't hold peace. That something is still haunting her. It wasn't just that I didn't show up for

Sabrina. It's that I didn't show up for her, or Mom, or anyone else. I let everyone hold the grief without my hands to help.

"I'd do it different if I could," I say as Kitana and Johnny Cage pop up on-screen, opposite each other, ready to fight. Even though it's the truth, it doesn't matter.

There's an alternate life being led somewhere else. One where Mom doesn't spend hours with the phone pressed to her ear, calling me over and over, because I'm ignoring her, a thousand kilometres away in a different city. Instead, I answer on the first ring and come home right away.

There's a timeline where Tracey doesn't have to spend every night alone. We sleep together in her room and wake up with the sun. We swear we hear Sabrina's voice from the bathroom. We cry together and aren't afraid of our sad, because we're alone and can stop pretending for everyone else.

In this timeline, Mom isn't split in two, one part readying her daughter to be buried and one part worrying about the one who's too far away. Instead, she gets comforted by my dad. She gets to be held the way she deserves, too.

In this timeline, I wash Sabrina's hair before the wake. And braid it in the way she likes. Me and Tracey get to imagine out loud which ancestors have travelled back to get her. We all go to the funeral together. We make sure the other one is eating. Our aunties rock us to sleep like they used to when we were kids.

In this timeline, maybe Tracey doesn't start drinking again. But maybe she does and that's okay, too, because love isn't conditional. Maybe my mom's heart breaks just a little bit less. Maybe the world doesn't grow dim, dim, dim.

Tracey sighs and nods in an absent way. Kitana and Johnny stand in an arena with a chain-link fence that has barbed wire at the top. In the reflection of the TV, I see a flap of wings in the living room window. I try to soften myself, to pull something out of her, to understand where we stand. "Anyways, I'm sorry. I heard you weren't doing great for a while. After the funeral."

Tracey tenses as Johnny Cage moves forward to attack first. "Yeah, well, seeing her was hard."

Mom told me Sabrina had an open-casket wake, just like kokum. The memory of me, Tracey, and Sabrina, hands clasped and standing side by side looking down at kokum in her casket flashes in my mind. I think about Tracey looking down at Sabrina alone.

"Seeing a dead body is never a picnic," I say. I try to get Kitana to block, but I'm too slow. Johnny doesn't let up, alternating between punching and kicking.

Tracey scoffs into her controller. "That's not what I mean."

"What do you mean, then?" Johnny is relentless, and Kitana tries to fight back, but her health bar starts to lower.

"Nothing," she says, almost sadly. "Never mind."

A month after Sabrina died, I saw her on the bus. It wasn't her, of course. But in one moment of forgetting, a moment in another life where I didn't lose her, I saw her. I stared at the girl, her brown hair and sharp face, long after I realized she wasn't Sabrina. I rested my eyes above her head and tried to blur my own vision. Tried to trick myself into seeing a ghost.

That was the only time I called Tracey after the funeral. I got off the bus before my stop and called. It rang twice and went to voicemail. "I saw her," I said into silence. "I saw her for a second on the bus." And before I knew it, I was crying. Wailing in the street. The sound of my sobs echoed back at me through whatever force connected my phone to Tracey's before it cut me off. She never called me back.

Kitana and Johnny Cage finally break apart, bouncing up and down in fighting positions. Tracey's fingers twitch. The bad part of me growls inside my stomach, bites at my insides.

"Mom said something the other day," Tracey says, her fingers moving along her controller as she speaks. "You were asking about a scar on Sabrina's collarbone."

I think about the thick, claw-like scar on the grey-haired Sabrina and on the Sabrina in the photograph on the lake. "Yeah, I don't remember it being there. But when I looked at a photo of us on the lake, the last summer before I left"—I swallow—"she definitely has one."

"She didn't," Tracey says. Her hands move in rhythm to Johnny Cage but her eyes don't.

I move Kitana carefully, trying to go in for a hit. "I'll show you the photo, I'm telling you—"

"You're not telling me anything about her I don't know better," she says, cutting me off. In her voice, I hear the rage I'm so used to seeing with her.

Johnny blocks Kitana's blows with ease. He moves forward as Kitana crouches back in a defence position.

I quiet and try to steady my voice. "Something might have happened—"

"And if it did, who do you think would know? Someone who left or someone who saw her every single day?" Johnny hits Kitana with a combo string that knocks her already-low health down to zero. Kitana dies and I say nothing.

We start another round. Minutes of silence go by.

"So you're not mad I didn't come back for Sabrina's funeral, you're mad that I left in the first place," I say quietly, trying to understand. Kitana readies herself again, but Johnny is already on her.

Tracey sighs again. "I'm mad about all of it," she says. Johnny hits Kitana with another combo string. "You did what you always do. You run. You hide. You don't deal and leave it for the rest of us."

"You can't blame me for wanting to leave," I say, my neck getting hot in defence. "You remember how this house was after kokum. I could barely breathe here. What was I supposed to do?"

"Deal with it!" Tracey yells. She puts down her controller and Johnny goes slack on the TV. "Like we all did. Together."

"It's unfair to ask that." I turn to her, forgetting any game we were playing.

"Unfair is bailing when shit gets hard. When people need you."

The heat moves from my neck through my chest. The quiet of the room presses against my ears. "So I should have stayed for what? To watch kokum and Sabrina get forgotten?" I yell back. "This is the first time any of you have even mentioned her. You're all living as if she never existed!" A lump like a fist forms in my throat.

Tracey is silent for a second, and her voice is sad when she answers, the sound of rage disappearing all at once. "How do you know how we've been living?"

I try to swallow down the lump, but it stays. I want to reply, but I know if I do, I'll start to cry, and I don't want to cry right now.

Tracey sighs and her face softens as she searches mine. "The truth is that you're just dealing with the absence of her now. We've already been doing it for a year. We haven't forgotten her, we've just been learning to live without her. Just like we had to do with kokum."

"I'm here now," I say. "I came back and I'm here and I'm trying."

"And why are you here?" Tracey's voice cracks. "You're not here for us. You're not here for Mom, who you're still punishing because you need someone to be mad at. You're not here because of kokum or Sabrina. You're here for you, because you needed something. That's what it took to get you home."

Kitana and Johnny Cage are still on the TV screen, abandoned and bouncing in a crouch. I feel ten years old again. And I know she's right.

Her eyes shift to the open window behind me. When she looks back at me again, her jaw is set, her stare steady. "Want me to tell you something you already know?" She picks up her controller again. "You're so mad at yourself that you've turned it into disdain for everyone else. And you think the shittier you are to us, we'll all have no choice but to be awful to you, to hate you right back. Well, I almost do."

I don't know what to say, so I say nothing. We play again in silence for a while. Kitana dies over and over. We fight in every arena. We listen to the instrumental music of *Mortal Kombat* and Auntie singing low from the kitchen. The smell of bacon eventually makes its way into the room.

"Breakfast is ready!" Auntie Verna calls from the kitchen.

"Okay," I yell back, my voice unsteady. I button-mash harder. On the screen, Kitana jumps back and forth and sporadically punches. Some land, some don't. Johnny is more controlled. He moves assuredly, knows patience, when to block.

"I did come back for me," I say, my voice shaking and low. "I was terrified. The dreams I was having . . . they weren't right."

I steal another look at her, and this time she feels it. "But I think they're done now and I want to make things better. With everyone."

She's silent for a few seconds. "Remember when we used to build forts in the woods next to the lake?"

Kitana's health bar has more red than yellow and my hands start to slip off the buttons.

Sometimes, Mom would let us miss school and take us down to the lake. We'd go to our camping spot, and she'd set up her beach blanket and romance novel next to the water while we walked through the trees, a bucket of nails and a hammer in hand.

"They were hardly forts. The structural integrity of those things was suspect," I joke.

Johnny starts to slow down, sporadic like he forgot his combo strings. Kitana hits him a few more times and his health bar starts to slowly empty. "Remember when Sabrina would disappear in the woods if me and you would fight?" Tracey went on. "We wouldn't even notice. One minute we were yelling at each other, and the next she was just gone."

I break my gaze from the TV for a second to look at my sister's face. Her skin looks soft, her eyes reflecting the bright of the screen. The sad truth of it is, Sabrina was always the glue between me and Tracey. We loved each other, of course, but our relationship was never as easy as each of ours was with Sabrina. She was always sure of herself in a way me and Tracey never were. I think we both clung to her for that. Without her, we were just two loose strings looking to be tied to something.

On the screen, Johnny starts to sway.

"We'd yell out for her but she wouldn't answer. We'd cry with worry. Retell all the bad stories about the woods. Imagine the bear traps she was stuck in. The wolves that took her away," she continues.

I want to let go of my controller and hold her. Rub her back or just touch her arm, anything to tell her I'm with her, but that kind of tenderness is out of reach for us. "She was always just being a little shit, though. She'd hide to scare us. She was never that far away."

"But we always stopped fighting," I say. "We'd stop to find her."

"This is the last time I'm calling you for breakfast and then I'm giving the rest to Atim!" Auntie's voice rings through the air between us.

On the TV screen, Kitana knocks Johnny Cage out in a KO,

my first win since we started playing. We both lay down our controllers at the same time, like an offering. She looks at me again and opens her mouth to speak, but then closes it. If there was ever a time to reach for her, to say something, do anything to start rebuilding this bridge, it's now. I stay silent, keep my eyes down, and head into the kitchen.

Auntie Doreen and Mom come back from town as me, Tracey, and Kassidy finish setting the table for breakfast. Auntie Doreen and Kassidy live out of town, but they decided to stay with us at the house while I'm here. We pass around eggs, bacon, and waffles. We don't talk about dreams, or what Auntie Verna told us that morning. We aren't ignoring it on purpose, that's just how this family holds hurt. If we paid attention to it all the time, it'd destroy us. Instead, we laugh, we tease each other, we eat. Hurt lives with us always. Like dirt under our fingernails.

I think harder about what Tracey said, that I'm only here for me. When I left, I thought the result would be twofold: I wouldn't worry about anyone anymore, and no one would have to worry about me. But now I see that's not how it works. I still had people to lose. I just became a full, clotted vein. And now I was back to ask them to heal me, to help me out of this mess I helped create. It feels bad to be loved this much when you don't think you deserve it.

The aunties pull out a deck of cards and a crib board as the last of the butter and spilled syrup are wiped from the table. I watch them play together, the smell of breakfast still hanging in the room, their laughter moving through me like smoke. Every now and then, Auntie Verna looks up at me and gives me a small, encouraging smile. Something inside me settles, some nerve, some jagged thing. I smile back and feel my eyes get heavy, a months-long tiredness moving across my body.

Eventually, I slip away upstairs and into my room. I close the curtains, though they're too thin to block the light out completely, and curl up on my mattress. The weight of the day sticks to my skin, and I close my eyes and breathe in the smell of home.

When I open them again, I'm staring into bright orange flames, heat full on my face. I jump, thinking the house has caught on fire, panic shooting through me. But I'm outside. The fire is contained in one spot, and people stand around me, swaying to the sound of country music.

A shock of remembering comes over me as I take in the rest of my surroundings: the curve of the giant gravel pits, the trees piercing the cloud-covered sky, the light dancing across faces and red Solo cups gripped in hands.

A lump of terror rises in my throat as I spot myself, Tracey, and Sabrina, plus a younger Kassidy, across the bonfire. I had been trying to convince myself, and my family, that the dreams had stopped. But somewhere in my gut I already knew: they hadn't gone anywhere.

The bottoms of my feet sting as I start to walk across the gravel, circling around the fire, until I reach the group of them sitting shoulder to shoulder in the open bed of a Ford pickup, a plaid blanket pulled across their laps.

"Can we leave? This spot is getting tired," Sabrina says as she glances around. I remember her wanting to leave as soon as we got there, but Tracey convinced her to stay a little bit longer.

Kassidy nods and hops off the truck, and dream-Mackenzie follows suit, pulling the blanket off everyone and throwing it into a bundle in the back. Tracey looks like she's about to protest but then doesn't. "Yeah, all right. It's winding down anyways and they keep playing this shit music."

I watch them make their way around the circle, saying their goodbyes, and then away from the party toward the water. Exhaustion spreads through me. I want to curl up on the ground until the dream ends, but I know that's not how it works. The four of them walk beside one another, and I follow behind slowly, watching the way their hair sways and catches in the bonfire light at their backs.

Then I hear Tracey's voice. "Let's go the short way through the woods!" And I stop in my tracks. My breath catches in my throat. I realize why I've been brought back here. A memory shakes loose.

This is the night Tracey ran into the woods and Sabrina went in after her. This is the night that, for forty-five minutes, they were lost to us.

"Fuck," I say out loud, knowing no one will hear me, and start walking again, quickening my pace to catch back up to them. I watch dream-Mackenzie crane her neck up toward the sky. Now I remember looking at the blanket of clouds, thinking about how dark it was despite the full moon. How it had gotten much darker compared to our walk over.

"It's too dark," Sabrina says. "We're going around."

"Are you scared of ghosts or something?" Tracey says, wiggling her fingers in front of Sabrina's face before Sabrina slaps them down.

"I'm scared your drunk ass will get us lost," she replies.

The dread rises in my chest as they walk further down the service road. I see Tracey, on the side of the road closest to the woods, look into the trees and then back to her siblings and cousin. From the side, I catch the grin on her face.

"Keep walking!" I yell. I run through dream-Mackenzie and Kassidy, static coursing through my body, and stop a couple feet in front of them. "Keep walking to the water. Don't let them go into the woods!" Of course, neither of them notice me. They all keep talking as they walk right through my useless body, and the wave of electric pulses fades again. The worst kind of nightmare is one where you know what is about to happen and you can't stop it.

I watch the backs of them again, walking away, and I see what I didn't that night: Tracey looks toward the trees again. The last bit of firelight from the bonfire, now yards away, catches the curve of Tracey's grinning cheeks. The dark pines she looks into sway in the breeze. A glint of white flashes in the treetops, something moving from one branch to another. Tracey freezes in place. Her face falls slack.

And then she runs. Tracey bolts into the trees before anyone has a chance to stop her.

"Tracey!" Sabrina yells, and turns to run after her. Dream-Mackenzie catches Sabrina's arm.

I feel again like I did that night, frozen in fear, as Sabrina looks back at dream-Mackenzie, all confusion. If there's one thing you're taught on the prairies as an iskwew, it's that you never go anywhere alone. This was always a warning we knew to be very real. *You aren't ravens,* Mom would say. *You are crows. You travel together everywhere.*

Sabrina holds dream-Mackenzie's stare for another second, and I groan as I watch dream-Mackenzie let her go. Sabrina sprints toward the woods yelling back over her shoulder, "Meet us on the other side!" And then she's gone, too, swallowed by the trees.

Even in the darkness, I see the blood drain from dream-Mackenzie's face. The air feels like a twig ready to snap. "Should we go after them?" Kassidy asks.

Dream-Mackenzie looks toward the dark woods and back at the road.

"Go with them," I plead at dream-Mackenzie, as I realize tears are welling up in my eyes. "Go in after your sisters!"

I see the hesitation in her face and remember thinking in that moment that we should be like Sabrina and follow without a second thought. But I let fear take over and pushed the thought away. "No, it's too dark," dream-Mackenzie says instead, her voice hollow. "They know the way. We'll meet them on the other side."

Even though I knew this would happen, my stomach drops when I hear my own words. They walk quickly and in silence down to the shoreline that leads back to the campsite. As I watch them go, I hear sounds coming from the trees and know that dream-Mackenzie can hear them, too.

We let Sabrina go in after Tracey alone. We let her go into the dark woods, and we didn't go in after her. I didn't even turn back when I felt the pang of wrongness in my bones. Because sometimes fear is so deep it convinces you that yelling sounds like the crunch of sticks, like the whip of tree branches, like the sound of boots running. We didn't go in after her. We let her become a raven.

I move to follow Kassidy and dream-Mackenzie. The darkness presses in on all sides as another realization washes over me. *I don't have to make the same mistake twice.*

I stop, then turn on my heel and start running toward the woods, toward my sisters. The trees are darker shadows, and as I get closer, I see icicles forming, dripping from branches like knives. I breathe hard and puffs of cold air form in front of my face. My skin prickles into goosebumps, and a heavy frost creeps along the ground.

A shiver runs through my body as I take a step into the woods and see, out of the corner of my eye, a sticklike figure move, quick and jarring. Two eyes blink open, staring out from the darkness. The eyes are a milky, unseeing white.

"You should have come in after me," I hear in the darkness. The voice is low, full of rocks. The eyes glow, moving forward from between two spruce trees, wolf lichen hanging from the frozen branches like limp hair. Clouds move above us, and the moon illuminates the rest of the creature.

I gasp. It's Sabrina. Her body is thin and pale. Her face sunken. The corners of her mouth have decayed away, holes where her cheeks should be expose her rotting teeth. Her long hair is entirely grey and falls across bone-thin shoulders. She brings a finger up to her cracked lips, a motion for me to quiet. Her fingers are nothing but tendons and bone.

I hesitate, but finally choke out a whisper, "I know. I know that now." I look around us. Dream-Mackenzie and Kassidy are out of sight, far away by now. The party we just left is quiet. Behind Sabrina, snow and ice crawl up the trunks of trees like pulsing veins.

"You should have come in after me," she says again, the rocks in her throat grinding harder, louder, "but you're a coward."

My feet are so cold they burn. "What happened to you?" I plead. "What happened to you in here?" My eyes dart to the woods behind her.

She cocks her head to the side and wisps of stringy hair fall forward. Underneath a tear in her flannel, the hook of a scar stretches up from her collarbone. "I found the hollow in her body," she says.

Something about the calm in her voice makes me nauseous and I feel like I'm going to gag.

"You know what I'm talking about," she whispers, taking a step forward, a tree uprooting. Her milky-white eyes trace my body. I stay frozen in place. "I see the hollow in you, too."

Another step. She's so close now I can smell her, like meat inside a freezer. "You should have come in after me."

Up close, I see the blue and purple veins stretching like webs under the skin that hasn't yet rotted away. She reaches toward me with bony hands. Before I can open my mouth to scream, I feel a familiar tug, like a rope on my spine.

I'm back on the bed in Sabrina's old room, sweating. When I exhale, a puff of white forms in front of my face in the sunlit room.

ᖃᒥᓗᑕᓐ

The first thought I have when I sit up is about death and how it makes a fool out of everyone. Even though I know these dreams aren't the same as dying, I can't help but let the thought worm in. Maybe dreaming is just a series of small deaths. At least, maybe it is for me.

I make myself as quiet as possible as I tiptoe to the bathroom, soak a towel in warm water, and bring it back to my room. I sit back on my bed and press the towel to the bottoms of my feet, still frozen from the cold frost of the woods. I can still feel the jagged points of gravel in my heels.

I curl into a ball and shut my eyes. No matter how I try to calm my breathing, the tightness in my chest won't ease. The dreams never left. Coming home wasn't the answer.

Sabrina's voice rings in my head. *You should have come in after me.*

Is this why Sabrina has come back to me in my dreams? Not because I didn't come back for her funeral, but because I didn't follow her into the woods?

I think back to my memory of that night. The sinking feeling of waiting for Tracey and Sabrina to come out of those woods close to the campsite. And they did come out of them. They were fine. Weren't they? We just got spooked by the woods and the dark.

The ache from my chest spreads to my limbs, a sharp static, like when I passed through my sisters in my dream. My body is waking up, remembering something my mind wanted to forget. Coming home didn't do anything but rip open a wound. And I'm still being haunted, anyways.

I try to make sense of the Sabrina in my dreams. My heart drops as I think about her walking right through me as if I were a ghost. Before she ran into the woods, she looked exactly how I remember her. But when I saw her again minutes later, she looked like a zombie, and she had the scar on her chest, like the Sabrina on the lake. What the fuck is happening?

I look at the time. It's 1 p.m., only a couple hours since I came up to my room. I pull out my phone and find Joli's number. The line rings three times before they pick up.

My shoulders lower in relief. "Hello!"

They laugh on the other end. "You sound so excited to hear my voice. You haven't been gone that long."

"I know," I say. "Things have been weird here."

"Have the dreams stopped?"

"No—" My voice breaks as I admit it. "I just woke up from another one."

"Fuck. What happened?"

They're quiet as I tell them everything that just happened.

"Jesus, okay," they say. "Any more texts from Sabrina?"

"Nothing since I left." A lump rises in my throat. "What the fuck am I doing wrong?"

They're quiet for a second. "Look, I talked to my mom, and I think we figured something out."

I swallow. Out the window, I see the three crows perched in the birch tree. They ruffle their feathers.

"It's about Sabrina. The grey-haired zombie Sabrina in your dreams." As they say Sabrina's name, their voice comes through robotic, like they're going through a tunnel.

"Where are you?" I ask. "You're breaking up."

On the other end of the line, Joli's voice cuts in and out, making it impossible to understand what they're saying. I look at my phone. My service is at full bars, but I get up and move around the room anyways.

"Joli?" I repeat into the phone, plugging my other ear with my finger. After a minute of trying, the line cuts and goes dead completely.

I try calling them back, but it goes right to voicemail. I text them and stare at the screen, waiting for a response. I message Joli on Facebook and Instagram and then lie down. I don't want to chance falling asleep again, but I don't want to face my family now, either. Do I tell them about my dream? Admit to the fact that coming home meant nothing except more trouble?

Eventually, I go back downstairs and try to fade into the background of the house. It's not that hard to do with so many people around. By dinner, I feel forgotten again, even though I'm surrounded by people. I eat quickly, my mind on the dropped call with Joli and the dream from my nap, and head up to my room again after saying quick good nights. I listen at the door until I hear the noise of dinner die down, plates being cleared, people leaving. The stillness of the house presses against my cheeks. Quiet is strange here, where the sounds of laughter, fighting, and crying live in the walls.

Only when I'm sure I'm alone again do I open the window to the night, letting the cool breeze sneak in. I put on an extra pair of socks and shoes I snuck up from downstairs. I pull on a sweater and my jacket and lie on top of the covers. I'm sweating, but I don't care. If I wake up in my dream again, being warm is the only thing I can control.

I wake up in darkness. I'm floating gently, like driftwood over waves. The smell of pine sap and soil hangs in the air. Hovering above me is the outline of a face with a sharp jawline and wide shoulders.

"Sabrina?" I say into the darkness.

"It's me, my girl," Mom whispers, brushing the hair off my face. Her hand pauses on my shoulder. I stay quiet and piece together the room around me. The sewing machine on the desk, the curtains limp against the window. I can hear the deep hum of the dryer downstairs. A dim light peeks through the window, highlighting Mom's open mouth and brown eyes. The smell of pine is coming from her, her soap maybe. I'm not in a dream.

"You awake?" Mom whispers again.

I nod and sit up. My jacket is unzipped and it falls down my shoulders.

"Let's go," Mom says. She doesn't say anything about me being fully dressed in bed.

The confusion clears as I get out of bed and follow her down the stairs.

Mom's already filled up a thermos of coffee and packed a lunch for the road. I don't bother showering. Instead, I throw on an old baseball cap of Dad's before following her to the car. It's not even 5 a.m. and the sun is just peeking up past the neighbouring rooftops. The morning smells like fresh dew.

We get into the truck in silence, the air still cold from the night before. It's been years since we've been alone together and even longer since we've gone scavenging.

"I didn't know you still did this," I say.

Mom shrugs and gives a hesitant smile. "Every now and then."

We follow drooping telephone wires through the empty streets and pass the gas co-op that signals the edge of town before Mom floors the truck, fields and trees whipping past our windows. We take another turn down a dirt road off the highway heading west, away from the rising sun, toward Grand Prairie. We pass more trees and fields in silence. Oil drills shaped like giant mosquitoes sit frozen still in the middle of tree-cleared land. When we were kids, we'd play a game of how many machine mosquitoes we could count when we'd go anywhere, especially if we were scavenging. The drills were always moving, dipping in and out of the earth like they were bobbing for apples. But I had never seen them all still like this, quiet, rusting ghosts.

The scavenging went back as far as I can remember. Mom would wake up my sisters and me at the crack of dawn, and we'd drive in what seemed like no particular direction, though Mom always seemed to know where we were going. For hours we'd listen to CDs, eat the road snacks Mom packed, fight or sleep in the back seat. Then we'd come upon an old house or barn, or it would come upon us. Sometimes Mom would drive through fields to get to where she saw, for a split second, a roof between tree branches. She'd take gravel roads and trails not meant to be driven on. Sometimes she would open up a locked gate with bolt cutters or take down a cracked wooden fence if there were no animals that could get out.

When we got to the barns or houses, Mom would park the car out of view of the road and grab an empty picnic basket from the truck bed.

"Remember," she'd say every time, "you can only keep what will fit in here. Stay clear of rotten wood and any stairs unless I say they're okay. And do not leave each other's sight."

Those were our only rules: don't take too much, stay safe, and stay together.

The houses were long abandoned but still full of furniture, toys, tools, and clothes. We'd go through everything. Mom would disappear and come back with an old chair, an ironing board, a broken picture frame. I never understood why she chose to take the things she did. Mom could look at something broken and rusted and see its potential, what could happen when she took it home and washed it, gave it a new face. That was Mom's gift, seeing things for what they could be, fixing the broken, making them whole again.

We were never allowed to keep photo albums, jewellery, or anything that seemed like it could be important to someone else. "Those were never meant for us," Mom told us once. "Leave them where you find them."

The trips lessened as we got older, and now I can't even remember the last time we went out together. The truck bumps along the highway as we drive in silence for a while longer. "Does Tracey ever come out with you anymore?"

"Oh, she hasn't been interested in coming with me in years," Mom says. She tries to hide the sad in her voice, but I catch it, the lilt that means she wishes it were different.

I open the lunch bag and see two sandwiches in ziplock bags, two apples, and a small container of almonds. I grab the sandwiches, open mine, and pass Mom hers. In between bites, I look out across the prairies, the budding green and yellow of wheat and canola already pushing up from the fields. Every so often, creeks flash out from the woods, cattails and reeds poking out through the blue water. No matter how far ahead I can see, it's still not as far as the land stretches.

"Why are there so many of these abandoned houses and barns everywhere?" I ask, trying to fill the silence. I don't know why I'd never thought to ask before.

Mom presses the brakes and her gaze moves to the ditch ahead of us. A doe and her fawns are camouflaged in the brush. I would never have noticed. It's amazing what the eyes forget to look for when they've been gone from a place long enough.

"I don't really know," Mom replies, slowing down a touch more before the family of deer dart further into the woods. She starts to speed up again. "The ones we used to find when you were younger were abandoned during the Depression, I think. A lot of places I've seen in the past year have been left much more recently, though."

"Yeah, but to leave all their things behind?" I think about the boarded-up businesses in town, the empty houses.

"It's just stuff." She shrugs and I look out the window again. Tips of trees rock against the sky.

"Where are we going, anyways?" I ask.

"Why do we have to be going anywhere?"

I think back to when kokum lived with us when she got sick. One time, she said she had to go somewhere and asked Mom for a ride. They got in the car and just drove around for hours, kokum pointing at roads and Mom driving down them, until they got lost. When Mom finally asked where they were, kokum laughed and said, "I don't know, my girl." Because sometimes it was easy to forget things like destinations. Mom just laughed with her. They trusted their gut, even if it got them lost. It was enough.

"We don't have to be going anywhere," I say. I look at her hand on the steering wheel, the dry cracks deep in her knuckles, and think about putting my hand over it. But I don't.

One time, near the end of winter, Mom took me and my sisters out scavenging. She took us to a different area going south, almost into Treaty 6. She went down dirt roads, took enough lefts and rights for me to lose track, until we came upon a small shack. We'd only just gotten out of the truck and were scoping out the side of the place when another truck pulled up. A white man with greying hair got out. He had wide shoulders and his trucker hat was pulled down tight to shield his eyes from the sun.

Mom didn't skip a beat. "Oh, thank god. Can you help us, sir? We got lost."

The man eyed my mother and looked over at us kids.

"This is private property, you know." He shifted to look around the truck, see if we had anyone else with us.

Mom straightened. "Don't know how we got so turned around."

The man moved closer to her, the snow under his boots crunching. "Where you looking to go?"

The rest of the exchange is foggy in my memory. But I remember him touching her arm, and Mom standing still, more still than I'd ever seen her, more still than any of the trees around us. There was a quiet to the air, too. Not even the birds were talking. Me and my sisters watched from the side of the shack. Mom's arms were straight along her sides, with one palm behind her, open toward us. The smallest signal telling us to stay back.

Their conversation was a low mumble, but I could hear Mom's laugh clear as day. Laughter is the best way to tell if nehiyawak are telling the truth, and hers was lying. She just wanted to put this man at ease.

Eventually, the man gestured to roads behind the trees, telling Mom all about the land she'd known her whole life, land that lived in her blood. He directed Mom's attention with one hand pointing and the other on the small of her back. She still didn't move. She smiled, but only with her mouth. She thanked him. He tipped his hat and left.

We left shortly after, Mom taking only a second to gather herself and then ushering us back into the truck, taking nothing. She was quiet as we drove away. It was back when she still smoked, and her right hand holding her Player's blue was shaking so hard she kept ashing on herself. The mound of ash sat for only a second on her leg before a gust of air from the open window blew it away.

She stayed quiet for most of the drive out of there, her eyes on the dirt roads and woods around us. There was a tension even in my sisters and me. It had never dawned on us before that we might be doing something wrong. I think it was Sabrina who asked Mom why we'd been on the man's property, and she replied, a little too roughly, "This isn't his property." She collected herself, lit up another smoke, then shook her head. "I knew we shouldn't have gone out today," she said between inhales. "I had a bad, bad feeling this morning."

She had ignored it, pushed it down, fed us breakfast, and then headed out the door. It dawns on me now that sometimes the bad isn't a hole, a lack, a place where something is missing. Sometimes feeling bad is a true warning, something that could save you.

Still, it was a long time until we went out again. And when we did, Mom pocketed the bear mace that usually stayed in the glove box and she showed each of us how to use it. Made clear that it was for animals of all kinds.

Now Mom and I pull up to an old barn with eyes that are big enough to see through, the sagging roof on one side opened up to the sky. Mom stops and puts the truck in park. "We're looking for more stuff for the craft room," she says. "You might have noticed it's looking a little bare."

I nod and we jump out, walk next to each other toward the building, checking the area, as usual. Long prairie grass and wild daisies brush against my jeans. Near the bushline, I spot wild raspberries. The air is thick with the sweet smell of them. I steal a sideways look at Mom and think that it's no wonder I mistook her for Sabrina this morning. From the side, they're near identical.

The hush of the morning settles over us as Mom buttons up her flannel and pulls her gloves out from her back pocket, sliding them over her hands before stepping into the barn. I lean against the doorway and sip from the thermos, watching her as she inspects the place, her eyes catching every crack and corner. At first glance, it looks like it's filled with mostly rusted tools, pinned to the walls like insects. Straw and empty shotgun shells litter the ground. Every now and then I spot an empty Pabst can.

After a minute, I step inside to follow Mom, the planked floorboards wincing underneath me, but she holds up her hand. "Not with those shoes."

I look down at my high tops. I didn't even think to pack boots. She'd never chance me stepping on a nail, so I shrug and crouch in the doorway, my back to the spine of the door frame.

Mom starts rummaging through a workbench and I notice a calm come over her. She is the kind of person who always seems on the way to somewhere else. She has that busy energy, like you just caught her in the middle of something, and if you didn't speak quickly, you'd miss your chance before she was onto the next thing. But when we were scavenging through empty barns and houses, wading in abandoned things, a stillness seeped out of her.

"Another dreamless night, I take it?" Mom asks as she moves to a corner of the barn, pulling out a broken fishing rod and a rake.

"Yep," I reply. I hold the truth of having had another dream yesterday ready in my mouth, but I don't let it come out. I feel like it's my fault that the dreams haven't stopped. If coming home wasn't the answer, then I must be the problem. "Something weird happened with my call to Joli yesterday, though. The line cut when we were talking and I haven't been able to reach them since."

Even from the shadows, I see Mom's eyebrows knit together. "Maybe they got busy," she says. "I'll try Dianne later."

"Okay."

In the quiet, I hear what I first thought was the sound of wind through the trees but I now realize is water. A creek must be nearby.

"You feeling okay? You've been going to bed pretty early since you got home." She steps closer to me, carrying a few old blankets full of tears and hay. "And this morning you were sleeping in damn near all the clothes you brought with you."

"It's a precaution," I say too quickly. I pull against the brim of my baseball cap. "And I've just been tired. The past few weeks are catching up with me."

She tilts her head, considering, but I can't read on her face if she believes me. Then I remember our conversation when I called her the first time to ask about Sabrina's scar.

"A couple weeks ago, you said you learned to stop dreaming." I pause to take a sip of coffee, trying to act more casual than I feel. "What did you mean?"

She sighs and throws the blankets back in the corner, readjusts one of her gloves. "When I was younger, I used to have these dreams." She looks up at the open ceiling. "Dead family members would visit me. People I knew in my lifetime, my own kokum, aunties and uncles. But also ancestors I only ever heard stories about, gone long before I came around. Sometimes they'd ask me to pass on messages or we'd just visit. But mostly, they'd tell me things that were going to happen. Bad things that always ended up coming true."

I nod. Even though it's different, I know the feeling of being in a dream that I can't control the outcome of.

"I didn't want it anymore," Mom continues, clearing her throat. "So I taught myself to stop. I trained my body to do the opposite of what it wanted. Found the pattern that led to dreamless nights, exhausting myself, taking risks I shouldn't have. Taking pills I shouldn't have. I made it so no one else would want to be in my mind or body. I didn't even want to be there, in the end. And then the dreams stopped."

Though I still can't read anything on her face, her voice has shifted in a way I don't recognize. Regret slips through her words like a needle.

"I'm sorry, Mom," I say, because I am, though I also catch myself feeling relieved. But in a moment, it's gone, and I feel a sudden ache to hold her. If any semblance of what's happening to me has happened to her, I know how lonely she would have been.

She shakes her head as if she's banishing a thought and goes back to looking through a pile of rubbish. She clears her throat and pulls out magazines and more beer cans, her back to me. "I keep thinking . . . what if I had just learned more about it? When it was happening, I mean. Instead of trying so hard to make it stop. Maybe I could help now. Maybe you would have wanted to confide in me and I could actually help." She pulls out something that was partially hidden under a pile of straw. A dress form with bullet holes through the chest. She examines every side of it with a tenderness I rarely see in her. She rubs dirt off the body's curves with the pads of her thumbs. Looks at it the way I imagine a surgeon would look at a body when they're figuring out how to fix a bleed.

I feel a pang of guilt. She had to hear about everything that was happening with me through Auntie Doreen. "I would have told you myself," I say. "It was just too hard—"

"I get it." She smiles. "I told my aunties more than I ever told your kokum."

"But you are helping!" I say. I stand up again, coffee spilling from the thermos as I move. I want to be more of a comfort for her. Want to take away her pain, instead of adding to it. Do something unselfish, for once. "It's stopped since I came home. I just needed to be here."

She looks at me, then back to the dress form. She nods slowly.

"I'm sorry about not coming home. Before. When I should have." I leave the apology hanging as we're both silent for another second. There's so much to be sorry about. She gives me a tight-lipped smile. It's then that I realize we have the same mouth. I don't often see myself in her, but I see it clear as day now. She comes toward me, the dress form under her arm like a surfboard. When she hands it to me, I'm surprised at how heavy it is.

"I sometimes wish that I could dream again like I used to. To see everyone again. For my body to be a home for Sabrina or kokum to visit. I taught myself to stop and now I'm afraid I can't ever get it back." She reaches for the thermos and takes a sip, studying the field outside the shack. "But another reason, one deeper than the rest, is so I don't have to feel the guilt anymore. So the regret of closing a door between the living and the dead stops eating at me like it does."

She puts the thermos down on the ground and moves back into the barn. She looks soft in the shadows. Like she's one of the tools that lives here. I grip the dress form tighter.

"Tracey says I'm punishing you because I need someone to be mad at."

Her forehead wrinkles in consideration but not surprise. "Are you?" She moves to a small bench and starts opening the drawers. I hear the clink and jingle of nails and screws.

"I wish you hadn't made it so hard to leave," I say. "You acted like I was doing the most unspeakable thing, getting out of here. There were days you wouldn't talk to me."

In the weeks leading up to my move, I would tell everyone

about the apartments I emailed about, the job openings I found, but Mom never said a word. She just gave me Dianne's number and told me she was expecting my call.

"I don't know what you wanted. I was still dealing with the death of your kokum." She busies herself in a corner.

"You didn't even come visit me," I say. As soon as I say it, I realize I've been holding that sentence in for years. My voice feels outside myself. "Not once in three years. And I asked you, a bunch of times."

"You don't know what it was like." She closes a desk drawer and turns to face me. "I had just lost my mother, and then I lost you. And Sabrina was . . . different. She didn't take the losses well, and I didn't know how to help her. I'm not saying I handled it all in the best way."

From above, I hear the click of talons on wood. Outside the open roof of the barn, a crow peers in at us, its head angled in attention.

"What do you mean, she was different?" In the two years after I moved, I spoke to my sisters infrequently. My calls with Sabrina were usually brief updates on our lives, but it always felt like there was something she wasn't telling me. When I asked Tracey about it, she said it was probably just grief. "You never said anything," I press.

"What was I supposed to say?" She opens her hands out in front of her. "It felt like everything hit her harder. Why do you think she never left town?"

Sabrina had been saving ever since she graduated high school to move to Edmonton. She wanted to start her undergraduate degree in science, to eventually become a botanist. She was at home with plants the same way Mom was at home with abandoned things, like each new discovery filled her up even more. She had the grades to get into any school. And she saved all her money from living at home and working. But then she never applied to any programs and never left. Whenever I asked her about it, she said she was just waiting for the right time. But then years passed and the time never got right.

"I guess . . . I don't know," I admit.

"I wish I could have been there for you. I wish I could have been there for them, too, because whatever I did obviously wasn't enough. So trust me," she says, turning to another part of the barn, dipping further into the corners, "you're not the only one punishing me. I am mad at myself every fucking day."

She starts to kick aside some pieces of wood. The calm that usually settles around her has evaporated. One by one, she starts pulling out lumber pieces that are still intact and throwing them to the side. I watch the dust from the wood and the rotting floor rise in puffs, catching the sunlight beaming in from the windows. Above us, the crow caws out into the woods. Somewhere in the direction of the trees, another crow answers.

"I know I have relationships to fix," I say. My words almost get lost in the sound of wood slapping against wood. I think about my conversation with Tracey.

Mom pauses, hands on her hips, breathing hard. She looks at me and then squints up to the ceiling. "Yeah," she says, wiping sweat away from her brow with the back of her gloved hand. "Maybe we all do."

I nod and shift the dress form onto my other arm, the heaviness of it starting to weigh on me. "Can I help you fix this stuff up? For Sabrina's old room?"

Mom sighs, but her smile reaches her eyes. She nods to the truck behind me. "Let's get packed up and out of here."

She grabs the planks of good wood and the thermos of coffee off the ground. As she walks past me in the doorway, I catch the smell of her again and try to hold on to it.

After we pack up, we take one final sweep of the barn. When she doesn't find anything else of value to her, we walk around the area, listening to the sound of the trickling creek, the bush noises around us. I smile at every new sapling we pass growing out from the old brush treeline. When we drive away, the shack in our rear-view mirror, I see the crow take flight, and behind it from the trees, two more follow in its wake.

ᒥᒉᑉᐝ

The musty smell of sawdust and exhaust coats us as we unload Mom's newest finds into the garage. It's the fullest it's ever been, with not even enough room for the truck if she wanted to park it in here. Lumber, half-stripped furniture, cans of paint, and tools cover the floor. It seems like Mom goes out more often than she said. She finds a place for the dress form and adds the planks of wood to another pile in the back of the garage.

"I'm gonna make a couple floating shelves," she says, answering a question I didn't ask. "Lumber prices are awful these days."

I nod as we walk toward the house together. The calm she had in the barn is gone, and she's already talking, detailing every project she has on the go and how I can help. I'm relieved to have something more to do here, to be preoccupied, to help in some way.

The aunties and Kassidy are in the kitchen when we come in. The sound of a bass guitar drifts down from upstairs.

"When did Tracey start playing bass?" I ask.

"Since she got bored of the guitar," Kassidy says, rolling her eyes. She comes to give me a hug, Atim at her feet.

"She still mess around with that shitty keyboard we found in the ditch that one time?" I ask, smiling.

"Why don't you ask her?" Auntie Verna offers. She's at the stove getting food ready for lunch. She's wearing a forest-green sundress, her glasses catching the light as she looks in our direction.

I give her a look and she shrugs innocently, flipping a grilled cheese on the pan in front of her. I bend over to pet Atim.

"Mom, can you try Dianne?" I ask. I keep thinking about the dropped call with Joli. They didn't answer any of my messages anywhere, and all calls keep going right to voicemail.

Mom nods, grabbing a piece of crust from the cutting board. Auntie Verna smacks at her hand with the spatula. After holding her phone to her ear for a minute, Mom's face drops into a frown and my stomach sinks.

"It went right to voicemail." She hangs up and tries again.

Everyone else, noticing the tension, pauses and looks at me.

"What's that mean?" Auntie Verna presses. Her long hair falls in front of her shoulders as she looks from me to Mom.

My mouth goes dry. "I don't know. I called Joli the other day and it cut out. Now we can't get ahold of them or their mom."

"It's probably nothing," Kassidy says in a rush. "Do you know any of their friends or family? Maybe reach out to them on Facebook."

"I'll call my cousin," Mom says with a nod. "Kass is right, it's nothing."

I nod but the air is tense. "Want to walk Atim with me?" Kassidy asks.

I hesitate, but the look of excitement on Kassidy's face makes me nod. "Sure."

Atim leads us out the back gate, tugging Kassidy forward on his weathered leash. His breathing is already laboured and short. She turns and glances back to make sure I'm following.

We walk down the sidewalk toward the back alley, grass already pushing its way up through the thick cracks. A slight wind has picked up, carrying the dry smell of soil and heat across our faces.

"I was thinking . . ." Kassidy starts.

"Never a good thing," I retort, smirking at her back.

She laughs and reaches back to nudge me. "Shut up." She keeps walking. "Things have been pretty heavy since you've been back. Maybe we should spend a day doing something fun? Go out to the lake, like we used to."

At the mention of the lake, the image of the grey-haired, rotting corpse of Sabrina flashes into my mind. The hair on my arms prickles and the levity of the moment evaporates.

"No," I say too quickly. "I don't want to go there."

Kassidy stops walking. Atim lets the leash go slack as he sniffs some rocks nearby. When she looks into my face, her own scrunches up in confusion. "Why?"

I search my mind for some kind of lie but panic works its way through my bones. "I just don't," I say a little too firmly.

"Fine," she says, her voice a huff of annoyance. She keeps walking and tugs on Atim's leash. "It was just an idea."

Guilt bubbles in my stomach. "Sorry," I say. "I just . . ." A deep need to understand my last dream forces the question out of my mouth. "Do you remember the last time we were all out there together? That night we went to the party?"

Kassidy's walk falters but she tries to hide it. "Bush parties start to blend together after a while."

I kick at a rock and remember the feel of gravel under my feet as I watched Kassidy and dream-Mackenzie walk away from my sisters, leaving them separated and alone in the woods. "I'm not talking about the party. Do you remember the walk home?"

Kassidy is silent. She watches Atim with careful attention and then studies the ground at her feet. From the road behind us, we hear a few cars pass. They sound like waves on a beach.

"Tracey," she says finally. She says my sister's name so quietly I almost think I imagined it. "And Sabrina. They went into the forest."

I swallow a mixture of relief and dread. A part of me was hoping that this memory was imagined. But I'm also grateful to hear confirmation that it actually happened. That it wasn't something I made up.

I inch closer to her and try to read the expression on her face, but I can't tell if it's sadness or fear. "I never thought about it," I say carefully. "After it happened, I mean. It's like I forgot, like there was something covering the memory. But since I've been home, it's all coming back."

Kassidy nods and we both watch Atim sniff a back fence.

"Okay," she says. "I think about it sometimes." She crouches down and pulls a treat from her jacket pocket, holding it out for Atim, who's just peed. Atim wobbles over and licks the treat into his mouth.

"Have you ever spoken to Tracey about it? Or Sabrina, before she died?"

"No," she says quietly. "How do you talk about something when nothing really happened? It was just scary for a second. It was dark and they were in the woods, and it took them longer to find their way out than it should have. We just got spooked."

"Plus, they were fine," I say, almost pleading. "They came out and they were fine."

Kassidy rubs Atim's head and gives his neck a scratch before standing up. When she looks at me, I understand her expression. It's not sadness or fear, it's regret.

"Don't you think something felt off, though? Like, it didn't *feel* fine?"

I try to remember when they came out of the woods. First

Tracey, and then, minutes after her, Sabrina. "Tracey was frazzled and scared. Sabrina, though, she was just so quiet," I say.

"Their clothes had some rips. Tracey's cuts. Like they had fallen or got caught in something," Kassidy adds.

I'm surprised at this detail, another thing I had forgotten. But I remember it now. There were scratches all up Tracey's arms. Small and thin, but enough to look like they stung.

The panic rises in my body again as I try to push the memory out. "Why didn't we go in?" I say, more to myself than to Kassidy. "Why didn't I just go in?"

Kassidy shrugs and leans over to put an arm around me. "We were scared, man," she says. Her words and her embrace don't feel comforting, they feel like salt on a fresh wound. I shrug her away.

She pulls her arm back and considers me. "Is that why you don't want to go?"

"Yeah," I say. It's at least a partial truth. "That's why I don't want to go."

It's then I realize that I don't want to be outside anymore. Talking to Kassidy about all of this. Thinking about this memory and all the mistakes I've made.

"I have a headache," I say. "I'm gonna head back."

Without waiting to hear her response, I turn back down the alley toward the house. I don't hear any footsteps behind me, so I know Kassidy and Atim don't follow.

When I get back to the house, I head upstairs without talking to anyone. My heart hammers in my chest. I vow to try harder to get rid of the dreams, to make them stop for good. If Mom could do it, I can, too. I figure it's best to keep away from my family as much as possible while I figure it all out. Less chance of them seeing through my lies.

Tracey is still practising her music. I pause at her doorway, next to Sabrina's old room, and listen. The bass comes out smooth and rhythmic. One thing we always had in common was our love of music. The thought of knocking on her door, going in and telling her everything, sits on the corner of my cheek.

I turn and go into Sabrina's empty room.

The afternoon light beaming in from outside spotlights my bed and unpacked suitcase. I set up my laptop on the desk, pushing the old sewing machine and basket of fabric to the side. Out the window, the crows sit on the birch tree. I try to block out the noise of my family drifting through the cracks of my door as I google the science behind dreams.

I find out that dreams happen in REM sleep cycle, which starts about an hour and a half after falling asleep. I drum my fingers on the old desk. So if I always wake up before REM sleep, I won't dream. I can stop my brain from being a place for dreams to grow.

I sigh and lean back in the wooden chair, obviously one of Mom's rescues. It looks newly painted, but the way it gives under my weight tells me its insides are old and worn. I stare at the bright light of my laptop screen and think about the Sabrina in my dreams and the one I knew in real life, the one who lived in this room, who nurtured me like a parent.

One time when we were teenagers, she snuck out to watch the stars with her friends. There was supposed to be an asteroid shower, and out here, the sky is the clearest you'll ever see, making a movie theatre of the sky. Me and Tracey asked to go with her, but she said no. "Go on the garage roof and watch for yourselves," she said, flipping her long hair back across her shoulders. "Can't I just do something on my own for once?"

We were mad that she wouldn't let us join, and we stayed inside and missed the whole show in the sky. To hurt her, maybe. We knew a loss for us was a loss for her, too.

When she came back later that night, she told us about it. She described the asteroids as looking like water ripples, like someone was skipping rocks across the sky. Even though we were angry at her for leaving us, she still told us. Still gave us a piece of that memory that was just hers to have. It wasn't until later that we found out she and her friends had taken mushrooms, that she actually felt, for a few hours of her life, like she was skipping across it all, too.

That was what I envied and loved most about her. She wanted to do everything. She wanted a taste of everything in the entire world. I think about what Mom said earlier today. That Sabrina changed in the two years between kokum's death and her own, two years of memories I'll never have.

My fingers start to move across my keyboard before the thought fully forms. I google "dream spirits." The first two links to come up on my search are "Signs Your Spirit Guides Are in Your Dreams" and "Dream Spirits Meaning." The first article is written by a white woman, a so-called Reiki master, and talks about the spiritual forces in our dreams. Largely unhelpful. The second one is about people's connection to dreams based on their birth chart, but since my mom never remembers exactly what time I was born, I know there's not much I can do with that, either.

After taking a "What Type of Spirit Guide Is Leading You?" quiz, I refine my search to "Cree dream spirits." I skim master's degree dissertations on traditional concepts of nehiyaw worldview as it relates to Cree cosmology and tradition. A Cree mythology website tells me that spirits can visit people in their dreams, but it doesn't say what these dream spirits are.

The chair creaks as I lean back into it. I study my hands hovering over my keyboard. They look the same as when I studied them in my shower, back in my apartment, when I first started trying to figure out what was happening to me. I thought it then and I think it again now: Why am I searching for the answers somewhere else?

Mom, Auntie Verna, Kassidy, and now me have all had strange things happen in our dreams. This has to be coming from somewhere in our blood, something that started long before us. I would do anything to talk to kokum right now.

I'm startled from my thoughts by a knock at my door. I slap my laptop closed.

"Mack, dinner's ready." Auntie Doreen's voice is muffled through the wooden door.

I look out the window and notice for the first time that the sun's already dipping behind the trees. I've been in this room all day. "I'm not hungry," I say too quickly.

She's quiet for a second but I don't hear her walk away. "I'm gonna make you a small plate," she says. "I'll just put it by the door and you better grab it, otherwise Atim will."

She leaves and I hear the laughter and the sound of chairs scraping the floor from downstairs as everyone settles in to have dinner together. A lump forms in my throat.

I don't want this. Whatever is happening, however it's happening—whether it's passed down or not—needs to end. Mom might regret her dreams leaving her, but right now, it's all I want.

A couple minutes later, Auntie knocks and I hear the sound of something being set outside the door. I open it to a full plate of food and a glass of water. I don't feel hungry, but I bring the plate in anyways. An ache forms as I hear another rumble of laughter from downstairs. *I just need to get these dreams under control,* I think to myself. *Then I can be a part of it again.*

I nibble on a piece of bread and go back to reading the dissertation. When my eyes start to get heavy, I set a timer to wake me up every hour, before the dream sleep cycle starts, and crawl into bed. Hopefully my stubborn blood can help, too.

At first, I have trouble falling asleep. I toss and turn on the blow-up mattress, now somewhat deflated from a couple of days' use. I turn on a podcast on my phone, but the voices grate in my ears until I turn it off. Finally, I stop trying to force myself into sleep and just lie there. I look out at the stars from my mattress and think about Sabrina skipping across the sky.

Sometimes, I pour her into memories she has no business being in. Six months after she died, I was on a run when a woman driving in her car turned too quickly into a street, crossing the road into oncoming traffic. She was T-boned by an SUV. The sky shrank in my vision, leaving just the two cars crumpled into each other like a fist in a palm. I was only a few feet away from the crash. I should have run to them to help. But I didn't, I just stopped in the middle of the sidewalk as the woman opened her door, unaware of the blood streaming down her forehead and across her arm, clearly in shock. Her eyes were wide and frantic as she looked around, and then her gaze settled and stayed on me standing there. Cars in both lanes stopped. Drivers got out, rushed to the woman, to the other man now out of his car and walking over to the crushed metal in front of him. I thought about calling an ambulance but my arms wouldn't move.

"I was just trying to get home," she said, still looking at me.

She had run her hands over her face, smearing the blood into stripes. Then it was like her face morphed completely and I was looking at Sabrina years earlier with paint across her face, when she had started painting the shrubs, trees, and flowers she learned about on her kokum walks. I don't remember the exact plants Sabrina painted, I just remember her face when she looked down at an empty piece of paper, her dark eyes tidal waves of earth, working through how to turn the empty into something else.

The bleeding woman looked at me in the same way.

"I was so close," she said. "I was so close to home."

And then someone draped an arm across the woman's shoulders and tried to guide her to the sidewalk. As they walked away, I reached out my hand, finally unstuck from my side, and my fingers looked for a minute like paintbrushes.

Finally, I do sleep. And just as planned, the alarms wake me every sixty minutes. The first couple of times, I wake easily. I stay up long enough to ensure that I'll start my sleep cycle over again, and then restart my alarm for an hour. But as the night goes on, awake and dreaming start to blur. It feels as if days have passed instead of just minutes. Sometimes, I forget where I am. Waking up in an unfamiliar room with a panic like I'm lost.

When my alarm goes off at 5:06 a.m., I stay up instead of trying to sleep again. I'm the first one downstairs, putting coffee on and cleaning up the remnants of a dinner I wasn't a part of. I'm exhausted, but I feel like the night has been a success.

The following days get gradually warmer. Like everything else on the prairies, change creeps in so subtly you don't notice it happening at all. Like when I was a kid and the town grew to twice its size from the oil boom. It happened in so many small ways until, overnight, everything was different. Queues everywhere took longer, more work trucks than cars filled the roads, the Cree boys who used to dance in powwows on the weekends started doing overtime at their new frack jobs instead.

But the days start to feel familiar. I work in the garage with Mom. Horseflies and bees follow us across the lawn as we alternate between outside and in, sanding and painting old furniture and bringing it outside to dry. I'm happy to have a ready excuse for why I can't hang out with the aunties when they ask. Mom doesn't ask questions or press me to talk. She jokes, but I know it's just to fill the silence. A gentle reminder that she's trying hard not to scare me off.

When I leave to take half-hour naps during the day, she doesn't ask about that, either. I find myself doling out lies like small favours, but she just waves them off. I can come and go as I please. As far as she knows, I'm safe and the dreams have stopped.

The lying is easy. When my eyes droop, I tell Mom the paint and varnish are making me dizzy. Kassidy and Tracey don't ask me to hang out again, and I don't blame them. Our last conversations have made it easier for us to avoid each other. The aunties don't ask why I'm quiet at dinner. No one mentions hearing my alarm go off throughout the night, every hour on the hour. If they do, I have a lie ready for that, too.

They ask me each morning if I had any dreams, and when I say no, they look happy. I make sure to have breakfast and dinner with everyone to get as close to normal as possible. The days feel as lonely as when I was in Vancouver, like I'm not fully here, but I tell myself I'm doing this for them. I won't be the person who comes home and brings more problems. I thought coming here would fix things, but that was a mistake. It was selfish. And now that I'm here, I don't want to make it worse.

One morning at breakfast, I feel Auntie Doreen side-eyeing me before she actually says anything.

"Okay, this is enough," she says, looking around at everyone in turn. The grey of her permed hair catches in the light. "This house has been sombre and quiet for days. We're going out to the lake."

I look down at the table, trying not to make any expression. "I can't," I say.

Everyone looks up from their plates except Kassidy. She keeps her head down and studies her food.

Tracey takes a bite of her eggs. "Why not?"

My face burns as I look at all the faces studying mine. "Ever since that drowning dream," I say shakily, "I haven't really felt like being around water."

Everyone nods their heads with understanding and goes back to their food, but Tracey looks at me for a second longer.

"Let's go out, then," Auntie Verna tries. She's wearing a blue jumpsuit today. "Karaoke at the Duster?"

Auntie Doreen whoops in agreement, but Mom is already shaking her head.

"I don't know if the bar is the best place for us all to hang out," I say, giving a nod in Tracey's direction. This isn't just an excuse not to hang out with everyone. I've never been to a bar with Tracey sober. I don't know what's okay for her.

"Yeah, probably not," Kassidy agrees. She likely wants to avoid all of us together as much as I do.

"I can go sing karaoke at a shitty bar," Tracey says. I'm surprised at her response. She looks at me and shrugs. "Might as well spend some time together."

As usual, I can't read anything on Mom's face, but Auntie Doreen seems to be able to. She looks at my mom and then to Tracey and reaches for her hand. "I'm not drinking, either. Just don't you dare desecrate the name of the Stardust again." She laughs and looks at Mom.

"You're only desecrating yourselves by going to that place," Mom says.

"*That place?* As I recall, a certain Loretta Cardinal used to run the Stardust. She was there every night, fighting anyone who looked at her sideways," Auntie Verna says. Everyone laughs. She loves throwing memory grenades and then just watching them explode.

Mom rolls her eyes and shakes her head. "You must be thinking of someone else," she says, getting up to take her half-finished plate to the sink.

Tracey tilts her head and grins. "Is that right?"

The aunties laugh harder.

"Oh, you don't know the half of it," Auntie Doreen starts. "One time, people started doing body shots, and your mom—"

"Okay, that's enough." Mom walks back over and nudges Auntie as she clears the jam and butter from the table.

"I'll tell you later," Auntie Doreen whispers, loud enough for Mom to hear. She feeds bits of bacon to Atim under the table.

"No you won't!" Mom calls behind her.

Every now and then, small snippets of stories about my mom in her youth bubble up. It's the only way we know anything about her life before us. From what we've pieced together, she was a hard one who was just as likely to whoop the aunties' asses for skipping school as she was to fight anyone who looked at her or her sisters the wrong way. But Mom would always squash the story before too much was revealed.

"So you're not coming, then, Lor?" Auntie Verna asks.

"God, no. None of you can hold a damn note, sober or otherwise."

Auntie Verna gets up to clear her plate, too. "I'm sure your lifetime ban from the place has nothing to do with your decision."

The aunties laugh again as Mom whips Auntie Verna with a towel.

"I think I'll stay home, too, since Mom's not going," I say. I'm glad the attention has turned away from the lake, but now I need another reason not to join.

"No, you go," Mom says from the sink. "It's been a full house since you've been home, and your dad has been working so much. But he finally has a night off. It'd be nice to have some alone time, just me and him."

Tracey rolls her eyes. "Gross, Mom."

"Yeah, you three are real buzzkills." Auntie Doreen pokes at Kassidy, who gives a half-hearted smile.

My brain churns, but I can't think of another excuse. I nod. I can come up with another lie before dinner. Maybe a stomachache, or a migraine.

Tracey catches my eye before looking away. "Okay, I'm done hearing about your alone time with Dad. I'm gonna get some laundry done before tonight, then."

I nod. "I'll try Joli. Again. Have you heard anything from Dianne or your cousin?"

Mom pauses washing the dishes and looks back at me. "I tried them both, no one has answered."

"You still haven't heard from them?" Auntie Doreen asks, her voice carrying worry.

"I'm sure it's nothing," Mom says too quickly, turning her attention back to the sink. "People are busy."

I nod and try to believe her.

"Clean this kitchen before you disappear, all of you." Mom waves her hand at us like she's casting a spell.

Auntie Verna gently pushes me and Tracey out of the kitchen, squeezing our arms. "I'll just do a quick tidy first." She winks at us. "I'll call you when it's time to help."

We smile at her, knowing she won't call us, and head out of the kitchen. Kassidy stays behind and feeds bits of leftover food to Atim, still avoiding my gaze.

ᐯᐳᗡᖾᐟ

We step outside after dinner. "It's gonna be a big one," Auntie Verna says. She squints up into the sky, her glasses making her eyes look big and round.

That's the thing about the prairies: It's honest. It'll tell you exactly what it's doing and when, you just have to listen. The day had been muggy and hot. The stickiness still clinging to the air tells us a storm is coming. When the wind stills, we know the thunder won't be long behind it.

I tried to weasel out of coming, but no one was having any of my excuses. In the end, I figured being out would help me stay awake longer anyways. Everyone's spirits seem lifted, even Kassidy is back to joking around. This might even be fun.

The wind chimes hang silent as we all stand side by side on the deck.

"Should we take some umbrellas?" I ask.

They all laugh.

"Living on the coast has made you soft." Tracey nudges me and starts down the deck steps. She's changed into black jeans and a blue button-up, dark blue lipstick on her lips. Kassidy wears a long-sleeved dress, her long, straight hair reaching to her lower back. The aunties wave back to Mom and Dad in the window before we're out of view of the house.

We walk the shortcut to the Duster, across the school playground and through the alley behind the 7-Eleven. It gets hotter as we walk, even though it's getting late. The night brings the smell of mud and deep-fry grease from the gas station.

"Keep your heads down when we walk past the Smith trailer," Kassidy says, pulling a curtain of hair over the side of her face.

From the trailer beyond the fence in front of us, we hear hollers and the faint sound of music.

Tracey laughs. "Which one did you break up with this time?" Kassidy gives a wry smile.

"You really are your mother's kid," Auntie Verna says.

Auntie Doreen slaps her sister's arm in fake admonishment. "So people fall in love with us easy. They can't help it, they're only human." She smiles and lights up a smoke, the flame from her lighter showing the blue and orange of her favourite Oilers sweater.

We all laugh again before Kassidy shushes everyone, quickening her pace past the trailer. As we cross the empty parking lot of the old breakfast diner, we finally see it: the bright lights of the Stardust, cradled in the backdrop of the woods. The symphony of croaking frogs from the nearby creek and the sound of music from inside mingle together in the dark.

The Stardust is the last building before the road opens to the highway, the first and last thing you see before heading north. The wood-slatted building is a hotel and lounge that's been around for as long as anyone can remember. The bar door is around the side and doesn't have a sign. But you don't need it—you just need to follow the sound of country music and the crash of pool balls kissing.

The Duster settles around us as we walk in. There are no windows, no clocks. Neon signs cast the worn-down bar top in bright red and green. It smells like oak and cigarettes, even though no one's lit a smoke in the place since the early 2000s, when it was legal. The only people inside are a couple of Métis men at the bar, the bartender behind the counter, and Ruby, the server and karaoke host who's been running the karaoke nights since the beginning of time. She nods to my aunties, and we walk to a lone booth in the back.

We slip onto the vinyl bench, its cracked skin catching on our clothes as we make space for one another. Tracey grabs a karaoke songbook and sits next to me.

"Kokum's booth," she says, flipping open the book.

"Kokum's booth," both aunties say in unison.

I look around and realize where we're sitting. I've heard the stories over and over. Sometimes from family or friends. Sometimes from people who I didn't know, but who knew my kokum. Of the seven booths in the bar, we're sitting in the one closest to the pool table and the two working slot machines. Legend has it, kokum would come to the Duster every weekday from 2 to 3 p.m., right before she'd pick up my mom and aunties from school at 3:30. It was the only time she would come into town, so she made it count.

She didn't drink. She'd just sit in her booth and chain smoke, alternating between sharking people at pool and playing the slots. She never went in on weekends when it got too busy with the young crowd. But there wasn't a person in town who could take her snooker title, at least not for long.

I've heard so many stories about her here, I sometimes forget I never saw her in this building in real life, since she died before I turned eighteen. But I swear I have. I swear I've seen her telling her jokes to the other regulars, the dirty jokes that Mom said she was never supposed to tell us, but always did anyways. I'm sure I saw her spinning her stories, the eyes of the Stardust on her like she was the world, which she kind of was. I swear I used to catch glimpses of her sitting at the slot machines, putting in a ten-dollar bill, her open-mouthed laugh swallowing the blinking lights.

"Hey, Doreen, Verna. Drinks?" Ruby asks from the edge of the table.

"Two waters for us." Auntie Doreen nods across the table to Tracey opposite her.

Tracey shakes her head. "I'll have a Pepsi, actually."

Auntie Verna orders Coors Lights for me, her, and Kassidy.

"Oh shit, Pat is here." Kassidy looks over her shoulder at a young Cree guy who has just walked in.

"I'll come back in a bit." She gets out of the booth and smooths down her hair with her hands. "How do I look?"

"Didn't you break up with his sister, like, yesterday?" Tracey says.

She rolls her eyes and smiles. "Don't be jealous," she says, and starts across the floor to the bar.

"Creator, is there no stopping her?" Auntie Doreen shakes her head as Ruby comes back with her tray of drinks. She slides them easily to each of us.

"Holler at me if you want to order food or anything," Ruby says, and walks away. I don't think I've ever seen anyone with food at the Duster before.

"You see how they've renovated the place?" Auntie Verna gestures to the huge disco ball hanging from the ceiling, just off centre from the dance floor, and laughs.

"What did I tell you about making fun of the Duster?" Auntie Doreen eyes her sister. "I miss working here sometimes."

"Yeah, sure. You must miss the way your shoes stick to the floor for an extra second longer than your foot. Or the lovely decor." Auntie Verna gestures again to the walls covered in old photos of the staff, posters of pinup girls, and a couple of mounted moose heads.

Auntie Doreen worked at the Duster when Kassidy was young. She quit after three months, said she was followed by ghosts whenever she'd close up. They'd bang pots around, whisper her name. The ghosts weren't the actual reason she quit, though. She said they were kind of creepy, but still, better company than most of the patrons. But the nights were long, and my cousin was still a baby.

We flip through the karaoke book and write down our requests on the backs of torn-up papers noting the Duster's old daily specials. I write down "Walking on Broken Glass" by Annie Lennox.

Auntie Verna looks at my paper and pushes her glasses up on her nose. "Your mom's favourite karaoke song," she says. "I see her in you sometimes. Small flashes. Like I've gone back in time."

I smile. Most people said this about Sabrina. Apparently, Tracey is the spitting image of their bio dad. "Walking on Broken Glass" was a song Mom used to play on road trips or when we went scavenging. She'd put it on repeat at the loudest volume our old truck could go, me and my sisters belting it out to each other in the back seat.

The aunties write down their favourite songs from Dolly, Garth, and Reba. Ruby comes by and collects the papers while one of the regulars gets up to sing some Elvis. We sing with him from our booth and he tips his beer to us. I feel the tension start to ease off my shoulders. The music, the hazy room, and my family together: I almost forget what brought me here.

"We're up next," Auntie Doreen says, smirking at Auntie Verna. "You two wanna be backup singers?"

"Nah, we'll wait. You two show off," Tracey says.

They smile as the Elvis singer finishes and they head up to the middle of the dance floor to claim their mics. They croon together, mouths open to the ceiling.

"You think that'll ever be us someday?" Tracey asks, nodding to our aunties.

I watch them move together, their bodies giving way for each other, the smiles they exchange in between verses.

"I hope so," I say, and I mean it. "We'll probably pick a better song, though."

The warmth of the Duster and the beer starts to settle into my cheeks. The walls breathe around us.

"I haven't seen you around much," Tracey says. Her head doesn't move but her eyes glance over at me.

I gather myself and lean forward on the bench. "I've been helping Mom. All her projects are going to start spilling out of that garage soon." I fake a small laugh. I think about all my lying, sneaking away for power naps. "Didn't think you'd notice too much, though," I add. "You're not around much yourself."

"Just because you don't see me doesn't mean I'm not around," she counters.

"Tapwe." I realize then how tired I am. A throbbing spreads from my temples down to my neck. It dawns on me how long it's been since I had a proper sleep.

"I just mean that it doesn't feel like you're really back." Her face sinks, cracking like the vinyl booth we've sunken into.

Behind us, I hear Auntie Doreen and Auntie Verna laugh together. Their voices coming over the loudspeakers sound like a crow's caw, one of the big, loud ones they use to call to their kin far away.

I push away my glass of beer and rub my temples, leaning my elbows on the table and taking deep breaths. The throbbing moves from my neck to the back of my spine.

"Whoa, are you okay?" Tracey's voice comes in warbled, like it's cutting in and out.

I nod and look up, try to focus my eyes on her. Her hair pushed back on her head falls to the side. Her round face squints at me as her blue mouth moves. The aunties continue belting into the microphone, their voices coming at me from further and further away. The sensation in the back of my spine starts to feel like tugging.

"I gotta get some air," I think I say, but I don't hear the words. I grab the edge of the table and try to stand, but as I step out, I feel the final tug.

>≡<

When my eyes snap open, the throbbing in my body has evaporated like a bad thought. The smooth nighttime water of the lake drifts in front of me, carrying the croaking of crickets and water beetles. I hear footsteps behind me. Kassidy and dream-Mackenzie are walking quickly toward the water like they're trying to rush without seeming like they're in a panic.

I feel a spike of nausea as I remember the last dream, the fear on Kassidy's and dream-Mackenzie's pale faces as Sabrina told them to meet on the other side of the woods. I remember this fear, too. In my own gut, all those years ago.

I already know that yelling out to them or trying to get their attention will do no good. So I swallow my words and follow them as they pass me. They alternate their worried glances between the woods and the shoreline.

Sand shifts under my shoes as I walk faster to keep up with them. From the woods, sticks and branches keep snapping, like something is following alongside us. Kassidy and dream-Mackenzie start walking faster. Every now and then, dream-Mackenzie says something comforting to Kassidy. I can hear now how empty it must have sounded.

As we get closer to our campsite, the sounds from the woods get louder. It's more than the crunch of boots and the whistle of the wind. A cacophony of whispers snakes its way out of the trees.

"Sabrina!" Kassidy yells into the woods.

"Tracey!" Dream-Mackenzie yells, too, but the darkness swallows the sound.

I remember this part. Screaming into the woods. Imagining every bad thing that could have happened to my sisters. While Kassidy and dream-Mackenzie frantically look into the trees, I notice the once-quiet and still water start lapping fervently at the shore.

"Where are they?" dream-Mackenzie says, turning to Kassidy. The whispers keep coming. "Do you hear that?"

And then the whispers turn into a scream. Dream-Mackenzie and Kassidy search the tree line for the only visible trail opening, a few feet in front of them.

"I'm coming in!" dream-Mackenzie yells into the opening of the woods. And just as she takes a step toward the trail, Tracey stumbles out. Her bare arms are full of cuts. Moss and sticks poke out from her hair.

"Tracey!" Dream-Mackenzie hugs her sister and Tracey's body goes limp in her arms. "Jesus, why did you do that!" Dream-Mackenzie holds her at arm's length and Tracey's confused face looks from dream-Mackenzie to Kassidy.

"What?"

"Why did you run into the woods? That was so fucking stupid."

Tracey blinks and looks down at her dirt-streaked coveralls and cut-up arms. Her chin is trembling when she looks back up. I watch from just behind, wanting nothing more than to reach out and hold them all.

"I don't know," she says quietly, almost childlike. "I don't remember."

"Where's Sabrina?" Kassidy says, her tone harder than she's ever taken with any of us.

Tracey looks back to the woods and then to us, shock in her eyes.

"I'm going to get Mom," dream-Mackenzie says, letting go of Tracey and starting toward the campsite, which was only five more minutes down the shoreline. I remember saying this and thinking that five minutes would be all it took to see the cluster of jack pines that would tell us we were safe.

None of them notice the water, now lapping angrily at my shoes. In my memory of that night, I don't remember this.

Before dream-Mackenzie takes two steps away, another rustle comes from the trees and Sabrina walks out. Her pace and expression are calm, as if she's returning from a nighttime stroll, but otherwise she looks in worse shape than Tracey. Her dark brown hair is knotted, falling across her shoulders, and her jeans and flannel are ripped.

I notice something else that I don't remember from that night: she's bleeding from somewhere on her chest, her flannel darkening with blood.

"Sabrina!" dream-Mackenzie yells. She runs back instantly, reaching out for her sister. She folds her into a hug, unaware of the blood. Kassidy falls into them, hugging them both. Tracey doesn't move.

"Are you okay?" Kassidy looks hard into Sabrina's face. It's emotionless. Her sharp jaw unmoving.

"That scared the shit out of us!" dream-Mackenzie says, hugging her harder. I can remember now that she was freezing cold to the touch. Dream-Mackenzie takes off her jacket and tries to put it around Sabrina, but she waves her away. Her eyes flit around, looking everywhere except at her sisters and cousin. That's the thing about the prairies: even in the dark, you can see for miles in any direction, so you don't have to look at the truth if you don't want to.

"Sabrina?" Kassidy asks gently.

Sabrina shakes them off and starts to walk back to the campsite without a word. The rest of them follow behind, the water now whipping angrily at their feet.

Tracey holds on to Kassidy as she walks, still looking around like she's confused about how she got there. They're together again. But not really. Not together enough to be crows.

I run up in front of Sabrina, wanting to get a better look at her. Her tattered and blood-soaked shirt sticks to her like she just emerged from the water. She has streaks of tears down her dirty face, and the blood has spread so much, her flannel looks black.

She stops walking suddenly. She stares right at me.

"You should have come in after me," she says. Her voice is cold and hoarse.

"You can see me?" I choke out.

She cocks her head to the side and, without looking down, tears away a piece of her shirt along the neckline, from the collar to her armpit. It's then I see where the blood is coming from: a deep crescent of skin gouged out underneath her collarbone. Blood trickles from the now-exposed wound.

"But you didn't," she continues, her voice shaking. "And look what happened." She holds out the blood-soaked piece of fabric she's just torn off.

"What do you mean?" I plead.

She stays silent and still. She looks at the piece of fabric in her outstretched hand, then back at me. Slowly, I reach out my hand and take it. When we touch, I don't go through her. She's freezing cold. She takes a step toward me and I notice her skin is whiter at the curve of her face, the beginnings of frost. She smells like freezer burn.

Dream-Mackenzie, Tracey, and Kassidy have now caught up to where Sabrina has stopped on the shore. She ignores them and keeps looking right at me. "You still aren't listening," she says.

I look at each of the girls but no one else seems to hear her speaking or notice the bleeding, missing piece of skin above her heart. I search and search my memory, but I can't remember Sabrina being hurt at all that night. Without another word, she steps easily past me and keeps walking, the others tailing her closely.

I hold the wet piece of cotton in my hands, cold with blood. "What do I do?" I yell at Sabrina's back. "What do you want from me?" I move to follow them, but as I do, I feel the tugging again. Without another warning, I wake up, my head resting against the cold, sticky floor of the Duster.

>═<

My vision is blurred but starts to focus as Auntie Verna, Tracey, and Kassidy's faces materialize above me. They are squinting in worry as their mouths move, but I still can't make out what they're saying. A ringing sound from somewhere in the bar echoes in my ears and then grows quieter.

"Move back." I hear Auntie Doreen's voice. "Give her some room to breathe."

The faces above me disappear and then hers replaces them. Her face is calm and she speaks slowly. "My girl, are you okay? Can you hear me?"

"I caught her before she hit the ground," I hear Tracey say somewhere out of sight.

Everything catches up to me slowly. My conversation with Tracey before I passed out, the dream-memory, Sabrina's words.

I sit up quickly and my head spins. Auntie Doreen rests her hand on my back to steady me. I realize that the whole bar is quiet, everyone has stopped to watch us. The back of my neck burns in embarrassment.

"I'm fine, I'm fine," I say, moving to stand up. "Really, I'm okay."

Auntie Doreen keeps one hand wrapped tightly around my arm and the other on my back as she leads me to the booth. Auntie Verna puts a glass of water in front of me as I relax into the bench.

"Should we call an ambulance?" Kassidy asks. Her and Tracey stand behind the aunties, eyes wide with the same frightened looks that I just saw in my dream.

"No," I say. "Just didn't have enough water today or something. I can walk back home."

Both aunties inspect me and my head, but once they are assured again by Tracey that she did actually catch me before I fell, they ease off.

"Okay," Auntie Verna says. "Let's settle up and get our stuff."

"We don't have to go now," I say, but even I can hear the desperation in my voice. I thought I had figured out how to stop the dreams. I was doing it. The past while of no sleep, of hiding away. I was training my body to be no place for dreams. "Everything is fine."

Auntie Verna's eyes trace around my body and I know she's seeing more than just me. And then her gaze shifts to my hands resting on the table. "I think we should get home and talk about the bloody rag in your hand," she says. "My guess is, it wasn't here before you passed out."

It's only then that I look down and realize my hands are balled into fists. Clutched in one of them is the piece of bloody flannel from Sabrina. When I blink, it doesn't vanish.

ᐅ ᒡᐦᐩ

The silence of the night cocoons us as we walk back home. Burnt-out streetlights loom like steel hooks and the air is still thick with heat.

Tracey holds on to me the whole walk, the bend of her arm a puzzle piece fitting into mine. The only thing guiding us is the pavement illuminated by a passing car every now and then and our bones knowing the way home. The town is quiet, like we're the last people on earth. Auntie Doreen chain smokes and Auntie Verna tries to hide that she's watching me. I grip the torn, bloody piece of clothing, worried it might disappear at any moment. But it doesn't. The smell of fresh blood hangs with us.

We move into the house quietly, ghosts sitting around the kitchen table. Tracey sits closer to me than she normally would. Kassidy puts leftover bacon and waffles from this morning in the microwave and pours us all glasses of water.

Auntie Doreen breaks the silence. "So you had another dream?"

I can't meet anyone's eyes, but I nod.

"This isn't the first one you've had since you've been back," Auntie Verna says. A statement, not a question.

My eyes burn as I nod again, yes. "I didn't want to say anything," I say. "I thought coming home would make them stop, and for a couple days, it did. But they started again. I didn't want to put more on everyone. I tried to make them go away on my own."

The microwave timer goes off and Kassidy clears her throat, taking out the plate with a tea towel. She puts it in the middle of the table with butter, Auntie Verna's homemade syrup, and a handful of forks, but no one reaches for the food. Atim, asleep in the laundry room next to the kitchen, whimpers low in his throat and wobbles out, curling up next to Kassidy's feet.

Both the aunties consider me for another moment. "On your own," Auntie Doreen says with a quiet sadness.

"This has never happened before, though," I say, another panic rising in my body. "The dreams always came when I was already sleeping. I've never passed out because of them. And this is the longest I've ever been able to keep anything." I hold up the bloodied piece of flannel still clenched in my first.

"Where did it come from?" Auntie Doreen asks.

Everyone stares at the rag.

"Sabrina. She was okay," I say quickly. "She got cut somehow and tore off this part of her shirt. She gave it to me."

I finally open my hand, which was stiff from clenching so hard for so long. I take a deep breath and set the cloth on the table. It doesn't disappear when it leaves my hand. My palm stays red with blood, though the strip of fabric has already started to darken and dry. Auntie Doreen scoops it into a large ziplock freezer bag in a quick instant and sets it next to the bowl of browning bananas on the counter.

"We'll talk about this more in the morning," Auntie Verna says in her gentle voice. She reaches out and grabs my hand, the one not stained with blood. Though the fear stays, I feel comforted by her touch. "I don't want to wake your mom now, and you know you should be the one to tell her, too."

I take a sip of water and nod. She's right. The aunties get up and hug each of us in turn. Auntie Doreen feeds Atim a piece of bacon before she heads downstairs to the spare room. Auntie Verna holds me for a second longer. "Get some actual sleep tonight," she says. "You need it." She turns to Kassidy and Tracey. "Watch her."

She disappears down the hallway to the back door and I swallow. Telling my mom will make it real. That I failed to stop the dreams, that this is something I still have to face. Even worse, I'll have to tell all of them about that night Tracey and Sabrina went into the woods.

Tracey and Kassidy ignore the forks and start to pick at the food with their fingers. Kassidy feeds another piece of bacon to Atim. I get up to scrub the blood off my hand in the kitchen sink.

"Kokum always said karaoke was healing," Kassidy says between bites of waffle.

"Karaoke and cards," Tracey says with a nod. A ghost of a smile passes across her face, the kind of smile that sneaks its way in when you think about the past.

"Is this why you've been avoiding us?" Kassidy keeps her eyes on her food while she asks this, picking waffles apart with her fingers.

I exhale and nod. "I thought I could get it under control. I didn't want this to be anyone else's problem."

"Why do you keep wanting to do this all alone?" Tracey says. She studies the plate of food and then my face. "See? This is what I mean. You're not really back at all."

I dry my hands with a tea towel. The bad still clings to my insides. Lying, dragging them all down into this bullshit. But I feel a relief at not holding this secret alone anymore.

"Tracey, give her a break," Kassidy says.

Tracey shoots daggers at Kassidy. "Isn't that all we do? Give her breaks? And she can't even tell us the truth."

Kassidy pauses a moment and looks from me to Tracey. "I'm just saying, I know the kind of safety that sometimes comes with having secrets."

She sighs and then tells Tracey what she told me. How her dreams can sometimes show her the future. How she's never told anyone other than her mom until now. As Kassidy speaks, Tracey fidgets in her chair. Her leg bounces like it does when she's nervous. When Kassidy finishes, Tracey gets up suddenly. "Fuck," she says. Her face hardens into a scowl. She walks quickly out the back door to the deck. Me and Kassidy exchange looks before following her and closing the door gently behind us.

Her back is to us, and when she speaks, her voice is low and firm. "Me and Sabrina used to share dreams," Tracey says into the night air. "It started when we were kids. She'd just be there, in my dream. Or I'd be in hers, I don't know. It happened for a while before either of us said anything in real life."

I walk up slowly behind her. "You dreamt together?"

"She always remembered the dreams exactly like I did. Everything," Tracey continues, looking around her like we might be overheard. "When we figured it out, this thing we could do, we knew we could never tell anyone." A flutter of a smile crosses her face at a memory she doesn't share, but in a blink, it's gone. "I saw her the night she died."

My hands start to sweat and my ears ring cold. Kassidy walks to the other side of Tracey. A protection on both sides.

"In my dream, I was in her car with her, watching her from her passenger seat. She told me she was going to be dead when I woke up," Tracey continues. "She held me. Told me that I shouldn't be scared. That I needed to be there for Mom."

Tracey looks like she's about to vomit. Her face sinks. "But I didn't want to wake up. I just kept my eyes closed and said, *not yet, not yet, not yet,* over and over. And she just held me like that. For the whole dream, she didn't move. When I woke up to Mom's scream from outside, I already knew."

I look down, ashamed again of ignoring Mom's calls that night.

Kassidy wraps an arm around her, but Tracey's eyes, dry and glossy, stay on the sky like she's with the stars. "Shit."

It's hard to breathe, but I don't know if it's from the humidity or what Tracey is telling us. Tracey runs her hand across her face, smudging her blue lipstick onto her chin. "I thought that would be the last time I saw her in my dreams. I thought that was it."

Somewhere in the distance, I hear the flutter of wings. A sudden realization washes over me. "You still see her, don't you?" I ask.

She answers so quietly I wonder if she's even spoken at all. "She kept coming to me after she died. Every single night. It was comforting, seeing her. But do you know what it's like to wake up and have to remember she's actually gone? It was like losing her over and over every single day." She pauses and breathes out a deep sigh. "When I drank, I didn't dream. And I just wanted the hurt to stop for a while."

My heart feels like it has stopped in my chest. I think back to our conversation in the living room while we played video games. "That's what you meant when you said seeing her was hard."

She nods. I think I hear the crows again, until I realize it's something else: a soft rumble of thunder. "But I couldn't keep that up," she continues. "When I got sober again, I figured she'd come back. She didn't. I thought I lost her for good."

She wanted the dreams to stop. Just like Mom did. Just like

I tried to do. I wonder if this is our family tradition—tamping down dreams before they have a chance to take shape, cutting off a part of ourselves once the fear sets in.

Above us, I hear another rumble and see the first crack of lightning, a small flash as it tests out the sky.

Tracey looks between me and Kassidy before continuing. "About a month ago, she came back." Her eyes start to well up and her body shakes. The rumbling in the distance gets louder.

"It's okay, it's okay." I put my hand on Tracey's back, crossing over with Kassidy's arm that's already there. A rush of wind comes from the north, warm on our faces.

When she turns to look at me, I'm surprised to see her laughing. Another crack from above, and her face brightens from lightning bigger than before. "Annoying little shit just doesn't want to leave us alone," she says, laughing harder.

I hear my laughter before I realize it's escaped my body. Kassidy starts to laugh, too, and we all fall into each other, laughing so deep in our bellies that it fills the space between us. We laugh until our cheeks are wet with tears and our stomachs hurt.

We quiet after a minute. Tracey shakes her head and grabs my hand. "Since you came back, she left again."

The rain starts to fall hard and fast around us. Sheets of thick drops cover us. The prairies, for all it can do, can't hold heat for long. It will always erupt, like a shaken bottle.

We all let out a shriek as if the rain is a surprise and rush back into the house. We stand on the rubber mat and laugh as our wet hair drips onto the floor around us. None of this is really funny. It's terrifying, actually, in a way that seeps into my bone marrow. But sometimes, laughter is less about what's funny and more about letting someone know you understand, that you're in on the joke together. We keep laughing, and I squeeze Tracey's and Kassidy's shoulders against mine, only for a moment, just enough for them to know I see them. Outside, thunder and lightning stretch across the black sky as if they have everywhere in the world to go.

After drying off, we all curl under the covers in Tracey's bed, the plate of breakfast food on the nightstand and Atim in between us. Our damp hair makes halos of grey around our pillows as we warm each other with our body heat.

"Do we have superpowers or something?" Kassidy asks. She crunches on a piece of dry, cold pancake.

"Nah," I say. "I already looked into it. We don't fit the bill. I guess we're something else."

They both nod like this makes a lot of sense. I think about these secrets we've all been holding tight to our chests like a bad hand of cards, trying to bluff our way out of losing it all. How did all of these dreams lie between us? In all of our sleepovers at kokum's house, in our own basements, in all the hours we stayed up talking and laughing, we never talked about our dreams. How deep is this denial of ourselves that even as children playing pretend, we didn't want to talk about them?

Kassidy looks at Tracey. "What happened in the dreams? Did Sabrina say anything?"

Tracey knits her brow in concentration. "The recent ones were different from when we used to dream together when she was alive, or even when she'd visit me in dreams right after she died. She was different. Like a hologram version of herself. Cold and fading away. She never said much." She looks at me again. "She just kept telling me to get you home."

I nod and twist a drying strand of hair around my finger.

"I'm sorry I didn't call. I didn't know how to listen, or whether I should tell you," Tracey says.

"It's okay," I say. "Trust me, I get it."

"The scar," she says, a seriousness etched into her face so deep she looks like Dad. "On Sabrina's collarbone. I wasn't just being an asshole the other day. She really never had one, I would remember it. We would remember it." She looks at Kassidy, who nods in confirmation. "But weeks ago, when she started coming back in my dreams, the scar was there. A thick, pink scar that looked like a claw mark."

I move some of the hair that's fallen in her face.

"I think something hurt her," I say. I take a deep breath and tell them about the dreams I've had since I've gotten back. The ones tied to the night at the lake with all of us. I tell them everything, all the things that were the same as the real memory and everything that was different: the snow, the troubled lake, and the biggest thing, Sabrina bleeding from her chest. As the words spill out of my mouth, I feel a dam breaking open inside of me.

"Her shirt was ripped when she came out of the woods," Kassidy says, her eyes searching the ceiling. "But she didn't have a cut on her chest and she wasn't bleeding . . . If it's as bad as you say, Mack, we would have seen. We would remember that much blood."

"Not all hurt is visible," Tracey says quietly.

"This all has something to do with that night," I say.

"I don't remember anything," Tracey says quietly. "I remember before and after. But everything inside the woods is . . . blank."

Kassidy runs a hand across Atim's back. "We should have gone in," she says, her eyes welling up.

When we got back to the camp that night, the four of us climbed into our small tent. The snores from the other tents told us Mom and the aunties were fast asleep. We silently changed into our long johns. Tracey gave Kassidy a pair of her sweats and a shirt. Kassidy washed Tracey's face with her sleeve dunked in water from a water bottle. Sabrina turned away from us to change. When she was done, she stayed quiet and climbed into her sleeping bag, turning to face the side of the tent. I lay next to her and rested my arm carefully across her side. Even through my long johns and her sleeping bag, her body was a brick of ice.

Tracey leans up on her elbow, rests her head in her hand. "The night she came out of the woods," she says, "something was different. She was strange right up until she died. She was quieter. Hardly even went out to the bush anymore. Stopped researching plants. I told myself it was grief from kokum."

"Did you still dream together?" I ask.

Tracey thinks for a moment. Her mouth twitches as she recalls these memories. "Yes. In our dreams was the only time I think I ever saw her happy."

We all lie in solemn silence. "Something happened to her that night, right in front of us," I say. "And we didn't even see it."

"We didn't see the snow or the raging lake, either," Kassidy says.

"Or this other creepy zombie Sabrina," Tracey adds.

"Then maybe that's what the dreams are for," I say. "To show me what we couldn't see."

"Wait," Tracey whispers. "In all these dreams it's been winter?"

At the mention of winter, a chill runs up my spine as I remember waking up in the woods in deep snow. The crawl of the ice as it overtook tree branches and the lake in a snap cold. "Yeah, even the early ones where I didn't see Sabrina yet."

Tracey looks between me and Kassidy before continuing. "Remember those stories we used to hear as kids about the wheetigo? They were always seen in winter, I think," Tracey says.

"Those were just made-up stories," Kassidy says.

"Just like stories about people who can see the future in their dreams." Tracey raises her eyebrows at her cousin.

"Wheetigo." I test the word out on my tongue. Dread blooms somewhere deep in my body as I say it out loud.

I remember asking kokum once about the wheetigo after hearing someone mention them. She let the cigarette smoke leak out from her teeth when she answered. "Wheetigo used to be humans. People who turned into monsters after eating their own kind."

"So they're cannibals?"

"There's more than one way to eat someone up. They feed off greed, and our world creates enough of that to keep them nice and full. That is why you never go off alone. You can't be greedy if you have your family to think about."

I had understood it as a lesson. A tale to scare us from going into the woods too far, walking alone at night, separating from each other.

Kassidy already had her phone out. "This website says the wheetigo are 'supernatural, cannibalistic monsters. Their appearance and powers differ in stories and across nations, sometimes taking on the look of animals or other people, in order to stalk their prey. Born out of greed and selfishness, they devour humans, often the most vulnerable. They are usually seen in the winter, and their hearts are made of ice.'"

"Seen in winter!" Tracey yells, and grabs on to my sleeve, her eyes wide.

"Where are you even reading that?" I try to peer over at Kassidy's phone screen. I don't want to believe it, but something in my stomach clicks into place.

"Uh, the internet, try it sometime." Kass squints harder at her screen. "I don't see any stories from around here, though. Just vague descriptions that change from one site to the next."

"There's got to be more," Tracey says.

"Well, I just started looking. Give me a minute, fuck." Kassidy's thumbs move quickly across her phone.

"So maybe Sabrina saw a wheetigo that night?" I say slowly.

"What does that have to do with these dreams happening now?" Tracey asks.

Exhausted, I shrug and lean back into the pillow. It takes me a moment to realize that I've started crying. The panic that's been brewing inside me has finally overflowed. But the tears are not a relief. They are not medicine. Questions swirl in my head. Is the wheetigo a lead? Or are we just grasping for anything to make sense of this?

I swipe at the tears running down my cheeks, a warning and a sign that this is nowhere near finished.

σⁿⅭᣔᑊ

The house is bone-still the next morning. Me, Tracey, and Kassidy walk down to the silent kitchen in single file. We've been awake for an hour already, looking up more information about the wheetigo, but not finding much more than we did the night before.

Mom and the aunties sit around the table, coffee mugs in their hands and the bloodied rag in a ziplock bag between them. The dried, crusty blood has stiffened the fabric. They all look up when we enter, as if they have been waiting for a while. Through the window behind them, I see the three crows in the birch tree.

I search Mom's face, but all I can read is that she's tired. The lines around her eyes reach back into her hairline. Auntie Doreen looks solemn and Auntie Verna offers a tight smile.

Auntie Doreen clears her throat. "We told your mom what happened last night," she says. "At least, what we saw."

I nod, and me, Tracey, and Kassidy take the empty seats across from them. Atim paws at Kassidy's feet until she picks him up and cradles him like a baby. Auntie Verna gets up to pour us all cups of coffee.

"The dreams didn't stop when you got home," Mom says.

I nod again, my throat closing up. Auntie slides the cups in front of us and presses her hand into my back as she passes to get to her chair. I feel a moment of relief.

I take a sip, the liquid burning the tip of my tongue. "I had one the day after I got back," I say. "I tried to hide it, and I tried to stop them from coming." I swallow. "It didn't work."

With another deep breath, I tell them everything else. About all the dreams, in sequence, and about how they are nearly identical to the memories of the night at the lake three years ago. Tracey and Kassidy add to my telling with their own details and versions, nodding and coaxing the story to finally spill out.

We tell them about what happened that night as we remember it. How Tracey's memory of being in the woods is blank until she came out again. The differences between the real memory and my dreams.

I didn't expect them to, but both Kassidy and Tracey also tell Mom and the aunties about their own dreams, the secrets they, too, have kept out of fear of not being believed, of not believing themselves, of feeling alone.

"You've all been able to dream different? All this time?" Auntie Verna looks softly between us all.

Mom's eyes stay on Tracey. "You saw her? After she died? Sabrina could visit you?"

Tracey swallows and looks down. "Until I fucked it up, yeah."

Mom looks at me. "Did you tell them about me?"

"No," I whisper. "It's not my secret to share."

Mom looks back at Tracey. "I used to get visits, too," she whispers. "When I was your age. From all my family members who died." She swallows. "I found a way to make them go away, too."

We all sit in the silence of this realization for a moment: that we've hidden ourselves from the only other people who could understand.

"I might have just made it all worse," I say finally, looking directly at Mom. "By trying to stop it."

"Shit," Mom says, her face cracking. "I knew there was something. I could feel it." She rubs her eyes with her callused hands. Auntie Doreen puts a hand on her back.

"I'm sorry for lying," I offer quickly. "I just wanted—"

"Not the most pressing thing right now," Mom interrupts. She gets up and walks to the kitchen window, her arms crossed in front of her chest. "Something happened to Sabrina in the woods. Something that changed her."

I pause and look between Kassidy and Tracey. They both nod. "We think so, too," I say. "What if it's a wheetigo?"

Mom's head snaps back toward us and Auntie Doreen leans forward, her permed hair swaying. "Mackenzie," she says slowly. "Why do you think that?"

I relay what me, Kassidy, and Tracey talked about last night and this morning. As I'm telling them about what we found online, something else hits me: "What if the grey-haired Sabrina is the wheetigo?" My voice comes out small, but it rings through the kitchen.

Tracey looks down at the table, biting her lip, as if she doesn't want to admit what she's about to say. "Wheetigo are shapeshifters. If they can appear as anything, why not Sabrina? It's obviously a good way to get to us."

My breath goes shallow and I wrap my arms tightly around my stomach, as if I need to hold my insides in.

Mom swallows. In the glint of the outside light, I see the tense and release of her neck muscles.

From outside, we hear the crows caw on the tree branch. "The crows," Auntie Verna says, turning to the window at the sound. "In the dream where they attacked Sabrina, you thought they were after her heart. But maybe they were after the heart of something that just looked like her."

My memory flashes to the cloud of black feathers I tore through to get to Sabrina. The feel of the crow's neck snapping in my hands.

"Okay, hold on," Mom says, holding her palms up in the air. "Let's not get ahead of ourselves."

"Should we go to the lake?" The words tumble out of my mouth before I have a chance to think them through.

"No, absolutely not," Mom says. "Not a chance."

"Everything points to there. What if that's what I'm supposed to do?"

Mom starts to pace the kitchen and Auntie Doreen swoops in. "We need to do some digging first," she says. "There were some stories about the wheetigo floating around years ago. I never paid them any attention then, but . . ." She hesitates. "I think we need to now."

Mom's pacing slows. Auntie Doreen reaches across the table and squeezes my outstretched hand. "This is a starting point. More than we've had to go off before. This is good."

I squeeze her hand back in thanks.

"So what do we do?" Tracey asks.

Mom and the aunties all look at one another and give a silent nod.

"We visit," Auntie Doreen says, "with people from here. Especially the old ones. We'll need to go with food."

"I'll get the baking started. You three can help," Auntie Verna says. "Loretta, do you want to be on baking duty with us or visiting duty with Doreen?"

Mom moves back over to the table. "Half the people in town don't even like Doreen. I'll take the lead on the visits."

Auntie Verna starts getting supplies together for baking, rattling off instructions for us, ingredients we need to replenish, while Mom and Auntie Doreen sit together and start making a list of people to call and pop in on.

"But what about this?" Kassidy says, nodding to the bloodied piece of fabric in the ziplock.

Mom and the aunties look back at the table. My stomach turns over. "This is the longest I've ever been able to keep anything I brought back. I don't know what that means."

"Keep it somewhere safe," Mom says. "Until we find out more."

I nod and she gives me a small smile. An offer of encouragement. We all move back to our tasks, the kitchen busy with work. Now that we're all carrying our secrets together, my breath comes easier.

The visits take days, as visiting normally does. Mom and the aunties are in and out of the house at all hours. Sometimes they come in together, sometimes alone. They grab food to eat themselves or to take to others, and then they're gone again, waving us off if we ask any questions. When they are home for longer periods of time, they close themselves away in Mom and Dad's room, talking on the phone to people from out of town.

For every house they visit, they bring the food we bake and cook or some of Auntie Verna's beading. Instead of gifts, some people ask for favours. One family needs to get their son a ride to the airport in Edmonton, one needs some stuff from Costco. No matter where the aunties go, they know how to value the information they're asking for. How to make sure the people who are helping us feel cared for in all this, too.

It's impossible to tell if the dreams will happen again, so we set up a system to be as prepared as possible. I go to bed every night in full winter clothes, and Kassidy and Tracey stay up in shifts to watch over me. Mom wanted to stay up, too, but we convinced her that with all the visiting and running around, she needed as much rest as she could get.

The time spent at each house or on the phone is counted by more than just minutes on the clock: it's stories, sharing food, laughing together. Mom says no when we ask to visit with them, because she needs us to take care of the house while they're away. Tracey spends a few hours each day at the detox centre, covering for Mom, since she only took off the first week of me being back. Me and Kassidy take over making lunches and dinners, making sure all the family who come over get fed. Dad helps until he has to leave for a few weeks to a job down south.

"Does he know?" I ask Mom as Dad drives away, realizing that he's never around for any conversations we have about the wheetigo or our dreams.

"He knows what makes sense to him," she says. "That you need help and we need to do the best we can to make sure that you get it. He didn't want to go, but we can't both take time off work right now."

A pang of guilt slides into my chest and I just nod. I feel like I've altered everyone's lives, shifted them into focussing on my own.

Me, Tracey, and Kass also get restless. We look up photos of Sabrina taken after that night on the lake up until she died. In all the photos, hard copies and digital, she has that deep scar under her collarbone whenever it's exposed. It's as if it appeared overnight.

"She was different," Tracey said again one day as we sat on the couch together scrolling through photos of Sabrina on her phone. She keeps repeating it, as if saying it over and over will make it make sense. "What if the scar is like everything else you can see in the dreams that we couldn't see in real life? Maybe it was always there and we just couldn't see it." The sadness cracks her voice.

We also study the blood-crusted rag, still in the ziplock bag, every day. We leave it on Tracey's bedside table for safekeeping, and part of me expects it to disappear every time I leave the room, but it's always where I left it.

Mom and the aunties tell us things they've been hearing. How the water on the lake is so low this year the fish are boiling alive, their dead bodies belly up in shallow pools. Creeks turning dry. Farmers' crops that just won't grow. Auntie Verna tells us the colours she saw around certain people. "You remember the Williers? Donna's side, not Brenda's. They weren't a very good colour. A scary tinge of orange. Stay clear of them for a while." It occurs to me that Auntie has always told us about people or places we needed to be wary of, but only now do I understand why.

Me and Kassidy sleep in Tracey's room, to make it easier for them to sleep in shifts watching over me and so we'll all be less alone. Even though I know they can't help, I go to sleep less scared with them around me. Grey-haired Sabrina doesn't come back. Instead, I dream of the lake. I am nothing. Not a person, not a living being. I drift through the air, formless. Every night, the lake gets closer and closer. Thrashing waves reach into the sky, the lake's body a deep blue. It moves like it's alive, like it has something to say, like it needs to get out.

But that's all that comes to me. I don't dream of that night in the woods or the crows. I wake rested, rooted in my body, a tree growing back after a fire. I tell everyone about these dreams and we all nod together, another puzzle piece that doesn't fit. We don't talk about it much, but it's not like before, like something that needs burying.

On the second week of visits, I wake up in the middle of the night from a gentle push on my shoulders, like someone trying to shake me awake. I sit up, expecting to see the outline of Tracey's or Kassidy's face hovering over me in the dark. There have been a few times where I shifted or twitched in my sleep, and in a panic, whoever was watching over me shook me awake to interrupt a dream. But now I'm alone.

Next to me, Tracey lies asleep, her breathing steady and deep. As my eyes adjust to the dark, I see the lump on the floor where Kassidy and Atim have fallen asleep, too. I check my phone. It's 3 a.m. Kassidy was supposed to be up for another two hours before Tracey's turn.

There's a warmth in the air around me and I feel like I'm being watched. That's when I hear the noise coming from the stairs: *shuk shuk shuk.* The shaking of coins in a tobacco tin. Like I'm ten again and kokum is on her way to the kitchen, ready to take someone's money at poker. My heart beats hard against my chest. I haven't heard this noise since I was in Vancouver.

It comes again: *shuk shuk shuk.*

I steady my breathing and swing my legs over the side of the bed, following the noise in the dark.

As I tiptoe to the stairs, I wonder if it's coming from the aunties and Mom, still awake. Earlier that night, me, Tracey, and Kassidy left them playing cards and drinking tea while we went up to bed. We had spent the night as we usually do: me and Tracey cooked us all dinner, the others filtered in from visits. They had travelled further north that day, visiting some of their great-aunts in Fort Vermilion. The drive had been long and they were exhausted, so we didn't ask any questions.

At the bottom of the stairs, I know immediately from the dark of the kitchen that everyone is asleep. I pause and listen again for the shaking, my ears straining against the stillness of the house, and wonder if I'd imagined the noise, the push against my shoulders. Then I hear voices coming from my parents' room.

My neck burns as I creep forward. A thin line of light beats in the darkness. The door is open a small crack. A muffled voice drifts out. I hesitate and look around before inching closer, avoiding the floor planks I know will creak, and tilt my ear toward the door.

"How does that have anything to do with it?" Mom talks low, an edge to her voice.

"Put it together." A tinny voice comes through the unmistakable sound of speakerphone. "The oilfield companies started coming in heavy to High Prairie and a bunch of other towns close by about ten years ago."

"It's the same time people started seeing the wheetigo." I'm surprised to hear Auntie Doreen's voice, but it explains the phone being on speaker.

"The wheetigo didn't appear here by accident. Greed lured them here, like bears to spawning fish. Or maybe they were turned here, created and set loose. Just like those damn pipelines, built underneath our feet and then abandoned."

I realize now who the tinny voice belongs to. Kokum Mary-Jane Bellerose. She still lives in East Prairie, a few acres down from kokum and mosum's old farm. Her horses used to graze by the road, never got spooked by cars.

I hear feet moving on Mom's bedroom floor. I know by the sound of the gait that Mom has started pacing.

"But what does that have to do with us? If the wheetigo feeds off greed, shouldn't they be haunting the oil companies, or whatever's left of them?"

"That's the point! There isn't much left of them." Mary-Jane sighs, then says more gently, "The hungry will eat anything when they're desperate. Greed isn't the only thing that can sustain a wheetigo. They'll sink their teeth into any type of sorrow. The lonely, the sick."

"The grieving." Auntie Doreen whispers the realization, but I hear it plain as day. The phone line is silent.

"Remember when Lesley had to get half her hand cut off?" Mary-Jane asks. Kokum Lesley, Mary-Jane's late sister, had a missing pinky and ring finger on her right hand for as long as I'd known her. I figured it happened before I was born but I never asked about it. "She was helping nôhtâwiy put the fence in when we were kids when she sliced her hand on the barbed wire. She didn't say anything, just left her hand in her sweaty glove and kept working in the heat. The cut festered, grew rank. A week later, it got infected. You never know what kind of hurt is lying in wait if you don't tend to it right away."

Auntie Doreen starts to respond, but I don't hear it. I slip back through the dark to the stairs. It's not until I'm in the safety of Tracey's room that I exhale and realize I'm shaking. My ears ring with Mary-Jane's words. Is that what Sabrina was? A casualty of a hungry monster that was brought here by something else? How cruel that we can't even hurt in peace, that we have no time to try to heal. We can't even grieve without something coming for us.

I crawl into bed, careful not to wake Tracey. I listen to the sound of her breathing as I close my eyes. Fall asleep to the image of snaking, clotted veins growing rotten all underneath my skin.

I get up a couple hours later with the sun and lie in bed waiting for Kassidy and Tracey to stir. Tracey wakes, turns to me, sleep still crusting her eyes, and yawns. "Whoa, what the fuck?" Her voice cracks from a night of rest and she sits up suddenly. "Kassidy! You didn't wake me for my shift!"

"What?" Kassidy says. Her head shoots up from her place on the floor, Atim snorting as he gets shaken off the covers. Her long hair covers her face. "What happened?"

"You fucking fell asleep," Tracey says, anger starting to redden her face.

"It's fine, it's fine," I say quickly, putting a hand on Tracey's arm. "Everyone is exhausted. I didn't even dream at all. Everything's fine."

"Oh shit," Kassidy says, Atim pawing at her legs. "I'm sorry, I don't even remember lying down."

"You guys, it's okay."

Tracey relaxes slightly. She gives an apologetic smile to Kassidy and then turns to me and stares more intently at my face. "What's wrong?"

Kassidy kneels forward against the bed, resting her chin in her hands.

"Nothing." The lie comes out too quickly, like an instinct. "I'm still just tired, that's all."

"Well, shit, don't worry us, then," Tracey says, her eyes searching my face for whatever I'm not saying. Mom and Auntie Doreen's conversation with kokum Mary-Jane stays at the back of my throat, but I swallow it down.

"We should get breakfast started," I say. "Mom and the aunties probably have another big day ahead of them."

We filter downstairs and make breakfast in silence. Mom and Auntie Doreen come into the kitchen, their exhaustion showing in the bags under their eyes, and pour themselves cups of coffee. Auntie Verna comes over shortly afterwards, dressed in a black-and-white matching sweatsuit. They kiss all of us in turn while we settle in at the table. The aunties and Mom start to talk amongst themselves, planning for the days ahead and who they still need to see, when the words I've been holding in spill out.

"Do you know anything else yet?" I ask in a rush.

They stop talking and all look at me. Kassidy and Tracey look up from their plates.

"I know you've been busy," I say, the back of my neck burning from their sharp gazes. "But do you have any leads?"

I look directly at my mom when I say this. Her eyes are soft and unreadable. I look at Auntie Doreen, too.

"We've heard some interesting stories," Auntie Verna says. She puts down her fork carefully. "They sound like they could be wheetigo sightings, but we're not entirely sure."

I nod and keep my eyes on Auntie Doreen. "Anything else?"

She looks at my mom. "No," Mom says finally. "We don't know anything for sure yet."

"We'll tell you as soon as we do," Auntie Verna says, pushing up her glasses. "We're doing all we can."

A hollow forms in my chest as I nod and look back down at my food. "I know," I hear myself say. "I know you are."

After breakfast, Tracey goes back to her room to sleep some more, and me and Kassidy settle in on the couch after we finish cleaning up. I want to tell them both about the conversation I heard last night. How hurt I am that Mom isn't telling us something, even though I know it makes me a hypocrite. But kokum Mary-Jane just confirmed what we suspected about the wheetigo, and even why it's here.

My thoughts are interrupted when my phone dings and lights up. I check the message, hoping for any kind of response from Joli, who I still haven't heard from, but it's from an unknown number. It feels like the couch tips underneath me.

Welcome home.

My ears ring and the phone feels hot in my hand. Without a

word, I turn the screen toward Kassidy. She squints at it. "Holy shit, that's her?"

I can only nod because my voice has stopped working.

"Let's get Tracey." She stands and I follow her out of the room, the calm morning vanishing as fast as a storm eats up a clear sky on the prairies.

Tracey is still rubbing her eyes awake as Kassidy and I stand in front of her, waiting. My phone sits between us on the bed. Tracey pushes her hair back, her eyes flitting between us and the phone. Outside, birds chirp from the roof. The sun beams through the window.

"What are you going to say?" she asks.

I stare at her. "I have no fucking clue."

"Okay." She shakes her head and takes a deep breath. "This could be our way of figuring out if this is really Sabrina."

"But we know it's not, right?" I say.

"Just in case," she says. "What if we're wrong about the wheetigo?"

I swallow back a reply.

"We shouldn't write anything," Kassidy jumps in. "Not yet. Let's tell the aunties first. They'll know what to do."

"No!" I yell suddenly. "We're not wrong about the wheetigo. And we're not going to the aunties and Mom."

They both look at me, confused. I sigh. "I overhead them last night, our mom and yours." I nod at Kassidy. "They were on the phone with kokum Mary-Jane Bellerose. She was saying that the wheetigo turned up at the same time as the oil boom, feeding off the greed of the industry or whatever. And now, even though the industry is dying, the wheetigo are still here, trying to find other ways to eat. They're feeding off the hurt, isolated, and grieving."

Tracey's face falls. "So what we thought is true?"

I nod.

"Why didn't they tell us?"

"Probably to find out more first," Kassidy says, her voice hopeful, though her face falls a second later. "Fuck."

"That's not fucking fair," Tracey says. "Sabrina didn't have anything to do with the oilfield. Why her?"

My eyes burn at the sadness in my sister's voice. The unfairness of it weighs heavily over all of us.

"I saw in a documentary once that crocodiles don't stalk their prey by listening. They feel the vibrations on the water," Kassidy says.

"Thanks, Animal Planet, but we're not dealing with a croc here," Tracey says.

Kassidy rolls her eyes at her cousin. "What I'm saying is they find their prey by feeling. Maybe that's how the wheetigo works."

"It feels the bad in us," I say. "It looks for people who are suffering. It feels their pain and targets them."

And what else is a hungry animal supposed to do? I think. I look at the broken faces of my sister and my cousin and feel a rage in my chest expand. Sadness is not so far from anger anyways. It's a flip of a switch. A trickle of water diverting from one pool to another.

"All we've been doing is sitting back and waiting for our moms and Auntie Verna to fix this for us, and they didn't even tell us the truth when I asked," I say.

Tracey's face hardens and she grabs the phone up off the bed. She types out, *If this is Sabrina, what was her favourite sandwich?*

She shows it to us and shrugs. "Unless anyone has any better ideas."

Me and Kassidy shake our heads no, so she taps send and throws the phone back in the middle of the bed.

"Okay, now let's not spend the next however many hours just staring—"

The phone lights up and dings. New message from unknown number.

I look at my cousin and sister before opening it, keeping the screen pointed toward the ceiling so we can all read it together.

Why haven't you been to the lake yet?

"Well, that's creepy as fuck," Kassidy says.

"And kind of rude," Tracey adds, looking around the room.

"Okay, so it's for sure not Sabrina?" Kassidy asks. "I mean, she didn't even answer the question."

I think about this for a second and Tracey shrugs. "I don't actually know what her favourite sandwich is anyways."

Kassidy rolls her eyes. "Well, then that question wasn't a great help, was it?"

"Okay, let me write back," I say. I type in a reply: *I've been home for a while. Why haven't you messaged?*

Three dots appear immediately under the message, appearing and then disappearing for what seems like forever. Then a new text appears.

I thought you'd have followed me by now.

The three of us look at each other.

"Where? The woods?" Kassidy says.

"I don't know," I say.

"Did you tell us everything? Absolutely everything that happened in the dreams, what Sabrina said to you?" Tracey says, turning to face me.

My mind races. I told them everything I remembered, but did I remember everything right? "Yes." The hesitation is in my voice. "I think so."

I type my reply: *What do you want?*

No dots appear underneath the text. Minutes go by, the phone goes dark. After a while, it lights up again. *See you tonight.*

I don't pick up the phone to reply. I know that's the end of it. My palms start to clam up. It's all happening again.

"We just need to get rid of it," I say, my voice too high.

"Getting rid of the phone won't change anything," Kassidy says.

"Not the phone, the bad." I grab my stomach, thinking that if the bad is anywhere, it's where I feel the pain the most. "If it's sensing the bad inside us, we just need to make it good again."

My eyes desperately search Tracey's and Kassidy's. Tracey looks at me in a way I've never seen before, and it takes a minute before I realize it's pity. "Do you think this is our fault?"

Suddenly, I can't look her in the eye and I'm staring at the floor, still clutching my stomach.

"The badness inside you, that guilt and shame and whatever else you feel, it brought you back home, didn't it?" Kassidy says. "I think that's good."

A lot of good that did, I want to say but don't.

"Kokum was the last of all of her nine siblings to die," Tracey says. Her voice is hard. "She outlived all of them, and she wasn't even the youngest. And you know what they all died from?"

My face grows hot in shame. I know very little about kokum's family apart from a few memories of seeing them at family functions when I was really little.

"Cancer," she continues. "Every single one of them. Not one lived over the age of sixty-five. They all went to residential schools as kids, two of them died there. The ones who made it out? Trauma grew in their bodies and killed them. They didn't ask for that. And neither did we. Don't you dare blame this on us."

"I'm not blaming anything on anyone. I'm just saying if we could change things, fix whatever part of ourselves the wheetigo wants . . ."

"Fuck the wheetigo and what it wants."

I feel a hand on my back, and I know by the pressure it's Kassidy's. "Plus, whatever bad is passed down, the good lives in our blood, too. We're fucking magic, man. Look at all we can do with our dreams."

Without warning, Tracey hugs me. She breathes into my hair and digs her chin into my shoulder.

"We are good," she says. "And we'll figure this out."

But the fear sticks to my insides. A warning I can't run from.

We stay in the bedroom together until the late afternoon. Finally, Kassidy suggests we go for a walk to clear our heads. It's hot and muggy again, the sky full of clouds bulging like blown glass. The town is sleepy, but a few people are out in the streets or their front yards.

"We can pretty much assume she's coming back to your dreams again tonight, right?" Tracey says as we pass the only set of traffic lights in town. The intersection connects the two roads where the grocery store and liquor barn sit. "Based on that creepy text."

"I think that's a fair assumption," I say. I kick a rock across the cracked sidewalk. I feel empty again. I don't want to go back to the dreams, where I'm alone, where I don't have the rest of my family to fall back on. "I just hate that I have no control over any of this. Other than dressing for minus-thirty degrees every night."

Kassidy wipes her sweaty forehead with her sleeve. "What if you took control back?"

"What do you mean?"

She stops in the street, so me and Tracey have to stop to turn around and look at her. "What if you took us with you?" Kassidy asks.

A crow lands on a garbage can behind her. "Took you where?" I say.

She rolls her eyes. "To your dreams."

"Yeah." Tracey jumps in. "You did it with your phone. What if you took us, too? So we can help."

The thought of having them there with me fills me with a sense of relief, followed quickly by panic. "No," I say. "No way."

"But—" Kassidy starts.

"I said no. I don't know what things can happen in these dreams. The worst thing I could do is bring you into them, too."

Kassidy looks like she's going to disagree again, but Tracey holds out her hand. "Okay," she says. She looks out hard into the distance and runs a hand through her hair, slicking it back against the heat, like she's trying to pull an answer from the strands. "What if you try to bring Sabrina back to us?"

"Like from the dead?" Kassidy asks.

"No, not from the dead," Tracey says. "The grey-haired, zombie Sabrina. The wheetigo. Bring it back from the dreams. You can't control what happens in dreams, but you know all the rules here, when you're awake. And you said she's the only other person you have been able to touch. The rest of them, or us, just go right through you. If you can grab wheetigo Sabrina and bring it back, we can deal with it here where we're in the driver's seat."

I nod and start walking again, slower this time, while I think about what they're suggesting. We cut through the grocery store parking lot, stepping over concrete barriers and shards of broken glass that twinkle like stars across the pavement. I spot the Welter brothers coming out of the grocery store. They give us a polite wave, but we just look past them. They're my age, and their dad went to school with our moms. Kassidy heard my mom and the aunties talking one day about how he used to bully them, call them names and hurt them in the big and little ways only white men know how to do. It's probably not fair for us to hate his children for it, too, but we do. Like crows who pass on revenge to their kin, we'll remember this hate forever.

"I'll think about it," I say after a few minutes of silence.

As we're walking back up to the sidewalk, a truck full of men drive past and holler at us out the window. Tracey gives them the finger and I think of Joli. If I could fly back to Vancouver, just to see them for a minute, I would. But I can't think about that now.

We walk past a boarded-up motel that had been running for as long as I remember. A piece of cardboard with "Closed" written across it in black marker is nailed to the front door. I think back to what Mary-Jane said to Mom and Auntie Doreen.

"The town is quieter," I say. "More closed businesses, vacant hotels. It's eerie."

"It happened pretty fast," Kassidy says. "As soon as there were no oilfield jobs anymore. People left, both townies and the people who moved here for work in the first place."

I remember Mom telling me a couple years ago about a few of our uncles moving their families away, chasing jobs. I've seen a lot fewer oilfield trucks since I've been home. I didn't realize how commonplace they'd been when I was growing up.

I look out at the streets around me. I'm surprised by a pang of regret, the kind that comes from finding out through the grapevine about an old friend who died. Even if you're disconnected from them already, it still hurts. It wasn't just my family I cut myself off from, it was this place, too. I don't know it anymore.

"Well, that's a good thing, isn't it? That the industry is dying?" I say.

"I don't think it's dying," Kassidy says. "Just moving. And they really don't give a shit about what they leave behind, do they?"

I think about the empty roads leading to old, abandoned well sites, the gutted woods clear-cut to make way for their trucks, now closed up and leading to nowhere.

"And all the so-called partnerships oilfield companies made with a bunch of the reserves. Saying they would get people jobs in exchange for access to reserve land. They got the land, sucked it dry, then abandoned it and all the people they made promises to when they couldn't use it anymore," Tracey says.

"Don't start talking about this on Facebook, though, unless you want everyone in town arguing about it in your comments," Kassidy says.

We find our way to the town's gravesite. We don't talk about going there, it's just where we end up. That happens a lot in this town, you get pulled where you need to go.

The cemetery is dry and open, not even as big as the parking lot of the Home Hardware across the street from it. Half of the space is still untouched land, waiting to be filled with bodies. The other half has perfectly spaced granite slabs in a line. Shrubs parallel the walkway that runs up through the centre to the back fence. Wild raspberry bushes have taken over the entire south gate.

Kassidy stops before the front gates. "We shouldn't go in there."

Tracey looks through the bars. "Why not?"

"We have enough weird shit going on in our lives right now. We don't need to be tempting any stray ghosts to hop on board, too."

We laugh but listen, taking every quiet precaution. We walk around the border of the graveyard instead, as if the rusted fence could hold back ghosts, if they even did want to haunt us. Tracey trails her fingers across the metal as we walk. We move off the pathway and into the ditch as we round the corner where the sidewalk ends. A few more cars honk at us as they drive by. We ignore them, grab pieces of long grass to chew while we walk. I take my phone from my pocket. No more messages from Sabrina. Tracey looks off into the cemetery again. "There she is." She points.

Through the gaps in the fence, I see it: Sabrina's gravestone is just inside. I can just make out her name, carved in grey rock. There's an etch of a wild rose, too, that makes it look like the rock has veins. Dried flowers and trinkets I can't fully make out cover the ground and the top of her headstone. A fungus grows around the base, too, that I notice isn't on any of the others. I wonder why no one has cleaned it off. A pine tree stands tall behind it, the small cones beginning to bud out from the branches. I inhale sharply. This is the first time I've been to her gravesite.

Like she can read my mind, Tracey wraps her arm around me. "I don't ever come here, either. It's a bit depressing."

I stare into the pine tree, imagining myself as the bark. "God, I just never stop letting her down, do I?"

Kassidy rests her head against my shoulder. "I think graves are more for the living than the dead. So we have somewhere to visit them when we want to."

"Besides, you're kind of getting your fill of Sabrina at the moment." Tracey smirks.

Me and Kassidy let out low laughs. "Come on," Kassidy says. "Let's get out of here, we look real morbid just hanging outside of the graveyard."

We wave at Sabrina's grave as we turn to walk back home, standing a little closer to one another than before.

ᓂ ᐅᐳ·ᐤ

By dinner, I agree to the dreams plan.

We talk it over with purpose, as if we were planning a holiday. We decide I'm going to try to bring the grey-haired Sabrina, the wheetigo, back from my dreams, and Kassidy and Tracey will stay up and watch over me. Try to wake me if it seems like anything is going wrong. We also agree not to tell Mom and the aunties.

"They want to keep shit from us," I say, "that's fine. We can have our own secrets, too."

The aunties and Mom come home at the same time, and the house fills with noise and laughter as uncles and cousins come by for dinner, too. They take up space in the kitchen and living room.

Tracey makes a big pot of mac and cheese for everyone, and afterwards me, her, and Kassidy sit at the kitchen table, trying to quiet our voices. Tracey shuffles a deck of cards curved at the edges, worn from hours of being played and passed from hands to hands over the years.

Every now and then we find a crinkled card, a telltale sign it has gotten wet and been dried again. Someone in the past must have spilled a drink on it, or left the deck outside by accident, collecting dew from the early morning. Mom's crib board, homemade from a piece of wood, sits in the middle of the three of us. The holes are all different depths and don't line up right, but it's our favourite board to play on. We can never remember who made it, some past relative or maybe mosum years ago. It's so smooth under the weight of our hands, like a stone that's been left in the water.

"What are you four scheming about?" Mom looks over from the kitchen counter, a half-eaten bowl of macaroni in front of her and a smile deep on her face.

Auntie Doreen is eating next to her and looks up, her own smile disappearing as her eyes glance around us. "There's only three of them, Lor."

Mom looks again and her smile disappears, a half snort and a shrug erasing what she just said as she turns back to her food. Auntie rubs Mom's arm and goes back to her own bowl. The three of us look at one another and then down at our cards again. Mom's slipup casts the absence of Sabrina over us like a cloud.

The worst part about missing someone is when you forget for a second that they're gone. When you remember, the pain hits you harder than before. Forgetting can feel like a gift, but a lot of the time it's just hurt lying in wait.

"So Kass and I will both stay up while you sleep," Tracey continues in a whisper, trying to leave the moment behind. She eyes Kassidy and emphasizes the word *both*.

"Yeah, yeah, I won't fall asleep again," she hisses.

"When the wheetigo shows up in your dream, like it says it's going to, just grab it and hold on until you wake up," Tracey finishes. She explains it like it's the simplest plan in the world. She starts to shuffle the cards, her hands more sure now than they were in my memory of us in the living room of kokum's trailer, pretending to be adults.

"Deal them proper," Kassidy says, eyeing Tracey. "Don't try and send any of that bad luck my way."

Tracey shakes her head and starts to deal out five cards to each of us.

I smile at their bickering. There's four ways to get bad luck in a game of crib. The first is something that could happen right from the jump: never touch your hand before it's finished being dealt. Sometimes the dealer will try to mess you up and throw one of your cards a little off, but don't take the bait. Be still. Let it sit until the dealer is done. Otherwise, you'll have bad luck running through you for that hand and maybe even a couple after.

The next way is only important if it's your crib. After you pick up your crib hand, but before you fan out the cards to check what you have, you have to lick your thumb. Just a little, not gross or anything. Use that thumb to fan out your cards, revealing your crib. If you don't do this, you're bound to have a cursed crib hand and you'll be lucky to get any points at all.

The third way is all about talking shit. You can trash-talk your opponent any way you want during a game of crib. Actually, that's a nice way to bottle up some of that good luck, which is hard to come by. But never mention skunking someone. To skunk someone in crib, you have to win by thirty-one points or more. Even joking about skunking someone will ensure that you're the one who never makes it past the skunk line. Trash-talk their hands, their family, even their haircuts, but don't talk about skunking.

The last way to get bad luck I can never remember, which is the worst luck of all. It's easy to avoid something when you know what you're up against, but it's a different story for something you don't know. I think this means that no matter what, you can never truly avoid bad luck, even if you know all the rules.

I gather my cards into my hand as Tracey finishes dealing.

"What if nothing happens?" I say it quickly, like I want to get the thought away from me.

Kassidy looks up from her cards but says nothing. Tracey stays silent.

"What if I can't touch her?" I press. "Or I can, but she doesn't come back with me?"

"If nothing happens, we're exactly where we are now. It's worth a try," Tracey says, finally. Her dark eyes stay glued to her hand.

We're silent for another second and then Kassidy sighs. "Whose crib?"

"Mine, I dealt," Tracey says.

Kass looks at her hand again and flicks one card toward Tracey, facedown. We play our first round, Kassidy and Tracey both moving forward, and then we all count our hands. "Looks like city iskwew is a little out of practice." Tracey nods to me.

"Yeah, just watch for the comeback." I count my measly six points and move my peg forward. Once we all count, Kassidy picks up the discarded cards and shuffles them while Tracey licks her thumb and counts her crib.

"Fifteen two, fifteen four, and a pair is six, thank you," she says, as she lays down the cards toward Kassidy and pegs forward again.

Kassidy shuffles the cards expertly. The deck moves quickly through her hands. The fanning of the cards together sounds like music.

"And what do we do if this works?" I ask.

"What do you mean?" Kass says, dealing without having to look at the cards.

"If I can bring this fake Sabrina, this wheetigo, back. What do we do when it's here?"

"We kill it. Jump it before it knows what's happening." Tracey fans her own cards out in front of her, tries to sound sure, but I catch her hesitation.

"That easy?"

Tracey shrugs. "Maybe it is."

The weight of responsibility wraps around my chest, sloshes through me like thickening mud. I only nod.

Kassidy deals out another hand and we quietly play a few more rounds, Kassidy and Tracey moving along the crib board while I slip further behind.

We finish the rest of the game without talking about dreams. We joke instead, take turns shuffling the cards and playing, passing the deck to the left, counting under our breath, our fingers tracing the holes in the crib board.

Aunties, uncles, and cousins come through the kitchen, some stopping to check who's winning, some just passing through. Atim settles under the table by Kassidy's feet. Our shuffling becomes rhythmic, a ceremony we've been practising since we were old enough to sit on kokum's or an auntie's lap while they played, teaching us how to count and add, what the cards and their signs mean. Our earliest lessons in how to be together.

Tracey wins eventually and we pack up the cards and crib board, tuck them away in a cupboard. Normally, we'd get tea and mugs ready for nightly chats with the aunties and Mom, but we say we're too tired. I go outside to say good night to Auntie Verna, who's looking at the moon.

"Look how bright, my girl," she says, pointing up to the sky. I look up at the crescent moon. It feels close enough to reach out and touch, to pull myself up and sleep in the curve of its chest. I forget my simmering anger for a moment while we look up at the sky together, the deep glow of the moon lighting up our upturned mouths. Before I turn back to head inside, I hug Auntie for an extra second. From behind her back, because I don't want to be looking into her face when she answers, I ask, "Auntie, what colour am I?"

I feel her heartbeat against my own chest as she holds me a little softer, swaying slightly in the night. She sighs. "I'm sorry, my girl, you haven't changed."

I nod and say nothing, so my voice doesn't give me away.

We sit in Tracey's room while the house sways under us. Every now and then, we catch the sound of footsteps, cousins giggling, aunties shushing, the TV turned up loud in the living room.

"It's weird how whenever we all get together, I still feel like such a kid," Kassidy says. She sits on the floor with two different kinds of nail polish in front of her. She paints her nails, alternating blue and yellow, slowly and carefully. "It's like I revert back to being twelve again. It's so annoying."

I smile from the bed. Having just spent years away feeling like I had to be a grown-up all the time, it's a relief to feel like a kid being looked after again.

Tracey laughs and lies back into her pillows. "Try living here. I always feel like this."

"What's it like to work with Mom at the detox centre?" I ask.

"It's nice to see her boss people around, other than me for a change." She laughs. "But I like it there. It feels good to be around people who I understand a little bit, and who I feel understand me."

Kassidy blows on her nails, the smell of polish filling the room.

"You should hear her and her band play, they're pretty good," she says to me between blows.

"You're in a band?" I smile and nudge my sister.

She runs a hand through her hair. "Hardly. It's just me and a couple friends who jam together."

"I call them Tracey and the Cuzzins," Kassidy says, laughing.

"Oh my god, we're not even cousins!" Tracey throws a pillow at Kass, who tries to block it with her elbows.

"Barbara is," she says.

"Second cousin, whatever."

We all laugh together while Kassidy puts the nail polishes away and settles into her bed on the floor. Atim grunts and curls up next to her. Kass and Tracey keep teasing each other and giggling.

"All right, chill out, both of you. I gotta get to sleep if we're ever going to do this," I say, even though I desperately want to keep listening to them bicker and tease. I don't want to think about why we're here or what we're about to do. I sit up and pull on the clothes I now wear every night to bed: heavy sweater, wool socks, jacket, toque, and winter boots.

Tracey grips the corner of the blanket in her fist. She props herself up on her elbow, watching me like she's trying to catch a magician in the middle of a trick.

"Awas," I say, sounding like our mother. "I'm not going to fall asleep with you watching me, creep."

Tracey smiles and smooths down the hair poking out from underneath my toque. "I read once that crows fight predators by banding together. Crow kin can hear a call from across the sky and fly in from anywhere," she says.

A wave of exhaustion washes over me. I burrow into the pillows. Kassidy turns the lamp off, plunging the room into darkness except for the sneaking light of the moon. I try to stay awake for a little while longer, but sleep pulls until I finally close my eyes and let it take me.

I'm looking up into a starless night sky. The moon is full and dull behind low-hanging clouds. A cold inches into my skin before I look around me. I'm standing in a clearing. Snow settles on the surrounding pines like it's trying its best to hide them. From their tips, icicles hang in long, perfect cones.

I search the trees while my eyes adjust to the dark. Instead of the panic I've felt waking up in the last few dreams, I feel oddly calm. "Okay," I whisper to myself. "It's okay." My breath comes out in a puff in front of my face as a shiver runs up my body. I zip up my jacket, saying a silent thank-you to myself for wearing it. This is the clearing that's been flashing in my mind every day for the past month. The clearing from the dream where I first saw Sabrina's body.

As my eyes adjust to the darkness, I scan the rest of the space, looking for any sign of a body splayed on the ground. A shock runs through me when I see her, even though I was expecting it. She stands upright on her tiptoes, almost floating, but still and solid among the trees around her. Her arms are spread out at her sides, wrists upturned to the sky. She looks like she's been propped up, like a scarecrow or Jesus nailed to the cross. It's not until I see the shoulder-length hair falling around her face that I realize it's not Sabrina in front of me. It's Tracey.

Tracey is wearing her coveralls, studded with leaves and twigs. She stares unseeing into the distance. Even from here, I see the milky white of her eyes, as bright as the snow underneath her. Before I can take a step forward, a familiar voice calls from behind.

"Sabrina!" It's Kassidy.

I search for the voice and see where it's coming from: a trail break opens to the lake, so close I hear the water lapping at the shore. The water is bluer than I've ever seen it. Kassidy stands on the shoreline, her back to the pulsing water, looking into the trees.

I wave my hands at her. "We're here!" I yell. She's so close, but she keeps peering through the bushes and then crouches, squinting her eyes like she can't see a thing.

"Tracey!" I hear a second person yell, recognizing my own voice. Then dream-Mackenzie walks up next to Kassidy, looking into the trees, too.

"We're in here!" I yell again, louder.

"Where are they?" dream-Mackenzie says, turning to Kassidy.

I yell again in frustration, but I remember looking into the trees from where they are, and I know they can't see anything. And just like in the other dreams, I know they can't hear me, either.

I look at Tracey's unmoving body and then back at the trail. The realization crashes over me like a wave. This is what happened in the woods. This is what I couldn't see from the other side of the trail break.

Snow crunches under my feet as I feel myself break into a run toward Tracey. She doesn't react. As I get closer, she lets out a yelp that sounds like a wounded animal. I run faster.

"Do you hear that?" Dream-Mackenzie's question is muffled under the sound of my footsteps.

I stop right in front of Tracey, her suspended body looming above me. I hold my breath and try to touch her. My hand goes right through her stomach. The tingling feeling shoots up my arm, and my stomach pulses with an ache. I can't help her.

The wounded animal noise comes again from her mouth, louder, more urgent, startling me into stepping backwards.

Another voice comes from behind me. "Tracey?"

I turn to see Sabrina coming out through the other side of

the bushes. Her clothes are torn and chunks of hair stick to her cheeks. Her flannel shirt slips off one shoulder and patches of sweat darken under her armpits. She breathes hard, like she's been running, and a cloud of cold breath forms in front of her face. But she's not shivering and she doesn't seem to notice any of the snow around her.

She looks around in confusion until her eyes focus on Tracey. "Oh my god, what—"

Her voice is cut off as Tracey starts to whisper, low and steady. I watch her mouth move, but I can't make out any of the words, even though she's right in front of me. Sabrina's face, confused only a moment before, goes slack. Her body relaxes, and she stares straight forward at her whispering sister. Her eyes, a moment ago their usual deep brown, go as white as Tracey's.

Without another hesitation, she starts to walk toward us. I look from the whispering Tracey back to Sabrina, and a sudden spike of exhaustion tunnels through me.

"Wait," I say weakly as Sabrina closes the distance between us. My voice comes out so small and desperate I don't even recognize it. I put up my hand, but Sabrina moves right through me as she reaches out for her other sister. Electricity courses through my body as she passes.

As soon as Sabrina touches Tracey, the whispering stops and Tracey's eyes shut. She collapses into Sabrina, as if her legs suddenly gave out.

"Tracey," Sabrina sobs. She blinks and her eyes are brown again and filling with tears. She gently lowers Tracey's unconscious body to the ground and rests her head on her lap. A force like someone leaning against my shoulders pushes me to kneel next to them. The air around us quiets. The only sound moving through it is the choked cries of Sabrina.

"Help!" Sabrina yells, the tears falling across her cheeks as she rocks back and forth, cradling Tracey in her arms. The tears form perfect lines down her dirty face.

As Sabrina searches the woods for help that won't come, I see Tracey's milky-white eyes blink open. Her mouth upturns into a smile. In one quick movement, she grips Sabrina's wrists with both her hands and sits up, pulling Sabrina's head to face her own.

Sabrina's mouth opens wide in shock, but before she can say anything, Tracey grabs her cheeks and stares, her smile never wavering.

"No!" I yell, trying to lunge at Tracey, but falling through her and hitting the snow hard. I turn just in time to see Sabrina's chin tremble. "Tracey?" she whispers, pleading.

"Kakepâtis," Tracey says, her voice coming out in a high-pitched screech.

"No!" I scream again, reaching out uselessly.

Tracey opens her mouth, and her teeth, sharpened into short points, close around the soft skin of Sabrina's throat. As she bites down, her body explodes into dust, glistening in the air.

Sabrina gasps, then goes limp. Her eyes flutter closed and she passes out on the ground. The dust settles like ash over her body. Her mouth, parted slightly, looks like it was in the middle of forming a word.

I move a trembling hand to touch her, and a sob breaks from my mouth as it goes through her once again. I keep it there for an extra moment, let the static in my hand live there since it's the only thing I can feel. I look closely to check if she's breathing and see the slight rise and fall of her chest. Before I can feel any kind of relief, I hear a crow's caw come from behind me.

When I look up, hundreds of crows are covering the sky. They fly over the clearing, coming from the direction of the water. They move so perfectly together, it's hard to tell one crow from another. They look like one giant shadow sent to swallow us up.

They start to descend and head right toward me and Sabrina. The sound of their caws reverberates in my skull as they get closer. Instinctively, I cover my head as they land, but they go right through me, too. Instead, they cover Sabrina's body, moving over every inch of her like they're searching for something.

"I'm coming in!" I hear dream-Mackenzie yell from the trail opening.

How much time has passed? From my memory of this night, me and Kassidy were only staring into the trail opening for a few minutes before Sabrina and Tracey came out. I feel like I've been in here for hours.

I look to the opening again and see Kassidy and dream-Mackenzie, the lake behind them still moving urgently. The crows' deep, guttural caws echo through the clearing.

I hear the branches breaking before I see Tracey stumble out of the bushes nearby. I exhale a sigh of relief to see her very much alive and breathing hard after I just watched her body explode into ash, before it dawns on me: the Tracey suspended in the clearing wasn't Tracey at all. It was just something using her shape to get to Sabrina. The real Tracey finds the trail opening and bursts out, toward the water, to Kassidy and dream-Mackenzie, to safety.

The jump and flutter of the crows brings me back to Sabrina's body. The birds hop around, exposing flashes of Sabrina's flannel shirt, her hair, her jeans. I saw this exact same scene in my third dream, but I hadn't known what happened before it.

I hold still as the crows, one by one, start to take flight, off Sabrina and into the sky. I feel the air move with the beat of their wings as each flies past, until only one is left. It perches on Sabrina's stomach, her chest pecked open and bleeding. Her heart beats into the sky. The crow seems to consider me for a moment and then stretches its beak behind its neck, preening. When it turns back to me, it has a single dark feather in its beak. It jumps toward me, only an arm's length away, and I stare, transfixed, its dark eyes reflecting mine.

Slowly, the crow bows its head and places the feather on the ground in front of my knees. Then it takes off, leaving me alone with Sabrina's body, her exposed heart. I brace myself and reach out for the feather. I'm surprised and oddly relieved to feel my hand close around the stiff, sharp barbs.

I can still hear the voices of Kassidy, Tracey, and dream-Mackenzie, but I tune them out. I squeeze closer to Sabrina, my knees making new dents in the snow. I can't help but stare at the open hole in her chest, the skin pulled back to expose the white breastbone. Her heart beats, the muscle squeezing together and expanding against her lungs. I swallow down vomit and blink away tears that have formed.

Suddenly, Sabrina's eyes snap open. I gasp and fall backwards, catching myself on my hands.

Before I can take another breath, she's standing. She looks around, disoriented, but quickly gathers herself when she spots the trail opening. Her chest is no longer open, but she's still bleeding, like the wound has been quickly stitched closed. She turns and runs toward the break, and I watch as she walks out to the girls on the other side, like she's completely unaware of what just happened to her.

A deep groan comes from the place where Sabrina was just lying. I look down and cry out when I see that Sabrina is still there. Except this is the other Sabrina, the wheetigo. Her face, ashen white, blends in with the snow underneath her. Her hair is completely grey and spread out all around her. Her lips are cracked and dry. Pieces of skin flake off her body as the rasping sound of her breathing escapes from her mouth.

I feel the tug at the back of my spine and remember why I'm here. I reach out for its hands, limp at its sides, and I don't go through them. Its fingers are icicles, so cold to the touch that they almost burn. I grip them so tight I worry they will shatter and I'll lose hold.

The wheetigo's chest is still open, and there is frost forming around the wound. I watch its heart turn blue and slow, slow, slow to a near stop. I'm trying to discern if there will be another beat as I realize its body is disintegrating before my eyes.

Sores sprout all over its face, red and raw, and then open into rot. Its skin starts to shrivel as its cheeks become holes and its teeth blacken. Its hair turns shock white as its body deflates like a balloon, till clothing outlines only bones. Roots start to snake up from the frozen forest floor and wrap around it, like the land is taking it back.

"Jesus," I whisper.

The wheetigo's eyelids open to reveal empty sockets. What's left of its mouth upturns into a smile. "You're trying to bring me back?" Its voice is low and hoarse in my ears. It sinks further and further into the ground. I watch as moss spreads over its limbs and mushrooms sprout out of its eye sockets and the rotting holes of flesh in its face. I try to brace myself, to keep the earth from taking me, too, but I stay holding on to its hands, now just bones. "Don't you see?" the wheetigo croaks. "You already brought me into your home. I've touched every one of them. I watch your sister while she sleeps."

A chill builds up through my spine. "Why are you doing this?" My voice is a cry.

Its mouth moves again, a disturbed gash. Its skull caves into the ground as the smell of rotting meat rises from what remains. "Kakepâtis," it hisses, like the screeched warning of a barn owl as it descends on its prey.

I feel the tug at the back of my spine and try to hold on, but its bones are thin and start to slip. One more tug and I'm back in Tracey's bedroom, pitch-black like the underside of a crow's wing. The warmth of the room hits me, and the smell of rotting meat is gone with the cold. The sound of winter woods is replaced by Kassidy's snoring.

It takes me a second to realize that I'm not in my bed. I'm still kneeling next to a body, but instead of snow, my knees dig into shag carpet as I lean on the edge of Tracey's bed. I can tell by the smell of her shampoo and the way her nose whistles when she breathes that it's her. She is sleeping on her back, stiff straight. Shadows bubble around her body, dark like spilled oil.

As my eyes adjust, I realize they're not shadows, but mushrooms. Lion's mane—mushrooms that only grow on dead or dying trees—grow out of her legs. They anchor her to the bed, sprouting up from the mattress and through her skin, like they would through a fallen tree. Moss grows from the floor, up the bedposts, and to the fungi covering Tracey like a blanket. Oyster mushrooms fan out along the sides of her body like quarter moons. Sabrina once told me oyster mushrooms can eat through anything, even hair. Tracey's skin, too, starts to crack, like bark rotting.

Then I hear it: a scream. Deep and loud and never-ending like a story you wish you could stop. It takes a minute to realize the scream is coming from my own mouth.

ᓂᐯ ᐅᕁᐃ

The scream crashes through the house like a high-rolling river. Kassidy is behind me first, jumping up from her bed on the floor. She holds my arms back as I try to pull the death-eating mushrooms off Tracey's body, except that they *are* her body.

"It got Sabrina, it got Sabrina, it got Sabrina," I yell, my face wet with tears and my voice breaking. On the bed, Tracey does not wake up, but her chest moves up and down slowly. I look into the shadows of the room, searching for the wheetigo. I held on to it, it has to be here. I thrash harder against Kassidy's chest, but her arms are pretzelled through mine to hold me still. I turn my head to look at the closet, the corners of the ceiling, the window curtains. As clear as it was in my dream, it has to be somewhere. It could be anywhere.

Atim barks at us from the floor as Mom and the aunties burst through the door. They throw on the lights, revealing even more of the grotesque form on the bed. Now we can see the mushrooms weep. A clear liquid seeps from their pores, their caps glistening like pus out of a wound. I taste the dampness of forest and the room smells like sweat.

We stand around the bed, shocked and unmoving. Mom cries

out and grabs Tracey's shoulders, shaking her. "What's happening to her?" Her voice is strangled with fear.

The mushrooms are flowering all over Tracey's body faster than we can think. She's almost completely covered under the layer of fungus. My ears still ring from my scream.

"Somebody help her!" Mom screams again.

Just as the mushrooms start sprouting up her neck, Tracey opens her eyes with a gasp. In the same moment, the mushrooms and moss vanish, leaving her body as it was before, the covers wrapped tightly around her like a cocoon. She swings her legs out and over the side of the bed, choking on her breath, feeling her arms and legs as if to make sure they're still there.

"What's going on?" We hear a voice from outside the room and then feet by the bedroom door.

Auntie Doreen rushes to slam the door behind us. "Nothing," she yells through the wood. "Mackenzie just had a bad dream."

We hear some grumbling and a few more sets of feet on the stairs as people resettle.

I'm still kneeling, trembling, next to Tracey. Kassidy's arms through mine have gone slack and she sits back with a tense sigh. Tracey's wild eyes find me first. "I was there," she says. "I was in the dream, too. The wheetigo pretended to be me to get to her. To get Sabrina." She grabs my shaking hands.

"Was this here before?" Auntie Doreen's voice comes from the other side of the bed. From the covers, she pulls out a single black crow feather. It's bent in the middle, as if it had been folded. The crooked shaft shines in her hand.

The blinking light on the coffee machine reads 2 a.m. We sit around the table and listen to the percolating machine spit out dark liquid while we wrap ourselves in quilts from the linen cupboard and breathe into the stale air. Mom paces the kitchen, Atim lumbering at her feet.

"You tried to bring back something that's been tormenting you in your dreams, to here? To real life?" Auntie Doreen says.

I shake my head. The idea sounds worse when she says it out loud. "We just wanted answers, to be doing something other than waiting. We thought if we brought it here, we'd have more control. We'd be able to *do* something." As soon as I say it, I see our mistake. How could we think we had any kind of control over this?

"And you didn't think to tell us?" Mom says. "Think about what could have happened. What almost happened!"

She looks at Tracey, who rubs her legs with her palms like she's trying to work out a stain we can't see.

"We're not the only ones keeping secrets," I counter. "You've been learning more and more about the wheetigo and you haven't said a thing to us." My voice comes out hard. I look between Mom and Auntie Doreen.

Mom stops pacing and looks at me, her jaw setting in a clench. "We told you we'd tell you when—"

"When you find out anything important?" I cut her off. "Like what kokum Mary-Jane told you?"

I see the surprise in Mom's eyes. Her and Auntie Doreen share a look. "Yeah, I heard." The anger leaves my voice, but the sadness stays.

"We tried to stay awake," Kassidy whispers, as if only to herself. She rocks quietly in place on her chair next to Tracey. "Me and Tracey. We weren't even tired. We were watching you, and then all of a sudden, everything went dark."

Tracey puts an arm around Kassidy. "I don't think we had a choice." They find each other's eyes, some silent thing between them. Tracey looks back up to our mom. "You didn't tell us something we should have known," she adds quietly.

"We're not kids anymore," Kassidy says, her worried eyes never leaving Tracey. "We're in this, too."

"They're right," Auntie Verna says softly.

Mom's jaw stays clenched and she starts pacing again. Auntie Doreen nods. "We're sorry. We do need to tell you what we've found. But first, what happened?"

My voice is unsteady as I recount the dream.

"I don't know how I was there," Tracey adds. "This wasn't like the other dreams I used to share with Sabrina. In those, we were each ourselves. In this one"—she swallows—"I was her."

Mom stops pacing and sits at the table next to Tracey. Her leg is shaking with nerves.

"I was in Sabrina's body, but I couldn't control anything," Tracey continues. "I saw through her eyes as she was running through the woods, looking for me. And then I saw me in the clearing. And I thought, only for a second, how strange it was that I was standing like that. On my tiptoes like I was floating, my arms spread. But then I heard it. The floating Tracey started whispering to come to her. She was saying that she was going to make it better. That she was going to make all the hurt stop."

She stops for a second as her eyes brim with tears, but none fall. "The next thing I knew, I was lying on the ground covered in crows. Everything went dark and all I remember is sinking, sinking, sinking. Roots worming through my body. Rocks and dirt in my mouth so I couldn't speak or breathe. I thought I was dead. Then I heard Mom." She looks at our mom, whose posture has gone rigid in her chair. "And I woke up."

Mom gathers Tracey in her arms. "I'm so sorry, my girl," she whispers.

"The wheetigo said it's already been in our home. That it

watches Tracey as she sleeps," I say. "I didn't bring it back from the dream tonight. It was already here."

Kassidy gets up suddenly and walks down the hallway, Atim at her feet. And then I remember something else. "Auntie Doreen," I say. "What does *kakepâtis* mean?"

She looks up from a crack in the table she'd been staring at. "What?"

I think I might be saying it wrong, so I slow down, try to enunciate the words. "*Kakepâtis*. It's what the wheetigo said to me before I woke up."

Her eyes go glassy and I hear the sound of Kassidy's feet as she sprints back down the hallway to the kitchen. She throws something down in the middle of the table: the ziplock bag with the piece of bloody fabric. "We already brought it into the house," she says, her voice shaking. "This has been on Tracey's bedside table every single night since the dream at the bar. This is blood from the wheetigo, not Sabrina."

Everyone stares at the ziplock bag. At some point, everyone had held it, examined it, wondered what it could mean. Mom holds Tracey a little tighter.

"Kakepâtis," Auntie Doreen whispers. "It means fool."

The fire rages too big for the firepit, but Mom adds more wood anyways. Our backyard lights up with the flames and the moonlight, shadows racing across the lawn. Mom burns the piece of fabric without saying a word, without procession or discussion. Auntie Verna suggested waiting until morning, but Mom refused to be in the house with it any longer.

We sit by the fire long after the bloodied cloth has turned to ash, pulling up from under the deck a bench and old camping chairs that haven't been used since last summer. Mom keeps shaking her head and mumbling that she should have known better, until she jumps up from her chair. "The feather," she says. "You brought a crow's feather back from the dream, too."

I think about the feather lying on the bed. The crow plucking it out of its own back and leaving it for me.

"We need to burn it. Where is it?" She turns to head inside, but Auntie Doreen puts a hand on her arm.

"Hold on, Loretta. It doesn't sound like the feather is bad like the bloody cloth," she says, then looks at me. "Mack, do you think the crows are there to hurt you?"

"I don't think so," I say. "The wheetigo didn't like the sight of them, either. I think they could be there to help?"

Mom doesn't look entirely convinced, but she doesn't go back into the house. She does stay standing, though, turning her back toward the fire to warm herself.

"So, what have you all found out?" Kassidy asks. Atim sleeps curled in her lap. Shadows of fire lick his back. "We need to stop keeping things from each other."

The aunties exchange looks but Mom keeps her eyes on the house. Auntie Doreen lights up her third smoke since we came outside. "You girls are right. This is a wheetigo."

Smoke envelopes my auntie's face as I sink back into my chair. Even though I knew this, especially after overhearing Mom and Auntie talk to kokum Mary-Jane, hearing the words out loud makes my skin crawl.

"We just wanted to be sure," Mom says, her voice quiet. She seems to say it more to herself than to any of us. "We needed to figure out how to get rid of it first. We were going to make a plan."

"We should have told you everything, as we were hearing it," Auntie Verna adds. "To figure it all out together."

Tracey squints in concentration. She runs a hand through her hair. "Is it true that the wheetigo are made by greed?"

"Yes," Auntie Doreen says. "*Wihtikowiwin* means greediness."

"It sounds like wheetigo sightings started happening about ten years ago, the same time as the oil boom. Sightings by the community were rare. Whoever and whatever it was feeding on was most likely situated in the camps or oil companies," Auntie Verna says. "The attacks on people in the community didn't start happening until more recently, since the oilfield has mostly shut down in this area."

I think about the toxic environment in the oil patch, the high depression rate among people based in camps for weeks and months on end, working every day. The way the industry changes men into worse men. The spike in missing Indigenous women, girls, and Two Spirit people with the rise of the industry.

"We don't know all the damage that was done to the land when people started extracting from it," Auntie Doreen continues. She holds her cigarette between her fingers, even though it's burnt down to the filter.

"Greed isn't the only way for a wheetigo to be sustained," Auntie Verna cuts in. "It might have been created by greed, but that's not how it's been surviving."

"It targets people who are vulnerable," Auntie Doreen says. "Any kind of bad it can get its hands on."

"It's hungry," Tracey whispers, rubbing her legs again.

"A bear doesn't normally go into a populated place to find food. But if it can't find anything to eat in the woods, it will," Auntie Verna says.

"Except this isn't a wild animal," Kassidy replies. "This is a monster."

"We think it works by isolating its victims," Mom adds.

"Might be why it tried to isolate you, Mack. Even cut you off from talking to Joli," Auntie Verna says. At the mention of Joli, a pang of sadness burns in my heart.

"The wheetigo is a shapechanger for a purpose," Auntie Doreen says. "It's how it lures its victims. Like a hunter who learns how to mimic a moose call."

"In the woods," Tracey says, "the wheetigo turned into me to lure Sabrina. And it's been Sabrina in all of Mack's dreams." She puts her face in her hands. "Fuck," she says, and looks at me, her eyes red and brimming. "It came into my dreams to get me to convince you to come back. Just like it used me that night when I ran into the woods."

Kassidy turns to her cousin beside her and gathers her in her arms. "It's not your fault."

Tracey sobs into her shoulder. "I don't know why I ran in there. I remember going in and coming out, but everything else—"

"You didn't have a choice," Mom says. "You said in your dream it was whispering to Sabrina to get her to go into the clearing. It did the same thing to you. It hypnotizes. It's how it has tricked other people, too."

"People who think they have encountered a wheetigo all tell similar stories," Auntie Doreen says. "They felt hypnotized, compelled to run off or be somewhere alone."

"There's people who have seen the wheetigo we could talk to?" Kassidy asks.

The aunties and Mom look at one another again. "No . . ." Auntie Doreen says. "Anyone who has ever been lured by the wheetigo is gone. Dead. That's why we wanted to figure out a plan for how to deal with it first."

A silence hangs in the air, only disrupted by the crackle and popping of the fire. Auntie Doreen flicks her cigarette, long burnt out, into the fire.

"It's family members and friends who told us the stories,"

Mom adds. "All the incidents seemed to happen in the woods or on the lake. One minute someone was fishing or swimming or hiking, and the next they were somewhere else. Off trail, deeper into the woods in a spot they don't remember running to."

We're quiet for another moment before she continues again. "The thing is, no one who was lured by the wheetigo died right away. They died about a year or two later. But their deaths are all strange. Unexplainable accidents. Sudden deaths."

"It makes a home in a person first, lives in their insides," Auntie Doreen says. "A place for it to stay while it slowly chips away at its host before it kills them completely."

A truck drives by the house and we hear music drift out as it passes. I stare into the fire.

"The Sabrina who came out of those woods, was she our Sabrina? Or the wheetigo?" Tracey's voice is low and shaking.

"She was our Sabrina," Auntie Doreen says. "Part of her must have been left in the woods, like you and Mackenzie saw. The Sabrina that came out was changed, but she was still our Sabrina. The wheetigo just became a part of her."

"Why the helpless, though?" Kassidy asks. "If it can hypnotize people and do all these things? Can't it take anyone?"

Auntie Doreen looks sad. "The wheetigo is like a parasite. It needs a host that's vulnerable, has something for it to feed off. Sabrina was in a bad place after kokum died. The wheetigo might have seen that and latched on."

I look at Mom. Her eyes have glazed over.

"We all felt something different about her," Kassidy says. "Why didn't we look deeper?"

We sit in awful silence for another minute before I clear my throat. "The people who you've spoken to, did any of their loved ones who were lured by the wheetigo say anything about weird dreams?"

Mom's leg starts to shake again. The aunties turn their eyes to the fire. "No," Mom says finally. "No one said anything about the wheetigo invading any dreams."

The fire grows for a moment with a breeze. I share a look with Tracey. What was it about us that allowed the wheetigo into our minds?

"What do we do?" Tracey says, her voice pleading.

"We think we know the way to kill it," Auntie Verna says. "We don't know for sure, it's just a theory. We only thought about it yesterday." She wraps her arms tightly around herself. "We have to destroy its heart."

"That's what the crows tried to do," I say, thinking back to the blue, frost-eaten heart barely beating in Sabrina's open chest as the wheetigo became a part of her. "They were trying to peck out its heart."

"How do we find it?" Kassidy asks. Atim snorts against her arm.

"We don't," Mom says in a hard voice. "We don't go after it. This thing feeds off the helpless and needy, and we are none of those things. We're all together now. We just need to keep being together and it can't touch us."

"Lor," Auntie Verna starts in her calming voice. "We know that's not true now. Look what happened to Tracey."

"We'll all just stay together," Mom says, her voice getting higher. "We have to stay together to stay safe."

Auntie Verna dips her head in response, the fire reflecting in her glasses. The thought of the dreams continuing forever hits me like an avalanche. Living the rest of my life like this would be like being buried alive.

"This thing took Sabrina," Tracey says. "We can't just do nothing."

"And even if it does leave us alone, who will it go for next?" Auntie Doreen says gently.

"I need to go to the lake," I say, my voice shaking. "I need to end this."

"Do you still think this is all about you?" Kassidy asks, almost shouting. "This is about all of us. We both should have gone in after Sabrina and Tracey that night. We're all in this."

"I know it's not all about me!" Suddenly, I'm yelling. "But I can't put anyone else at risk—"

"No one is going anywhere," Mom shouts over us both. Behind her, the sun peeks up over the trees. Exhaustion shows in the creases on her face. "I'm not losing anyone else." Her voice cracks, like she's been holding this thought her whole life and it has finally broken free from her body. Everyone goes silent. "This is bigger than all of us. We need more time to figure it out. We can't get Sabrina back. We didn't know enough to protect her. Now that we do, I have to protect you."

"What if we don't have time?" I ask. "These dreams have hurt me, hurt Tracey. Almost killed us."

At the mention of this, Mom crosses her arms over her chest. Auntie Doreen puts her head in her hands.

"Let's regroup in the morning," Auntie Verna tries. "We're all tired. Let's get some rest, come back to it later."

"We'll find another way," Mom says. "But until then, we do nothing." She looks directly at me. "If you dream again, you stay as far away from it as you can. Run in the opposite direction and keep running until you wake up. Until we figure something out. We will figure something out." She grabs her blanket slung over her camping chair and heads across the lawn to the house.

Auntie Doreen lifts her head. Bags weigh heavily under her eyes. Auntie Verna sighs. "I'm going home. I'll come back after a bit of sleep and cook a late brunch." She gets up and hugs and kisses everyone before heading out the back gate.

Me, Kassidy, and Tracey get up to help put out the fire.

"I'll do it," Auntie Doreen says, sighing. "You all go in to bed."

Kassidy kisses her mom and carries Atim back into the house, Tracey right behind her. I stay back, grabbing a pail from the garage and filling it up with water from the outside tap. Auntie follows me with a pail of her own, moving slow like she's wading through something deep. The morning starts to creep in. Birds are waking up in the backyard tree. The sky pinks around us. "Auntie," I start. "Does anything happen in your dreams?"

I've been wanting to ask her ever since everyone else admitted theirs. As far as I can remember, she has never said anything about her own dreams, but I've never asked.

She watches me pour my bucket of water on the firepit, smoke sizzling into the air around us. "You know," she says, "I knew about Tracey and Sabrina visiting in their dreams when they were kids. Sabrina told me."

I'm surprised. Neither Tracey nor Sabrina ever told me.

She pours her own pail over the fire, too, slower, making sure to get all the edges of the pit. "And I knew about your mom, too. She told me when we were younger, but no one else. There's a real honour in being the kind of person people can tell even their most terrifying secrets to. Someone who can help other people hold the heavy stuff."

I think about how Auntie Doreen was the first person I told when the dreams started. How I didn't think twice about it.

"No, my girl, I can't do anything in my dreams," she says, "but fire needs wood and wind to burn, right?"

We watch the dark embers glisten against the water and she hugs me. "Wait, so you *are* a goddamn dream oracle, then?" I say, thinking back to our first phone call about my dreams, which seems like years ago now.

She hits my shoulder and we laugh before climbing the porch steps to the house together.

"It also means I'm the first to get the best gossip." She winks, nudging me.

We leave with the blossoming sun at our backs as we head into the house, the day already feeling long and never-ending.

ᓂ �·ᕈᖽᐧ

In Tracey's room, her and Kassidy are still awake in bed when I walk in. I crawl in with them, my clothes still on, and they make room for me.

"Are you okay?" I ask Tracey. Even though she's lying down, I can tell she's anxious. She's jiggling her foot under the covers and her eyes are wide. The big brown of them takes in the room.

"I can't stop thinking about it," she says. "The feeling of being pulled under, awake, but not being able to move. Plants and bugs moving through my skin. Like I was dead."

Kassidy rubs her arms and sighs. "I hope they figure something out soon," she says, nodding to the doorway.

"No," I say. The words spill out of me in a whisper. "We're not going to wait for Mom and the aunties to fix this. I'm going to the lake. Tomorrow morning." The angry shoreline flashes through my mind, burns into my stomach. "I don't think the wheetigo will wait anymore."

Tracey nods. "If you're going, we're coming."

Before I open my mouth to protest, Kassidy jumps in. "It wants people alone, remember? We're coming." She stares at me until I nod. For a moment, I feel relief that I won't be doing this alone, but then dread rushes like water into my lungs. Tracey's gaze follows mine to the crow feather on the bedside table.

"The crows went for its heart," Tracey says. "We should, too."

"I've never killed anything before," Kassidy says. "I don't even like touching raw meat. It's gotta be one of you."

Me and Tracey look at each other. I already feel out of breath. I'm not sure I'll be able to do anything. But I know we have to try. "I'll think of something," I say.

Tracey jiggles her foot faster. "Should we tell Mom and the aunties first?"

My instinct is to lie. My tongue moves to the back of my teeth before I hesitate and catch it. I've been lying since before I got home. Lying kept me away from my family. Lying almost got Tracey killed. Lying isolated me. I look at Kassidy and she gives a shrug. "We have to tell them," she says.

I nod in reply. "But they can't come with us," I say, thinking of the look on Mom's face before she left the fire. "It's not about pushing people out," I say quickly when Kassidy looks like she's about to disagree. "I'm not doing this alone. I have you two. But that night was about us four, and I think that's how it has to end."

As we lie in silence, I think about the wheetigo being called here, or maybe created, by greed. Did it ask for this, or was it forced into the life of a monster? I know what it's like to be made into something, to not be sure if the hole in me was always there or if it was carved out over the years. My anger toward the wheetigo is partly pity, which isn't the same as forgiveness, not really. But I'm surprised to feel anything soft toward something that has created so much hurt for us.

My eyes drift as I feel carried by the weight of the blankets and the sounds of my sister and cousin falling asleep beside me.

I sleep restlessly. Dreams don't come, but a fear gnaws at my insides, making me twist and turn. I slip between being awake and asleep until late in the afternoon. Kass and Tracey are still sleeping when I sit up slowly in bed. Their resting faces turn up into the open space of the room and, despite everything we've already been through, I remember how hard and fragile we all are. A shadow from a bird flying past the window blinks their faces into darkness for a second, and I look at the feather on the nightstand.

I move through the bedroom with a building panic that we're out of time. I forget to put on a sock, half brush my teeth. Even though I told Tracey and Kassidy I'd wait to go to the lake, that still seems too far away. The urgency of our lives flows through my body. I slip down the stairs to the kitchen, and I hear the sounds of Mom and the aunties already: the opening and closing of cupboards and the hot hissing of the coffee pot.

Auntie Verna and Auntie Doreen hold mugs to their faces as they talk. Atim sits on Auntie Doreen's lap. Mom stands at the counter, looking out the window, cradling her yellow baking bowl in the nook of one arm while she stirs a wooden spoon with the other.

"Good morning, my girl." Auntie Doreen holds out her arm and I hug her quickly.

"Morning," I say. I sit down next to her but quickly get up again. I start sorting the recycling by the back door, my heart thrumming. I feel like I have to keep moving, like every second is time wasted. The opportunity to catch the wheetigo off guard feels like it's slipping further and further away. Haunting my dreams forever isn't even the worst thing it could do.

"I made brunch," Auntie Verna says. The plates of pancakes and bacon sit on the counter next to Mom, still stirring her bowl. "I can make you some fresh eggs."

"No, thanks," I say. My stomach is tight, collapsing in on itself.

"How did you sleep?" Auntie Verna asks, her eyes checking me over.

"Fine," I say. I take in all their faces in the afternoon light of the kitchen. They still look so tired. My heart twinges with nerves at telling them we want to go to the lake without them, that we are going to face the wheetigo alone. The impulse to lie, the one that wants to make things easier, comes over me again. What am I waiting for? Tracey and Kassidy are still sleeping, the aunties and Mom don't know anything yet. I could go to the lake myself. End this without putting anyone else in harm's way.

I finish the recycling with a buzzing in my ears as I run through the budding plan. I swallow, even though my mouth is dry, and smooth down my hair. "Can I borrow the van?" I ask Auntie Doreen. "Just to run uptown."

She eyes me and looks at my mom, who nods. "Sure," she says.

Mom is still cradling the bowl with one hand, the spoon sticking out the side. Her eyes find mine. "Help me quickly before you go."

The smell of sweet dough wafts through the air. It's the smell of my childhood, mornings standing on a chair at the counter, Mom or kokum giving me a small, dollop-sized piece of dough to play with while they baked.

"I'll help you when I'm back. I'll be quick." I give her a half smile before trying to move again, but she reaches out and holds on to my arm with a gentle firmness.

"My hands are too sore to knead this. Damn arthritis, you know." She looks at me with the same firmness of her hands.

I stand next to her as she sprinkles flour on the counter. A cloud of white dusts her hands, resting in the cracks, showing all the sore spots she tries to hide. She turns the dough onto the counter and nods toward the round, beige mass.

I wash my hands while she pours herself more coffee and grabs a chair from the kitchen table, sliding it next to the counter to sit with me while I work the dough.

My thoughts are racing. The familiar pillowy texture pours into me. I push my palms into the dough, thinking about the fastest route to take to the lake. I punch it with my other hand and turn it over onto itself.

"Don't rush the dough," Mom says. She puts another hand on my arm. "It'll turn out too dense. There's no need to hurry."

I turn the dough over more slowly, careful to trap air like Mom and kokum taught me.

"About this morning," Mom says. "I'm sorry I exploded like I did."

Her voice is soft, and I notice the shift in her posture since this morning at the fire. She's no longer tense and agitated, though the hardness of her eyes holds mine.

"Nehiyawak are supposed to be less controlling with their babies, you know. When someone is born, they become their own person. Have to be trusted to make their own choices. Parents are supposed to just help when they need it. I've always had a hard time with that part. The letting-go part. I'm a bad Cree sometimes."

I nod and hold the dough firmly, thinking back to kokum's kitchen. Her baking bread, making Mom knead the dough while she took cigarette breaks. I breathe a little softer, let the dough move through my hands, a memory in my blood kicking in, telling me when to turn it, when to fold and stretch. Every now and then, Mom leans over and pokes it, waiting for it to tell her when it's time, and I see my kokum in her, her finger feeling the dough, too. "Slow down," she says. "What else have we got to do with all this time but get it right?"

I knead slower, relaxing into the motion. The thumping in my chest eases. Finally, I feel the bread tighten and I ask Mom to feel it. She pokes the dough and smiles. "That's perfect."

Mom covers the dough with a tea towel to proof. The aunties sit at the table, Auntie Verna wrapped in a blanket and Auntie Doreen wearing one of Mom's old bathrobes. They're working on a crossword puzzle together. I hear feet on the floor upstairs, Tracey or Kassidy waking up.

"Still need the car, my girl?" Auntie Doreen asks, not looking up from the crossword.

The keys next to the coffee pot catch a glint of the outside sunlight. "No," I say. "I'll go later."

I watch the crows through the window while Tracey tells our mom and aunties our plan. I listen to the careful calm of her voice, the way that it doesn't shake. She sounds more sure than I feel. The crows outside ruffle their feathers and the wind catches their wings, shaking them slightly on the waving branch. I bring my attention back to the kitchen, to how Kassidy stands so close to Tracey that their shoulders touch, to the way Tracey uses her hands as she speaks. I catch Mom's mouth twitching like she's been stung. Auntie Doreen and Auntie Verna listen quietly.

"The wheetigo can hurt us," Tracey ends with a sigh. "We can't just let it anymore."

"Why can't we be there, too?" Mom says, her voice pleading.

"This is just something that we need to do," I say finally. "I know it in my gut."

Mom looks like she's about to say something, but she catches herself. She holds my gaze for another moment before nodding. Auntie Doreen rubs Mom's back and Auntie Verna gives us an encouraging smile. "We'll just have to do what we can from here, then."

We spend the rest of the afternoon in quiet, everyone's minds knitting together, thinking about what tomorrow might bring. Mom and the aunties stay glued to our sides, cuddling us on the couch, arms around us while we sit at the table. Their bodies become extensions of ours.

Mom cooks us dinner while the aunties help us pack our bags. I'm reminded of how important our aunties are to our survival. Truth be told, I was never a very good camper. Whenever we'd go out to the lake, I would always forget something. It was the aunties who made sure we would be okay. They pre-prepared meals, coordinated where everyone would sleep, made sure we all had enough blankets and pillows. Uncles followed orders, kids made things harder on everyone, but aunties carried the magic that made it all come together.

It was the same now. They make sure our bags are packed with the necessities: some granola bars and fruit, a blanket, extra sweaters, mace, a lighter. Auntie Verna gives us her buck knife and shows us how to use it. She puts it at the top of Tracey's bag. Auntie Doreen whispers prayers we can't hear against our backs.

"Never, ever leave each other's side," Mom says, her eyes pausing on each of us. I've heard her tell us this a million times in my life, but this time is different. "Not for anything."

Before we head to bed, they each hold us for a minute longer. They kiss us, loving us up like rain filling a barrel. Heading up the stairs, I catch a glimpse of outside. The sun setting against the horizon has cast the sky in a deep yellow and green.

Me and Tracey crawl into bed quietly and Kassidy collapses into her bed on the floor. "I don't know if this will work," she says. Her voice hangs in the quiet of the room.

"Me either," I say.

"I'm scared," she says.

"Me too," Tracey agrees.

As we lie in the room, wide awake, I think about the times me, Tracey, or Sabrina had nightmares as kids. We'd lie together in the dark, clutching whoever was scared. We held pieces of one another's shirts in our small hands. There wasn't anything any of us could do if the nightmare came back. But we clung anyways, and it felt like enough.

I wake up to the feeling of pressure against my chest, like someone is pushing down on me with their full weight. Tracey's body is floating upright in front of me. Her face is tensed up, pained. Her lips pull tight across her teeth. Her eyes are closed, but her lids twitch and flutter like she's trying to will them open. Her hair stands up on end as if it's full of static. She's close enough to touch.

I think for a moment I might be transported to the woods again, but when I try to reach out to Tracey, my arms stick to my sides. I try to kick my legs, but nothing happens. A familiar kind of fear muscles its way into my body as I realize this is a darkness dream. The last time I had one was three years ago. When I woke up, Sabrina was dead.

I'm trying to slow my breathing when I notice the frost crystallizing on Tracey's body. It starts at her feet, growing like mould across her skin, inching its way up her legs to her torso and neck. Her eyes move more rapidly, like she can feel herself being overtaken. I try the countdown to wake myself up, but nothing works. The more I try to move, the heavier the pressure against my chest grows. It's getting harder and harder to breathe.

Watching Tracey now reminds me of the moments after someone dies, the helplessness of it. How I imagine Mom felt as she cradled her dead daughter in her arms for ten minutes before the ambulance showed up, trying to feel for a pulse even though there was no life left in Sabrina's eyes. Like when Mom told us about kokum dying and we just had to stand around and try to understand it. That's what this is like.

As the frost starts to reach her cheeks, I feel a sudden rush of oxygen and I breathe in as deeply as I can. The breath shakes me awake and I sit up in a sweat in Tracey's bed. Tracey is already awake and staring at me.

I'm panting and coughing, afraid I won't be able to get enough oxygen in. Tracey gulps in air, too, and looks as scared as I feel. Sweat drips off her face.

"I couldn't . . ." she says, searching my face, fear inching into every corner of it. "I couldn't get to you."

Tears pool in her eyes as she reaches out to me. She grabs my arms and pulls me into a hug. "You were just floating there and I couldn't move, I couldn't get to you. A frost grew on your body like it was disappearing you." Her grip around me tightens as I realize that she saw what I did, too, except I was the one disappearing before her eyes. "But I'm not going to let it," she says against my hair. "I'm not going to let it swallow you up."

I bury my head into the nook of her neck. Was the dream showing us something that was going to happen? Are we walking into something that's going to devour us?

I breathe her in and try to hold it, commit the feel of her to memory. I was wrong. The only thing worse than the moments after death have got to be these ones: the moments before.

After the darkness dream, me and Tracey lie in bed holding on to each other under the covers, waiting for the sun to wake up from behind the trees.

I get dressed while keeping Tracey in my sight the whole time. The horror of watching her freeze stays fresh in my mind. The crow feather still sits on the bedside table. I carefully lay it across my palms, tracing the vane with my fingers, straightening the shaft where I had bent it in my grip. I think about the crows that have been following me since the dreams started, both in real life and in the dreams, the protectors who I now understand have been by my side from the beginning. I tuck it into my backpack. "I'll meet you two downstairs," I whisper. "I'll put our bags by the back door."

Tracey nods and heads to the bathroom down the hall. As she closes the door, Kassidy, who had woken up and started getting ready in silence, grabs my arm. In the quiet of the bedroom, I feel the wind pick up outside. The sun peeking through the window highlights her face and I realize how much she's grown up.

"Don't go in the water," she whispers.

"What?"

"Don't go in the water," she says again, louder. More urgently. She looks around. The lines around her eyes harden. "Just listen and trust me. I had a dream last night and . . . Just please. Whatever happens today, don't go in the water."

I try to laugh, to ease the tension. But she keeps looking at me until I nod. She squeezes my arm once and turns back to change. I quietly head down the stairs, my thoughts racing.

Within minutes, we're all by the back door, ready to head out.

"What the hell?" Kassidy whispers, looking into her sneaker.

Me and Tracey look into ours, too. Small mounds of crushed herbs sit in the heels of our runners. Tracey smells hers. "Sage," she says, and gives a small smile of relief. I wonder which auntie did this. Or if it was Mom. I imagine them circling around our shoes before bed, pinching sage between their fingers in the darkness to put a protection at our feet, not knowing exactly what was going to happen, but still wanting to be a part of keeping us safe. We all put our shoes on, thinking about this love running into our heels.

The road from my parents' house to the lake is in the shape of a hooked thumb, a hitchhiker pointing to the past. Kassidy drives us in her mom's van, the dreamcatcher and air freshener swinging in the rearview mirror as we back out of the driveway. I sit in the front seat and Tracey climbs in the back, wading through McDonald's wrappers and dog toys. Kassidy plays the Garth Brooks CD but turns it down low. We drive without speaking, as if there isn't anything left in the world to say.

We move slowly through town, but as soon as we hit the highway, Kassidy speeds up, the flat plains flowering open around us. The fields are starting to thicken with the yellow of canola and wheat, they'll be ready for baling in a few more weeks. We crack the windows and the air of farmland drifts in.

We take the left turn to Grouard. The single-lane road weaves through bush and prairie land, leaving a plume of dust behind us. The rocks pinging under the car sound like they're part of the music. We come up to the bridge over the river, where a couple of people are hanging fishing rods over the edge of the barrier. They nod at us as we pass. Later in the day, kids will sit and fish with their family here, coolers in between them holding ice or their lunch.

"Remember that time at the lake when Tracey got so mad at us she tried to walk home?" Kassidy asks, breaking the silence for the first time. "She only made it here before giving up and waiting for us to come by in the car." She laughs into the steering wheel.

"I wasn't mad, I was annoyed," Tracey says. "You've all been pissing me off from day one."

I look in the rearview mirror and see the edges of my sister's mouth quiver as she tries not to smile.

We take the first right after the bridge: a dirt trail into the brush.

"Damn, look at all the witch's broom," Tracey says, pointing to the tops of the trees lining the small trail.

I look out my window, tree branches slapping against the sideview mirrors. The balsam and birch are all stripped of leaves when they should be full. Witch's broom, a dense cluster of shoots and thick stems, have formed at the tops of most of the trees I can see. If it wasn't for their discolouration, I might have thought they were nests. But witch's broom is bad for the woods. It latches onto the tree like a growth, takes its nutrients, and distorts the tree's own sense of healing. Tricks the tree into thinking it's dead until, eventually, it is.

Kassidy parks the van when the trees get too thick to drive through. We climb out slowly, careful not to open the doors too wide and hit the brush around us. The sun is out in full, the heat beats against our skin. Kassidy slaps her arm. "Fucking mosquitoes."

We head to the front of the van, dry brush crunching under our shoes. The sound of twigs snapping reminds me of the noises that came from the woods that night.

"There used to be trails over here," I say. I point to a spot that used to lead directly from where we parked to our campsite by the lake. The aunties were able to park two or three cars along this small trail. We could never drive all the way in, so we'd have to walk the rest of the way through the brush, but the trails were well worn back then.

Even though the trees around us have thin, sparse branches from the witch's broom, the dogwood and dwarf birch shrubs cover the bottoms of the tree trunks and scatter over the forest floor, making it hard to see through. Grouse and sparrow sing in the background, their voices slipping through the wood.

"I haven't been out here for years, not to this spot, anyways," Tracey says. She wipes her forehead with the back of her hand. The hair on her arms glistens with sweat. "Not since that summer."

"No wonder," Kassidy says, swatting another mosquito.

"Let's get to the water," I say, moving past them in the direction I know in my blood, the way to the lake. "We'll just have to make our own way."

We step over prairie crocuses and into the bushes, our shoes crunching on dry pine needles and moss. We only take a few steps before the ground suddenly clears into a perfectly cut straight trail, wide enough for us to walk in single file. On either side of us, gnarled pine trees line the trail like the audience at a funeral procession. They look as though they've been dead for years, the branches hanging limp off the trunks. Pine sap, thick as paint, bleeds out from the bark. The dirt below us is a deep red, not like any soil that I've ever seen around here. At the end of the trail, a glint of blue water: the lake.

I stop, Kassidy and Tracey right behind me. A wave crashes in my stomach.

"Do you hear that?" Tracey asks.

"What?" Kassidy replies. They're both whispering.

"Nothing. It's completely quiet," Tracey says. "I could hear birds before, and bugs. Now, nothing."

I hold my breath and listen. The woods are silent. There's not even a rustle from the wind in the dead pines.

Kassidy stands right behind me, and Tracey is behind her. In a row, we clasp one another's hands. Me at the front holding Kassidy, Kassidy reaching back and holding Tracey.

Since I can't reach Tracey, I take the feather out of my backpack and give it to her. She puts it behind her ear.

I open my mouth to tell them I love them but stop. A lump in my throat threatens to release a sob. They both look solemnly at me. Tracey's dark eyes catch the light, and she nods for me to move forward.

U<ᑯ">ᔑᐠ

My steps on the red dirt make no sound, as if the earth has swallowed the noise down. I hold on tight to Kassidy's hand behind my back but keep looking forward. The twisted branches to our sides snag our clothing. My pulse quickens as I try to slow my breathing. *We're almost there,* I think. I can see the blue lake just a few yards in front of us.

As I take another step, I realize it's harder to move, like my feet are stuck in mud. I lean forward, gripping Kassidy's hand harder, willing my legs to push on.

"Mackenzie, the trees," Kassidy whispers. I look to my side and see that the dead trees, already so close to us, seem somehow closer. Their branches finger our hair, reaching out for us.

"Keep moving!" I yell without looking behind me. The earth moves under my feet, inching us backwards. I start walking faster, but the air grows thicker, making it harder to breathe. The trees move closer and closer together, squeezing so tight we have to walk sideways to keep from being squished between the trunks. Bark and branches scratch at my cheeks. The smell of decaying wood fills my nose.

Tears well in my eyes as I push harder toward the water, my legs heavy under me. I hold on to Kassidy's hand like my life depends on it. Like her life depends on it. Our palms are slick with sweat, and it feels like she's being pulled away, but I hold on tighter, the opening in front of us so close. The weight of trunks presses into my back and sternum, but I push toward the lake and fall out of the brush, pulling Kassidy out behind me.

We spill right into our old campsite. My knees hit sand and I bow forward, take in a huge gulp of air. I stare into the lake and listen to the sound of croaking frogs across the water. To my right, the three jack pines cluster next to the shoreline, like they always have. The sound of birds chirping in the distance fills me with relief.

I almost laugh as I turn around. Just like before we went into the woods, the trees look completely different from the outside. They are half dead from this side, too, the witch's broom merging at their tips. The brush is thick and hard to see through. There's no sign of the trail we just came out of, just bushes hiding what's inside. Kassidy kneels facing the woods, her hand outstretched and unmoving. Tracey is nowhere to be seen.

My hands shake as I turn Kassidy to face me. Her face is sunken. She stares forward, eyes wide and unblinking. "I couldn't hold on to her. She slipped." Her hand shakes. "I tried to hold on, but the trees. They pulled her away."

I look back to the woods. A swallow lands on a branch in front of us and chirps.

"Kassidy, look at me." I try to keep my voice even as I grab her shoulders. "We have to go back in. We have to find her."

She looks through me and nods. I help her up and we grab hands. The swallow takes flight. Before we can step forward into the brush again, we hear a splash from behind us. When I look back, I see her. Wading in the cool water, her hair pulled into a single, tight braid, Sabrina stares at us from the lake.

The earth moves around me like a tremor. I blink sweat out of my eyes to make sure it isn't a trick of the light. But every time I look again, she's there, standing in the water up to her hips, the tip of her braid soaked to a paintbrush point. Her face is emotionless, soft-surfaced like the water. Right below her collarbone, a claw-like scar glints in the light.

"Do you see her?" I ask Kassidy. "Sabrina?" My voice shakes as I step toward the water, sand shifting beneath my shoes. Sabrina smiles with empty eyes.

"Mackenzie, don't!" Kassidy yells from behind me, grabbing my arm with both of her hands.

I shake her off effortlessly. Something feels wrong, but my feet walk me into the water, my shoes slipping slightly on the algae-covered rocks. "She's here," I say. The cold water soaks my ankles.

"Mackenzie!" Kassidy yells from the sand.

I keep going toward Sabrina. The water splashes up across my calves. Sabrina's mouth is moving, saying something I can't hear. If I could just get close enough to hear her. I wade in up to my thighs, the water sticking my clothes to my skin. Sabrina is like driftwood, every ripple toward her moves her further out into the lake. I think of kokum waking up on the blow-up mattress. Like her, I don't recognize anything around me.

"Is it really you?" I yell across the water.

I'm closer to her, but she's going in deeper still, the water now up to her chest, her braid a snake floating around her. Up close, she looks pale and older than I remember. She nods and her lips keep moving, whispers I can just barely hear. I keep going, the water up to my shoulders now. Behind me, Kassidy yells something, but I can't make out those words, either. I have a feeling I'm forgetting something, but I can't remember what. It's on the tip of my tongue.

"I'm sorry," I whisper across the lake. "I'm sorry I didn't come in after you."

Under the water, I feel a rush, like a wave pulling me back to the shore. Sabrina stops talking and bites down on her lip, a half-moon of blood prickles to the surface.

"You left me." Her voice cracks when she speaks. Blood smears on her teeth. She looks so deeply into my eyes I think she's looking right into my skull. She bites her lip again. So hard, she bites right through, as easily as if it were a soft piece of cheese. The chunk of flesh dangles to her chin, held only by a thin piece of skin. The blood is rushing now, running down her neck.

"Stop!" I yell, and move forward. My feet can no longer touch the bottom. I kick my legs against the molasses-thick water.

"You left me there to rot," she yells again, in a voice that's not her own. Her tongue darts out and flicks the hanging chunk of lip into her mouth. She bites the dangling piece of skin and doesn't even chew before swallowing. As she floats in front of me, her hair comes out of its braid, turning completely grey. Her cheeks sink into her face.

I feel like I'm going to throw up. The wave underneath me pushes again, harder, urgently, toward the shore. I kick slower, my legs tired. Water splashes up into my nose and mouth. Kassidy's voice comes in again, but it's quieter now, fading. The thing I'm supposed to remember feels so close.

"All of this pain can end." Sabrina's voice pulls me back to her. "Just come to me." She brings her hands up from the water, one reaches for me and the other moves toward her dripping mouth. Her teeth tear at the base of her index finger and slowly peel her skin until it tears off at the nail, like she's peeling the skin off a banana. She turns her face up to the sky and swallows, her throat glistening with blood as it moves.

For a moment, the world is quiet. It would be easy to give up, to go to her. My legs are made of stone. My head bobs under the water. It's so peaceful under here, how did I ever think it was lonely? I swallow a mouthful of lake water. How many of my ancestors have been in this lake? How many are here now? I kick and break the surface again. The water in my eyes blurs the floating form of Sabrina in front of me.

"Come to me, you can sleep now." Sabrina's voice rises across the water. I blink and try to clear my vision. She has peeled the skin off her entire finger. A gush of red on her hand. Exposed muscles and tendons shimmer in the sun. Her eyes are white holes in her head.

A caw, deep and guttural, floats across the sky. A black cloud in the distance, behind Sabrina's floating body, is moving toward us. She hears it, too, and when she turns away to look at the crows, everything rushes in at once: the cold of the water, my exhausted, thrashing legs. This Sabrina in front of me is not real, it's the wheetigo. Its blood blooms in the water. Panic spreads through me.

When it turns back to me, it cocks its head to the side.

"Kakepâtis," it shrieks as it shoots upward. It hovers just above the surface, water falling like rain around it. Its eyes are trained on me for another second before it turns and darts through the sky toward the woods.

Before I have a chance to look back to shore, a wave pushes me up so I no longer have to struggle to swim. I watch the back of the wheetigo as it escapes and see the giant murder of crows following it in the distance. A hand behind me grabs my arm.

"Move!" Kassidy yells. How did she get so close so fast? She pulls me backwards and moves her body underneath mine to keep me afloat.

A memory in my gut triggers and I swim. My arms cut through the water and my feet kick and kick. Without stopping, I turn my head to the side to breathe. I don't feel out of breath or afraid of drowning. It's as if someone else living inside me is pushing my limbs through the water. All I think about is getting to the shore.

Kassidy swims next to me until we get close enough for my feet to find the lake bottom. I push against the rocks, and the lake pushes us to shore, too.

We make it to the sand and I vomit onto the ground. My eyes sting with the tightness of retching. I collapse onto my back, staring at the sky. The crows have thinned to a straight line over the woods, heading away from us. Their caws come in even louder, like they're calling to their kin a half a world away. And then another sound, a screech: the wheetigo in the woods.

Kassidy looks toward the trees. "Tracey." Her voice is a trembling whisper and everything clicks back into place.

"She's alone," I say. "We left Tracey alone."

The wheetigo did it again. It separated us. My mom's stern voice echoes in my head. *Never, ever leave each other's side.* I am a fool. Once again, I let her go into the woods alone.

We throw ourselves into the woods without thinking. The pine and brush stick to our wet clothes. Kassidy's hair is matted from the sweat and water. We hold on to each other's hands and know without saying it that we can't let go.

The woods are not the same woods we stepped out of. The single red dirt trail has shapeshifted, replicating into identical paths shooting out in every direction.

"Fuck!" Kassidy yells. "Where do we go?"

She turns to me, fear cracking all across her soft face. I look down each trail, my breath coming in short gasps. My heart beats in a panic. A crow's caw brings my attention to the sky. The dark plume is flying east of the shoreline. I grip Kassidy's hand tighter.

"This way," I yell, leading her in the direction of the crows.

We're running soundlessly on the red dirt again. The trees on either side of us stand at strict attention, reaching toward us with their branches but staying in place for now. The air stays thin and our legs pound against the ground.

We follow the sound and shadow of the crows until we pass another trail, its mouth opening out to the water. Sunlight on cool blue winks at us as we pass. I hear Kassidy mumble something as we run. Another trail opening, another flash of water. Kassidy speaks again, and this time I catch what she's saying: two. She's counting the High Prairie minutes as we run toward Tracey.

We pass two more trail openings before I see the snow. It's just frost at first, a white fuzz on the tips of tree branches. Then we're running through fresh powder, the soft thump under our shoes echoing with every step. Icicles start to form on the trees. The bushes and shrubs are blanketed in white. Our heaving breaths transform into clouds of cold air. The crow's caws are behind us now, we've outrun them.

We keep running the snowy trail until it opens into a circular clearing, like a mouth opening into a scream. The snow here is packed hard as ice. This is the clearing from my dreams.

Tracey stands in the middle with her back to us. No more than ten feet in front of her is the wheetigo. Its hair, thin and white, is wet across its shoulders. Its skin sags off its bones, loose like a deflated balloon. It stands like Tracey did in the clearing in my last dream: floating on its tiptoes, hands spread to its sides, wrists up to the sky. Blood drips from its fingers and mouth where it bit away its own flesh. It's whispering low and soft to Tracey, something I can't make out. Tracey steps forward slowly.

I stare in shock until Kassidy shakes me, jostling me into a run.

"Tracey!" Kassidy yells as we sprint to her side.

The wheetigo's eyes don't leave Tracey. As we get closer, I see that the blood dripping from its open wounds has turned to icicles. Its body is coated in a soft, white frost. It whispers faster, more urgently. Even being closer, I still can't make out what it's saying.

We reach Tracey just as we hear the caws from overhead, the murder having caught up with us. They sweep over the clearing, casting the white forest floor in shadows. Tracey's eyes, trained on the wheetigo, have gone white.

"Tracey, stop!" Kassidy grabs her arm, but Tracey shoves her back. Kassidy's eyes go wide in surprise. The wheetigo's mouth moves, its blood-red gums glistening into a horrific smile.

I step in front of Tracey, try to get between her line of sight and the wheetigo. "Listen to us!" My voice trembles as I shout. "That isn't Sabrina. It's the wheetigo."

Tracey's stare doesn't break. She grabs my arms and shoves me aside with a strength I didn't know she had. Her hands feel like ice. She keeps stepping closer.

Me and Kassidy each grab one of Tracey's arms. I dig my heels into the snow, screaming with the effort of holding her back, but Tracey shakes us off like we're nothing. Kassidy sobs as she gets up again, refusing to stop, trying to pull Tracey backwards, slipping and falling with each tug of her arms. I stand up again, too, and for a second, I watch the strain and fear in my cousin's face as she tries to hold on. I feel just as useless as I did in my dreams, when suddenly I have an idea.

Without wasting another second, I lunge at my sister. Instead of grabbing her arm again, I open the pack hanging low on her back. The zipper rips with the force, sounding like a swarm of bees in the winter woods. Granola bars and a piece of fruit fall to the ground, but what I'm looking for is lying on top of her sweater: Auntie's buck knife.

The crows' caws fill my head as Tracey comes within arms'

reach of the wheetigo. I grip the knife handle with one hand and pop open the buckle from the leather guard with the other. The silver blade glints in the light.

As I take a step toward the wheetigo, it reaches out for Tracey's face with its bleeding hands, muscles exposed. But just as it's about to make contact, it stops. The garish smile leaves its face and its white eyes narrow in confusion.

In the next second between cocking the knife over my shoulder and bringing it forward, the wheetigo's arms tense, trying to close the gap between its palms and the sides of Tracey's face, but nothing happens. It can't seem to touch her.

I lean toward the wheetigo's outstretched arms, throwing my entire weight behind thrusting the blade into its chest. It lets out a howl like I've never heard before. Blood like freezing rain runs over my hand, still closed around the handle. I let go and stumble backwards. It grasps at the knife sticking out from its chest.

As soon as the wheetigo's focus on her is broken, Tracey's eyes flash back to their usual deep brown, and she collapses into Kassidy, still pulling her back with all of her strength. They fall together onto the frozen ground as the wheetigo howls.

The caws come again, so close above us I can feel the air from their flapping wings.

"Pull her back!" Kassidy yells, and my frozen feet move. I hook my arm underneath Tracey's armpit, and together we drag her away from the wheetigo, who has collapsed to the ground. A circle of blood spreads in the snow around it. The murder descends on the wheetigo's body, covering it in crows.

Snow scrapes underneath me as we keep pulling Tracey further away. The screeching sound of the wheetigo is quickly overwhelmed by the crows' cawing, and then there's no sound at all.

We watch from the snow, clutching one another like the forest might still pull us under. One by one, the crows start to take flight again, and when the last few leave, there is nothing left. No blood, no feathers, not even an indent in the snow as evidence. Even the buck knife is gone.

We lie together and cry, our faces dirty and wet. Slowly, finally, we help each other up. We walk without speaking, back through the trail. Kassidy counts down four of kokum's High Prairie minutes to get us back to our spot.

We wash ourselves off in the lake. Kassidy wades in up to her neck, dips her head under, and bobs in place. Tracey walks out until the water is waist deep, and I stay close behind her. I know the threat is gone, but my body is still stiff and ready. The water gently rushes across me, cleaning off the red dirt and leaves.

The jack pines sway in the breeze and the sky is alive with sound. Frogs croak in the distance, mosquitoes buzz around my head. From far off, I hear birds. When Kassidy dips her whole body under again, I copy her. I let the cold lake hold me and I'm not afraid.

When I break the surface, Tracey and Kassidy are facing me. They look like how I remember them as kids.

"What happened in there?" Kassidy asks.

Tracey's eyes search the water. "I don't know. When I got separated from you two, I tried to keep going toward the water, but the trees pushed me somewhere else and I got too turned around. I wandered through the woods for a minute or maybe an hour. Then I saw the clearing." She swallows. "And Sabrina. She was standing there and she started to talk to me. She said if I just came to her . . . she said she could make it better."

"Could you hear us yelling? Or feel us grabbing you?" I ask.

"I could hear something, but it sounded so far away." Her eyes start to water. "I'm sorry."

"It's okay," Kassidy says. "The same thing happened to Mackenzie. She walked right out into the water. Damn near drowned. I couldn't make out what the wheetigo was saying to either of you, though."

"Why couldn't it touch me, then? I was right there in front of it." She runs her fingers through her hair as she says this, stroking the crow feather.

"I think we had some protection," I say, nodding at the feather. Tracey grabs it from behind her ear and holds it in the palms of her hands, searching it for answers. I watch my hands float in the water, washed clean of the wheetigo's blood, and marvel at how they shapeshift between the moments when they're submerged and when I raise them above the surface again.

"We're going to have to get Auntie a new knife," Kassidy says.

"I'm sure she'll understand," Tracey says.

Suddenly, I start to cry. The tightness in my chest I've been feeling all along lifts off and leaves my body. An undercurrent surges and I'm pushed toward Tracey and Kassidy. I wrap myself in their arms and we float like that for a minute, buoyed by the water gently moving underneath us.

"We need to get home," Kassidy says, pulling away and wiping the tears from her full cheeks. "I'm tired from saving both your asses all damn day."

We laugh and the water carries it. We're shaking when we get to shore, as the cold and shock of the day drips from our skin. We stand for a moment to let the sun dry us. I trail behind Tracey and Kassidy to take one last look out at the water. I think I see something floating in the middle of the lake. A raft with a bird, someone waking up to something familiar, finally.

⊲ᑊᑫ ᓄᐅᐁᐧᕼᑊ

We stand at the gate of my parents' house as though we're seeing it with new eyes. When we walked through the woods again to get back to the van, the forest was changed. It was almost how I remembered it: thick, full of life. Birds flew into nests and the trails snaked through and connected like veins. The brown soil stuck to our shoes. Some of the witch's broom at the tips of the trees started to fall, too. Whatever death the wheetigo had brought to the place seemed to be leaving, though it would still take a while to fully heal.

We drove back home in silence. We rolled down the windows and let ourselves dry off in the breeze. Every now and then, I'd look over at Kassidy driving and then in the rearview mirror at Tracey, just to make sure they were both still there.

"How do we explain what happened?" Tracey rests her hands on the gate and presses her cheek to the cool metal. Closes her eyes against the sunlight. The feather is still stuck behind her ear.

"I dunno but we better figure it out fast. We know what happens when we try to keep something from an auntie." Kassidy laughs and the sound cracks open the air.

The aunties are busy in the kitchen when we walk in. The kind of busy that tells us they were just watching us from the window. Auntie Verna is stirring a pot on the stove and Auntie Doreen wipes down an already clean counter. Mom doesn't try to pretend anything. She sits at the table, staring at us as we walk in.

She looks at us with a worry that catches me in the stomach. She takes in our damp clothes and hair. Atim wakes up from sleeping at Auntie Doreen's feet and runs to Kassidy, whining until she picks him up.

"We did it," I say. My voice comes out quiet, my throat still sore from the lake water and vomit, from yelling and crying.

Mom stays sitting as Auntie Doreen and Auntie Verna rush over and hug us all in turn. When they let us go, Mom gets up from the table and wraps us all in her arms. She sobs against my neck. For a while, we just stand there, the sound of her crying filling the kitchen and seeping into every pore in our bodies.

"Let's get you cleaned up," Auntie Verna says. "You can fill us in on everything after." As she gathers me in her arms, she whispers in my ear. "You're all looking yellow, yellow, yellow, my girl."

Mom starts the bath for me while I sit on the closed toilet seat. Tracey hugs us and goes right up to her room. Kassidy stays with her mom and Atim. I want to tell my mom what happened but exhaustion weighs my mouth closed.

"Astam." she motions for me to feel the water. Its warmth spreads across my outstretched hand. Mom smooths out my hair and kisses my forehead before leaving, closing the door behind her.

I let the bathroom fill with steam before undressing and crawling into the tub. Sitting in the hot water, I search my skin. This time, I'm not surprised at anything I see.

As soon as I wake up the next morning, I call Joli. They answer on the first ring.

"Mackenzie?"

Relief spreads through my body at the sound of their voice. "Joli, are you okay?"

"Of course I'm okay, are you okay? I've been texting and calling you and literally all of your family."

"We've been texting and calling you."

"I haven't gotten anything."

I sigh and tell them everything.

"We fucking knew it," they say when I finish. "My mom and I. We didn't know it was that wheetigo thing. But we knew it was something bad looking to trap you. No wonder it blocked us from talking."

"It did a pretty good job of making me feel alone."

They're quiet for a second on the other end of the line. "So are you coming back soon or what? Don't make me get on a plane to the prairies. You know open skies make me dizzy."

I laugh. "I'm booking my flight for next week," I say. "I also want to learn how to swim."

"Dear Creator, I cannot imagine you in the ocean." They laugh again. "But I'll tell you what, if you want to learn, I know someone who can teach you. I don't have the patience for a sentimental Cree like you."

I laugh and we keep talking. The distance between us shrinking down. When I get off the phone, I book a flight back to Vancouver for the following week. Mom calls the aunties and uncles and tells them when to come around for my goodbye dinner.

"You don't need to call the whole damn crew, I'll be back for another visit in a couple months." I laugh and nudge her. "Besides, we don't have enough food for all those animals."

Mom shoos me away and picks up the phone again to call another relative. I go to the living room, where Tracey is playing video games. She doesn't look up when I come in, but nods at the TV. "Want to play?"

She's playing *Zelda,* so we'd have to put in something else.

"Nah," I say. "I just wanna watch you. Where's Kass?"

"Her and Auntie went to town," she says, not taking her eyes away from the TV.

I sit and watch her play for a while. Her mouth twitches a little as she concentrates. The clicking of her fingers on the controller and the background score to the game eventually lulls me to sleep.

When I wake up in my dream, kokum is sitting on the couch with me, watching Tracey play. The world is shadowed here, and it moves slower, like I'm treading water. She smells like cigarettes and coffee. She smiles and the white of her teeth glint in the sunlight. "Hi, my girl," she says, looking over at me.

"Hi, kokum." A hole in my heart deepens at the sound of her voice.

"God, she plays a lot of video games." She laughs and shakes her head at the TV.

I laugh, too. "This is really you, right?"

She smirks. "The one and only."

I can already feel the tears forming. My eyes search around her.

"Sabrina's fine," she says, reading my mind. "Don't you worry about her. Me and mosum came and got her when it was time. We've been holding her ever since."

"Do you think she'll ever come back? Tracey thinks she's lost her forever." I look at Tracey again, her eyes still glued to the TV.

"Oh, she's been back. She likes to shapeshift and keep an eye on things."

I don't trust myself to say anything without crying. Instead, I reach out to touch her. I imagine my hand moving through her body, like what happened in the other dreams, but instead it hits her arm with a soft thud.

"Hey, what the hell." Kokum pulls back her arm and rubs where I hit her. "That's elder abuse."

We laugh and I reach out again, this time more slowly. Kokum waits, watching me and rolling her eyes at my carefulness. I grab her hand and feel the softness of it, just like I remember. No one has hands as soft as hers. I entwine our fingers and lay my head against her shoulder, breathing her in and out.

"You can't take me back with you, my girl," she says, though I already know. "I have to get going, I just wanted to come by and say what's up."

I laugh and wipe my tears on her sweater. "Is this a lesson?" I ask, because sometimes it's hard to tell.

"No," she says, and holds me closer. "I just wanted to be somewhere quiet with you." She smiles, letting go of my hand and moving my face off her chest. "I miss you."

"I miss you, too, kokum. Every day."

She perches on the end of the couch and holds on to my arm, giving it a squeeze. "Tell your sister I love and miss her. My Kassidy, too. Don't tell the other ones you've seen me, though, they get jealous."

She winks at me and I nod, feeling the tug of awake.

The couch pillow under my face is drenched in sweat or tears, I don't know which, and Tracey is watching me from the floor. "It happened again, didn't it?"

I wait for the rest of me to return to my body. Slowly, my breath starts to come back and my thoughts catch up from the dream world. I watch Tracey looking at me with the same intensity she uses to play her games, when everything is at stake. I can still feel kokum's hand on my arm when I tell Tracey, "Kokum says she loves and misses you. She still has the softest skin."

Tracey gathers me in her arms and we cry into each other. From my neck she says, "I can still smell her here." This time our tears are more ceremony than sad.

The day before I leave, Mom helps me pack. I don't have enough clothes to need help, so she just refolds everything I had already put in my bag. Over the past week, she'd been moving more things into the room, even put up some of Sabrina's old drawings. The dress form, the bullet holes filled and patched but still visible, sits in the corner of the room, the varnish glossy against the sun streaming in from outside.

I look at Mom and see the same hurt in her eyes as when I left the first time. The kind of hurt she's been taught to hide.

"I mean it, Mom," I say. "I'll be back again soon."

She looks at me and hesitates. From a grocery bag at her feet, she pulls out a small bottle of sand. "From the lake," she says, and shrugs like it's nothing at all.

I think about the truth of my absence over the last two years. I left to get away from a hurt I didn't want to handle.

I wrap the bottle in a sweater. "It wasn't the wheetigo," I say, "that made me make the choices that I did. It might have tried to burrow in my body, but I was already fucking up. I created all that hurt. Not coming back for Sabrina's funeral and not being here for all of you. I still have healing work to do."

She pulls me into a hug and we hold each other tight. "What, you think you were off the hook or something?"

We laugh and I breathe her in deeper, try to commit her smell, the feel of her chin on my shoulder, the strength of her, to memory.

"I saw kokum the other day," I say.

I feel her body tense and she pulls back a little, looks into my eyes.

"She didn't have anything to say, really," I rush on. "She just wanted to, um, say what's up."

Mom looks at me for another moment, her lined face unmoving, and then bursts out laughing. I laugh with her. We both hold our stomachs and laugh and laugh until I ache all over.

"What a real asshole," Mom says through tears.

Eventually, we hear the bustle downstairs getting louder as the house fills with family.

For my last supper, Mom and the aunties pull out all the stops. Everyone has brought one of my favourite dishes: perogies, mac and cheese, shepherd's pie, bannock, a big pot of chicken noodle soup. We all eat in the small kitchen, filling the table and counters. We eat off each other's plates, standing up, one hand on our cups and another around the arms of a cousin or auntie. Tracey and Kass stand on either side of me, and we move together like a unit. Dad has come home from working away, and his eyes water every time he looks at me. The house hums against my back as I lean against the wall: someone singing. When I look around at everyone, I feel inside of it all.

After dinner, we play cards. The cousins have a table of crib going in the living room, while the adults play poker at the kitchen table. We bet quarters that come from one another's pockets, not caring so much about winning, not really. Eventually, people start to trickle out to head home or to land in various places around the house to sleep. The aunties stay behind to clean the kitchen, talking to each other in whispers and laughter that can be heard down the hallway. The whole place smells like sweat, and it's warm even though most of the windows are cracked open, like even the heat doesn't want to leave.

After dinner, me, Tracey, and Kassidy walk to the 7-Eleven.

We say it's to go get snacks, but it's mostly just to be together. A nighttime breeze drifts across my skin, carrying the deep prairie mood: a steady breath of soil and pine sap, a hand brushing across our cheeks like it's saying it's okay to feel swallowed up every now and then, and a deep, deep sigh of relief. The sky is a smudge of pink.

We walk and talk and listen to the cars passing by sounding like rushing water. In the ambulance sirens from across town, I hear the sounds of the city calling me. In Kassidy's jokes, I hear Joli's teasing. As we move around town, I feel like the mountains are a little closer and the ground underneath us has the forgiving surface of sand. Our steps sure, our laughter carrying itself across the streets. I feel us come together, crows again.

We pass a truck parked out front of kokum Louise's trailer, boxes and garbage bags full of clothes packed tight into the bed of the truck. My heart sinks at the thought of her moving, this old woman who has lived down the street from us for as long as I can remember. And then I see her sons, my parents' age, come out the front door, followed by their kids. They each grab a box or bag and head back toward the trailer. They're teasing one another, and they wave at us as we pass. Relief settles over me. She's not moving out, someone in her family is moving in. I think about the forest by the lake that's already started to repair itself and smile.

At the 7-Eleven, we get slushies and beef jerky. We take the alleyways back to the house, curving along side streets, wanting to take our time with this last night together. Along the gravel road, I see the glint of a small, blue rock and pick it up. I hold it up to my sister and cousin. "Doesn't this look like the ocean?"

They stop in the middle of their conversation and study the rock between my fingers. Kassidy smirks. "It looks like a blue rock."

Tracey smiles and nudges our cousin. "You're just saying that because you've never seen the ocean."

They laugh and kick up some dust as they continue walking, talking about their plans to visit me in the fall. I put the rock in my pocket and make a mental note to give it to Joli when I'm back in Vancouver. I feel the smooth stone between my fingers and think about the past week.

After we got back from the lake, we all slept for days, exhausted from the fear that had been building in our bodies for weeks. Then we went to the cemetery to visit Sabrina's grave. Tracey brought a rock from the lake and placed it in front of her gravestone next to a line of other rocks that already rested there. She brought one every time she visited. I remembered when she told me she didn't visit often and thought about saying something to her. But sometimes love means boundaries. A moose shedding its antlers means it's always a changing thing.

We killed the thing that killed Sabrina, but it didn't fix anything. It didn't make the sad feel less enveloping. It didn't stanch the grief still pooling inside me. At her grave, I said a prayer for her, and a plea for myself. That I would be better, stop running, stop hiding when it all got hard, which it would again.

I still hold a piece of the bad inside me. I used to think enough love was supposed to wipe all the bad clean, but I don't think that's true anymore. The truth is, I'm brimming with love. The love pouring from the tip of kokum's finger when she pointed out wapanewask. The love in Auntie Verna's eyes when we got a good bingo. In Mom's hands carrying the other end of a pile of lumber. I have so much love I'm sick with it. But there will always be bad living alongside it, etched under my skin. Living with bad doesn't make me bad, though, it's just there like everything else.

I breathe in the prairie night and run my hand through my

hair, coming away with a few loose strands and laying them on the ground at my feet. As I start walking again, I notice a flash of something in the trees in front of Kassidy and Tracey, about a block away. I think I see a glint of white move from the tip of one tree to another. But when I blink, there's just a slight breeze rocking the trees innocently against the backdrop of sky.

Kassidy and Tracey's laughter pulls me out of my thoughts.

"What do you think, Mack—could Tracey be much of a city iskwew, like you?" Kassidy takes a sip of her slushy.

I look at Tracey grinning, a smile I haven't seen from her since we were kids. "Nah," I say. "She's too bush for that."

We laugh together again, Kassidy walking a little closer to Tracey, their arms brushing against each other as they move. I glance back to the trees, but when I'm sure I see nothing, I quicken my pace to catch up to my cousin and sister, a streetlamp illuminating the curve of their cheeks.

Acknowledgements

Forever grateful to the lands on which I wrote this book: unceded Musqueam, Squamish, and Tsleil-Waututh territories, Treaty 6, Treaty 7, and Treaty 8. This is a love letter to ayahciyiniw sâkahikan—the place I will forever be no matter where my feet are.

This book started as a dream, something that lived in my mind and then worked its way out. It would not have been possible without the following people:

Mary-Jane Cardinal, Eileen Smith, Robert Smith, Don Smith. You live in every word I write.

My first editor, Aeman. We made this together. Thank you for your kindness, insight, and honesty.

Margo, Jenn, and Marika. Thank you for your edits, brilliance, and never-ending support.

Steph. Where would I be without you? Thank you for fighting so hard as my agent and my friend. When I look in my corner, I'm honoured to know I'll see you standing there.

My niblings Thomas, Sadie, Briella, Liam, Kye, Noah, Harper, Caroline, Stella, and Alfredo. This future is for you, my sweet precious angels.

My parents, Loretta and Brent, and siblings, Amanda, Garrett, Stayce, and Ben. My aunties: Auntie Missy, Auntie Nancy, Auntie

Mena, Auntie Lesley, Auntie Joli, Auntie Lissa, and Auntie Diane. I learned to organize, love, and lead by watching you all. Auntie Doreen, thank you for always patiently answering my questions and helping me with my basic nêhiyawêwin. My cousins, and in particular, Kassidy. Thank you for sharing your dreams with me.

Ele and Liz, my best and oldest friends, thank you for reading my shit poems when I was only thirteen and still insisting I had something to offer the world.

Ashlee and the Brady family, in particular Rosemary, Cowboy Greg, and Grandma. For being the best second family I could have ever asked for.

Forever grateful to my first readers who assured me this book wasn't a wash: Jocelyn, Brandi, and Ben. The broads Jocelyn, Rachel, Selina, Mallory, and Mica. My beautiful friends Molly, Cara, Kiri, Serena, Justin, Sam, Edzi'u, Whess, Jillian, Adrienne, Brittany, Alana, Alicia, Carleigh, Burhan, Emily H, Jason, Justy, Jyles, Brandon, Kara, Dustin, Bri, and Jane. Gillian, I will remember you forever. Jade, thank you for the line "What have we got to do with all this time but get it right?"—I live my life by it.

Banff pals Oubah, Lue, Zoe, Salma, and Georgina. Thank you, Shyam Selvadurai, for being a wonderful mentor in the mountains. An ocean of love to Eden Robinson for telling me in the first reading of this manuscript to "go deeper, go darker," and for giving me the crystal that fucked up my dreams in a good way.

Indigenous Brilliance babes Karmella, Jónína, Patricia, and Emily DO for being medicine when I needed it most.

NDN Mario Kart crew: Arielle, Jaz, Conor, Billy, Dallas, Evan, Elliott, thanks for keeping the discord lit and me alive over the pandemic.

Emily, jaye, Matt. What can I say except I love you? Thank you for filling my life with joy.

Jackson, through letters to you, I learned to write.

Acknowledgements

To the Cree & D crew and all my DND pals, for sparking joy and creativity in me when I didn't think I had any left. Big ups to Katherena, Cherie, Leanne, Eden, Josh, and Marilyn for giving the biggest auntie energy and paving the way for dreamers like me. Thank you, Lisa Bird-Wilson and *Grain,* for being the editor and magazine to first publish "Bad Cree" as a short story.

Thank you to the Writers' Trust of Canada, the Canada Council for the Arts, and the Banff Centre for Arts and Creativity for providing me the space, funds, and support to create this novel.

Hiy hiy to everyone who has supported me along the way. Not just with this book, but in all other creative and non-creative projects that brought me here.

A Note About the Author

JESSICA JOHNS is a nehiyaw-English-Irish auntie and member of Sucker Creek First Nation in Treaty 8 territory in Northern Alberta. She is an interdisciplinary artist and award-winning writer.